She could wait
no longer

Slowly Sam groped for her purse and slid her hand around the cold, comforting piece of steel.

The footsteps were cautious. Padded. Coming directly for them. But she couldn't tell from what direction.

She and Scotty had fallen on the sidewalk, a half block from the motel. The streetlight was behind them, illuminating their forms. The hunter was in darkness while Scotty and she lay in light. And, like any hunter, he was coming in closer to make sure the prey was dead, not just wounded.

It wasn't going to be easy. She would have to shoot with one hand over Scotty's body into the darkness at a moving target that she could not clearly see. But it was the only chance they had.

The footsteps were coming closer....

ABOUT THE AUTHOR

M. J. Rodgers lives in Malibu, California, and commutes to Los Angeles each day where she works as a manager for a major corporation. She has traveled extensively around the world, having both lived and worked in Europe, Asia and the Middle East. *For Love or Money* is her first novel.

For Love
or Money
M. J. Rodgers

Harlequin Books

**TORONTO • NEW YORK • LONDON
AMSTERDAM • PARIS • SYDNEY • HAMBURG
STOCKHOLM • ATHENS • TOKYO • MILAN**

To Jerdan,
the hero of all my dreams

Harlequin Intrigue edition published November 1988

ISBN 0-373-22102-9

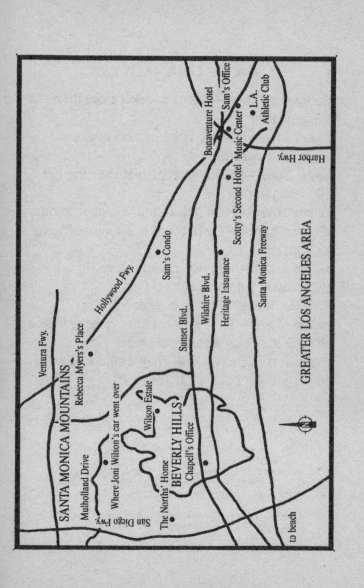

GREATER LOS ANGELES AREA

SANTA MONICA MOUNTAINS

BEVERLY HILLS

Ventura Fwy.

Mulholland Drive

San Diego Fwy.

Rebecca Myers's Place

Where Joni Wilson's car went over

Wilson Estate

The Norths' Home

Chapell's Office

Hollywood Fwy.

Sam's Condo

Sunset Blvd.

Wilshire Blvd.

Heritage Insurance

Bonaventure Hotel

Sam's Office

Music Center

Scotty's Second Hotel

L.A. Athletic Club

Santa Monica Freeway

Harbor Hwy.

to beach

N

CAST OF CHARACTERS

Samantha Turner—She unraveled more than she bargained for.

Scott Lawrence—The circumstances were beyond his control.

Isabel Kane—She loved Joni as if she were her own daughter.

Peter Taswell—Now heir to the Wilson millions.

Walter Chapell—He handled much more than legal affairs.

Monty Larkin—He was about to put an engagement ring on Joni's finger.

Rebecca Myers—Friend or enemy?

Julian Harris—He decided what the story would be after the body was discovered.

Claire and Colin North—They would stop at nothing to get back what Joni took.

Chapter One

"I've got to know if my client of yesterday is the same woman who was found dead today."

Warren's voice, blaring over the telephone, drowned out the television noises in Scotty's room at the Bonaventure Hotel in Los Angeles. But, despite the volume of his partner's voice, Scotty was confused. Confused and a bit surprised at the apparent unraveling of the other man's composure.

"Who's been found dead, Warren? Who are you talking about?"

"Joni Wilson. The heiress. Haven't you seen this morning's TV news?"

"No. We had a late night at the convention. I just got up and turned the set on. Wait a minute. A local news report is coming on right now."

Scotty directed his attention to the program.

"Joni May Wilson, the twenty-four-year-old daughter of deceased millionaire Gregory Wilson, was found early this morning in her burned car, in a deep ravine below Mulholland Drive. Miss Wilson's body was taken to the coroner's office where an autopsy will be performed.

"Miss Wilson was the sole heir to the estate of her father, who died of a heart attack two years ago. The estate is rumored to be in excess of twenty million dollars."

A photograph of the heiress, her long, straight hair curving around high cheekbones and a full, smiling mouth, flashed behind the newscaster. Scotty recalled seeing her picture in the newspapers. Society column, probably, although he couldn't remember the particulars. He pressed the mute button as the announcer went on to another story. He spoke into the telephone receiver.

"Are you saying that Joni Wilson was a client of ours?" he asked now, genuinely puzzled.

For a moment there was silence on the other end of the line. Scotty could almost picture Warren pacing jaggedly between the two secondhand oak desks in the small San Francisco office from which they made their livelihood. When Warren finally answered, he sounded confused, as though he needed to reconcile something to himself.

"She said her name was Jane Williams. But I can't believe she was a different woman with exactly the same face, the same hair. They've got to have been the same. So why did she pose as somebody else?"

Scotty knew the questions weren't directed at him. Warren was just thinking aloud. Whatever the mystery concerning the heiress's death, his partner's meandering wasn't making things any clearer for Scotty. He was patient, however. He knew his tall, handsome partner was not the strong, silent type. He would be more than willing to unburden himself. Any minute now.

"It was just after you left for the convention yesterday. Around nine-thirty."

Warren paused again, and Scotty decided he needed prodding. "What happened?"

"She arrived."

Scotty recognized the telltale wistfulness in his partner's voice. It was the same reaction he had to every attractive woman he saw.

"I can still see her. She stood in the doorway with the light from the hallway catching her hair. Incredibly rich brown hair cascading over ivory shoulders. Form-fitting white dress. A vanilla ice-cream cone with one end dipped in chocolate.''

"Perhaps you could provide me with a less-subjective description?''

"Somewhere in her twenties, five foot five, no more than a hundred and ten pounds, light blue eyes, long dark lashes, long, straight, dark brown hair with bangs.''

"What did she want?''

"Well, when I asked her how I could help, she told me she was missing and had to be found.''

Scotty frowned. "She said she was missing?''

"It threw me off balance for a minute, too. But it makes sense. Or at least it seemed to when she explained it.''

A line had drawn itself between Scotty's sandy brows as Warren went on with his story.

"She said her name was Jane Williams and she told me this somewhat plausible story of how she was orphaned at two. It seems she and her parents were on a holiday on the East Coast when the bus they were on crashed. Must have been a terrible accident, because most of the passengers were killed, bodies burned beyond recognition, including her parents'.''

Questions began swarming through Scotty's skeptical mind. Apparently Warren understood the reason for his partner's silence.

"I know what you're thinking. But it could have happened. She said the police had trouble identifying the dead. Just Jane and three other passengers survived. The others didn't know Jane or her parents. And although she was only about two, Jane knew her name and the fact that she and her parents were on vacation.''

"Did she say how long ago this happened?'' Scotty asked.

"Twenty-two years.''

"Then she'd be the same age as the heiress. Where did she and her parents live before they went on this vacation to the East Coast?''

"She couldn't be sure. She had memories of looking out over water and a huge red bridge her parents insisted was golden."

"San Francisco. The Golden Gate," Scotty said.

"Yes. It's what she finally concluded, or said she decided when she was about fourteen."

"What happened to her after the accident?"

"She was adopted by a couple in New Jersey. They died a year ago."

"If she grew up in New Jersey, what brought her to San Francisco? Why did she come to our firm for help?" Scotty asked.

"She said she was attending the funeral of her adopted mother's sister. The woman lived in Oakland. She told me she had decided to take the opportunity to try to find out who she really was—you know, as long as she was in the neighborhood. She only had yesterday, and then had to fly back to New Jersey."

"Did you get the name of the woman in Oakland?"

"No. I didn't think it was important at the time."

"How did she choose our firm?"

"Found us in the yellow pages. Liked the name—Riddle Investigations—and the fact we guaranteed results, or we'd give her her money back," Warren said.

"So you ended up giving her her money back?" Scotty asked.

Warren muttered under his breath. His next intelligible words took Scotty by surprise.

"That's what makes this so incredible! I didn't have to give her money back. I found out who she was! Or at least I thought I had."

"Okay. Give me the highlights," Scotty said.

"It was simple really. I just reasoned that if her family came from San Francisco as she thought, then a birth certificate for a Jane Williams would be on file in the County Hall of Records. Frankly it didn't take a private investigator to gain access to the birth records of twenty-four years ago. I just gave the clerk a bit of a come-on, and she let me look at whatever I wanted.''

Scotty knew Warren wasn't boasting—just stating the facts. He never seemed to have any trouble getting what he wanted from women. Physically Warren was a heart stopper. But his using women bothered Scotty, even when it didn't seem to bother the women.

Scotty's introspection was interrupted by Warren's continuing his story of Jane Williams.

''...certificate said a Jane Marie Williams was born twenty-four years ago to a Paul and Beatrice Williams of Church Street in San Francisco. Paul Williams was listed as a gas company engineer. It all seemed to fit.''

''Did Jane Williams seem happy with the identification?'' Scotty asked.

''Yes, very. She was grateful. I got her a certified copy of the birth certificate. We went out to dinner, had a few drinks and ended up back at her motel. She had great legs and—''

''Spare me the details. What time did you and your client part?''

''Just before six-thirty. She said she had to catch a plane for New Jersey.''

''And you didn't hear from her after that?''

''No. And it wasn't until I got up this morning and saw the TV news that I realized Jane Williams and Joni Wilson were the same person. I mean, they've got to be, which means she lied. She lied to *me*.''

Scotty was amused. His partner seemed more upset by the fact that Jane Williams had lied to him than that she was dead. After all the lies he had heard Warren dish out to women, he found it amazing that Warren could possibly be offended when he found himself on the receiving end. Still, he had to admit that the story of Jane Williams was an intriguing one. He considered the facts quietly for several moments. Warren waited patiently on the other end.

Why would Joni Wilson, an heiress, pull such a charade? Why would she want the birth certificate of another

woman? And why come to his firm? His and Warren's pri-
vate-investigative firm wasn't exactly the first choice of
people on the social register.

Then again, maybe theirs was the perfect firm. Who
would ever believe that Joni Wilson had been a client of
theirs? Scotty was having a hard time believing it himself.

He had a good imagination, but before he let it run wild,
he'd better discover if it really had been Joni Wilson who
paid Warren a visit the day before.

"You have the paperwork on the Williams case?"

"Uh . . . I didn't finish it."

Scotty shook his head. No use in reminding his partner of
basic procedure and the need for paperwork. It never did
any good. "All right," Scotty said. "Jot down all the facts
now as you remember them. We can check the airlines to
determine if a Jane Williams flew out to the East or a Joni
Wilson to Los Angeles. Then, with the facts we have about
the child born twenty-four years ago as Jane Marie Williams, we might be able to get a lead on her whereabouts. In
any case, we can try."

"You think this is worth pursuing?" Warren asked.

"I don't think we have any choice. If it was Joni Wilson
with you, she was playing a strange game. And we supplied
her with false identification. People who want to hide their
true identities often do so for illegal reasons, so I'd say we'd
better investigate to insure we're not accessories to a crime."

"What do you want me to do?" Warren asked.

"Check the airlines first. Then go to the gas company.
The birth certificate identified Jane Williams's father as an
engineer there, so maybe they have a record of his employ-
ment. It might give us a lead."

"Okay. What are you going to do?"

"Well, as long as I'm in L.A., I might as well check with
the local police. I've already given my workshop speech. The
convention is over as far as I'm concerned. I'll grab some
breakfast and see what I can dig up here."

"Do you think her death was an accident?"

Scotty got an unwelcome mental image of the young woman with the long, dark hair plummeting to her death. He shook his head. "I don't know, Warren. Let's find out."

DETECTIVE SERGEANT Samantha Turner of the Los Angeles Police Department drove to the business address of Walter Chapell, attorney-at-law, with less enthusiasm than she reserved for a visit to her dentist.

An August sun already sizzled in the bright morning sky. A radio newscaster warned of temperatures in the nineties. And, as usual, the air-conditioning in the unmarked police car was on the fritz—like her relationship with her boss, Lieutenant Mansfield.

She glanced at the storefronts as she entered the Miracle Mile of Wilshire Boulevard. Expensive shops. Her face squinted into an uncharacteristic frown. The day had gotten off to a bad start: first having to block a pass from Mansfield, and now a journey into the life-styles of the rich and famous. She envisioned nothing but problems. Experience had taught her that the rich considered themselves above the law by the mere fact of their money. Intolerant of the rights of others, yet demanding and insistent of their own rights, as though money sanctified their actions.

So what case did Mansfield stick her with? The death of the rich socialite. Just what she needed. He knew her record, how she felt. The man was just getting back at her for refusing his advances. A subtle harassment and one he knew she could never prove.

Nine years on the force. Nine years of hard work and struggle to get into plainclothes. To prove her worth as a detective, pass the sergeant's exam and be assigned the cream of investigation—the homicide division.

And after all that, she got stuck with a Neanderthal boss like Mansfield. The kind of guy who thought taking a risk meant getting more than ten items through the express line at the grocery market—and who thought all women were up for grabs. She'd set him straight on that score, however, but it seemed he'd been punishing her ever since.

Sam exhaled her frustration. Dwelling on her fate wasn't going to do any good, and she'd just have to accept it. She had to rub elbows with the snobs again. Her first appointment was with the family lawyer at his Beverly Hills address.

Well, she thought, maybe it wouldn't be too bad. Sometimes lawyers were more reasonable than the rich clients they represented.

She tried to deep-breathe her agitation away. Play the nice, polite detective. Get in there and do her job, no matter how much those people turned her stomach.

Her suit jacket lay beside her on the seat; it was much too hot to wear in a car without air-conditioning. Her tanned arm extended from the end of her short-sleeve blouse to rest on the open window. It was a strong arm for a woman. She had worked to make it that way. Exercised to keep herself fit.

She pulled up behind an old Ford, which was crawling along. Sam glanced at her speedometer. Twenty miles an hour. Something was wrong. Nobody traveled so slowly unless they were forced to. She tried to see if there was something delaying the car, but its bulky design and small back window prohibited her view. She got a look at the driver, who was an elderly man....

It all happened so quickly. In sudden dread, Sam watched the vehicle in front of her crawl across the intersection through a red light. From her peripheral vision, she could see the black sports car, speeding along the street to her left and heading directly for the ancient vehicle and its driver. She hit her own brakes, feeling helpless to stop what was about to happen and hoping against hope that it wouldn't.

The driver of the black sports car must have seen the old Ford only a moment before the collision. Sam watched a look of horror descend on his young face. He hit his brakes as his car careered out of control across the intersection,

broadsiding the hapless Ford only a few feet in front of
Sam. Her heart leaped into her throat, her ears deafened by
the sound of screeching tires and metal, as the two vehicles
spun madly across Wilshire Boulevard.

Chapter Two

Scotty witnessed the traffic accident from a block away. Only one person immediately upon the scene seemed to be doing any good. A woman in a businesslike skirt and blouse had put a blanket over a person lying on the sidewalk and was administering CPR to another. Scotty pulled his car to the curb and hurried over to see if he could help.

His quick glance at the occupants of the two smashed cars was enough to convince him that even if they were still alive, to get to them would require a crowbar. He turned his attention to the woman whose back was to him as she knelt next to the pedestrian victim. He got a glimpse of thick, black braids circling her bent head and the light, golden skin of her neck.

"May I help?" he asked.

At first he didn't think she was going to answer. But after a moment, she looked up briefly from her life-saving effort.

"I'm police. An ambulance is on the way. Please disperse the crowd and keep the streets clear for emergency vehicles."

Those were the only words she spared him before returning to her CPR. He leaned down and touched her shoulder reassuringly before he turned to scatter the growing gathering of curious spectators.

He shouted his commands with authority, and the crowd reluctantly dispersed, and cars began to move along. A marked police vehicle pulled up to the curb, lights flashing. Scotty returned to the woman.

She was standing over the victim and didn't seem to have noticed Scotty. She had grabbed her suit jacket and was draping it over the lifeless form on the ground. Gently she picked up the hands and placed them beneath the jacket, then stood up. Scotty tried to swallow the lump of pain sticking in his throat. "I'm sorry." His words sounded awkward to his ears.

At first Sam ignored the words and the man standing next to her. It was her training that finally broke through, which told her to focus her attention on the living. She turned to look at the stranger who had come to her aid. Although she was tall, five foot ten, she found herself looking up into his eyes, the color a mixture of light and dark gray. His straight, sandy-colored hair was a mixture of brown and blond. While his cheekbones and jaw were sharp, his mouth was sensitive, and maybe even a little sad. It was a face of contrasts, and Sam had to fight her sudden curiosity.

"Thank you. I appreciate what you did. I—"

Sam's comment was interrupted by the wailing arrival of an ambulance, and she left Scotty's side to help with the accident victims. He followed, but was intercepted by two uniformed officers, who encouraged him to go about his business.

As he reached his car, Scotty looked back, his eyes straining to catch a glimpse of the tall, black-haired woman among the bobbing heads that lined the sidewalk. But she was gone.

SAM HAD DRIVEN SLOWLY back to her office, made her report and gone to the washroom to clean up. But the image of the dead person could not be washed away. Her years on the force hadn't made dealing with such tragedies any easier. The innocent victims were the worst part of police work.

She dried her hands. It was time to begin investigating another death. It was one even worse than the ones she had just witnessed, because this one had been deliberate. Planned and executed by another human being.

As she walked back to her office, she thought again about the stranger who had come to her aid. She regretted not being able to thank him properly. She could still hear his deep voice raised authoritatively, ordering the curious on-lookers to go about their business.

"There's someone waiting in your office, Sam," her clerk said.

"I don't have time to see anyone. I just came back to the office to give a report to the traffic group and wash up. I never made it to my appointment with Chapell. Give him a call for me, will you? Tell him I've been delayed, and I'll be there in twenty minutes."

"But, Sam, this guy told me he was here about the Wilson case. Something about knowing what the heiress did on the day she died. Are you sure you don't want to see him?"

Sam paused. She was tempted. She knew very little yet about the dead heiress. Perhaps it would be prudent to talk with this person first. If he knew Joni Wilson, he might be able to shed some light on her death. The more information she had before tackling the lawyer, the better.

"All right. Call Chapell. Tell him I'll be there in forty-five minutes. And hold my calls. What's this guy's name?"

"Scott Lawrence."

Sam's visitor's back was to her when she entered her office, and he seemed to be studying the items on her desk. Her immediate impression was of broad shoulders and the light shining off of his sandy-colored hair.

"Please sit down," she said. "I'm Detective Turner. You have some information for me concerning the Joni Wilson case?"

Her visitor sat down, a look of surprise in his gray eyes and a small smile playing about his mouth. He was appar-ently waiting until he saw recognition dawn on her face, too.

"Hi. Nice to see you again," he said.

Sam stared at Scott Lawrence as though the *Enterprise* had just beamed him down.

"You're the man from the accident! What's going on? What do you have to do with Joni Wilson?"

The man's look made it pretty obvious to Sam that he was just as surprised to discover that she was the same police officer he had helped with the accident.

"It seems we have more in common than perhaps we both anticipated. I'm a private investigator from San Francisco. My name's Scott Lawrence."

Sam motioned her visitor to a chair and sat down behind her desk. She was still trying to get over her surprise.

"It's nice to meet you, Mr. Lawrence. Now, what do you have to do with Joni Wilson?"

Sam watched the man openly studying her, a speculative gleam in his eye. He seemed to like what he saw, and she felt a little uncomfortable.

"I think my partner may know what the Wilson woman did the day of her death."

She could almost feel, as well as hear, the deepness in his voice, which seemed to vibrate down her spine. She tried to concentrate on what he was telling her. "Why," she asked, "do you think the activities of Joni Wilson would be of concern to the police?"

The slight smile had traveled to his eyes.

"Because of the word Homicide on your door."

Of course. She should have known. When he found out the case was assigned to her, he had also realized the death wasn't an accident. It was the only way he could have known because nothing had been released to the press.

Sam smiled in capitulation and leaned back in her chair. "All right. There's no use in denying it. I'm interested. Tell me what you know."

The gray eyes kept their disconcerting gaze on her. "I'm interested, too, and getting more interested by the minute. Perhaps we can find a way to satisfy both our interests. You share with me. I share with you. Was the heiress murdered?''

Scotty's question made it clear to Sam what the man was up to. When she told him what he wanted to know, he would tell her what he knew. She had been caught off guard. She had made an assumption that his cooperative spirit at the accident scene could also be expected on the Joni Wilson case. She had been wrong.

She leaned forward in her chair. It was her turn to look him over more carefully. He was dressed casually in a light-colored sports shirt and slacks, but that was the only part of him that was casual. Everything about his posture, his gestures, was formal and confident. He was more than assured of his bargaining position. Still, she had dealt with this kind of information blackmail before and knew how to handle it.

"Mr. Lawrence, withholding evidence from a police investigation is a serious offense. One that can result in your license being lifted, and that's just for starters. I hope I make myself clear?''

She eyed him pointedly. His smile was as open and unwavering as before. She couldn't help noticing the look of appreciation in his eyes as they dwelt on her face, then followed the curve of her neck to her arm. She looked away from them before they went any farther over her anatomy.

"Well, Mr. Lawrence?''

"I haven't withheld information. I've come forward ready to give the information, but then, my partner knows the specifics. You could ask him, but I don't think it would be worth your while. He may not remember much.''

There was no concern in that deep voice; in fact, it almost roared with good humor. Her threat had made no impression at all. And Sam had a pretty clear idea of what would happen if she tried to question the partner. No doubt he would either be conveniently unavailable or decide he didn't know anything after all.

She bit her lip in frustration. This man had her and they both knew it, but at least he didn't seem to be gloating about it. He almost looked guilty as he asked her again, "Can you tell me the circumstances—accident or murder—of the heiress's death?"

He sounded as though he thought the fight was over, but Sam knew otherwise. She may not win this round, but the best this disturbingly attractive man before her would get was a draw. "No, Mr. Lawrence. I cannot. It seems our conversation has come to an end."

He didn't seem upset. Or even disappointed. He simply stood and offered his hand. His smile was warm and even looked sincere. His face of contrasts seemed to match his personality.

"I'm sorry I'm not able to be of more help," he said. "And vice versa. Here's my card. No hard feelings?"

Sam looked into his lively gray eyes and wondered why she couldn't remain upset. He was deliberately withholding information that might be crucial to her case. She wanted to dislike him, but feeling the warmth of his hand in hers as she looked into his smiling face made it impossible.

"No hard feelings," she said. Much to her surprise, she meant the words. He held her hand a moment more before he let it go and walked confidently from her office. Sam watched him leave with feelings that could have best been described as torn.

She picked up her purse and headed out of the building toward her car. She still had to see Chapell, but she knew she would have trouble getting her mind off Scott Lawrence.

Part of her wished she could jail the self-assured private investigator for his lack of cooperation, his blatant, overt attempt to blackmail her into giving him information. Yet another part of her was happy she couldn't lock him up. The part that remembered the warmth of his look, the deepness of his voice as it vibrated down her spine, his irresistible self-assurance. What an irritating man!

Chapter Three

Sam reached the lawyer's address in one of the main business sections of Beverly Hills.

Walter Chapell's offices were on the second floor, with a glass, double-door entry, a waiting room complete with leather couch, healthy plants and thick carpeting. An extremely plain receptionist sitting behind an incredibly beautiful oak desk looked up inquiringly.

"Sergeant Turner, L.A.P.D.," said Sam.

One plain finger pushed the button on the intercom and the colorless mouth repeated Sam's message. A male voice instructed she was to be admitted.

To Sam, Walter Chapell resembled a woodchuck: squat and chunky with a large, pointy nose, squinty, wide-set eyes and a receding chin covered by a narrow beard. He was gnawing at a skinny cigar, brown and splintery-looking like a stick of wood.

"Sergeant Turner? Please take a seat," the short man said. "You mentioned something to my secretary about wanting to see me concerning Miss Wilson's tragic accident?"

Nothing in Chapell's tone or manner hinted he felt there was anything all that tragic about the death of Joni Wilson.

"I'm afraid you're under a misconception," Sam said. She paused deliberately.

The cigar twisted between the lawyer's sharp front teeth. "You haven't come here to discuss Miss Wilson?" he said.

"Yes, I'm here to discuss Miss Wilson. But you've indicated that Miss Wilson's death was accidental." Sam paused a second time.

"Not an accident? Then what?"

"Then murder."

Chapell quickly responded to that little bit of news. His eyes blinked and his mouth dropped open. Sam was glad to see he could feel something, even if it was only surprise.

"I don't believe it," he said.

Sam reminded herself again of the need to convey pleasantness.

"Well, the L.A.P.D. does. So naturally we are interested in who could have benefited from her death."

Any vestige of civility vanished from the lawyer's face. "Why isn't the Beverly Hills Police Department investigating this matter? Miss Wilson was a resident of this city."

His voice was challenging, like a feudal lord confronting a trespasser. Sam imagined he would probably prefer to have one of his buddies in the Beverly Hills police force handling matters for him. She felt a surge of delight in being able to disappoint him.

"True, Mr. Chapell. But sadly, Joni Wilson was murdered within the city limits of Los Angeles. So I'm afraid you'll find the L.A.P.D. has jurisdiction in this case. You were her lawyer, is that correct?"

Sam took out her notepad to ensure Chapell understood the visit was official and any comments he made would be on record. The woodchuck eyed her pointedly before he condescended to respond.

"Yes. I was employed by Greg Wilson, Joni's father. Since his death I have taken care of matters for his daughter. But you must tell me how Miss Wilson was murdered. I understood from the news report that her body was found in her car in a ravine?"

"It was. The body and vehicle were badly burned. Not, however, by the crash of the automobile."

Sam deliberately paused again, ostensibly to cross her legs, but really to closely observe the interest of the listener. Chapell was on the edge of his seat.

"It may interest you to know," she said at last, "that ninety-nine percent of cars do not burst into flames when they go over cliffs. Hollywood has to set them ablaze for effect on television or movies. Just like the murderer did to Miss Wilson's car after he or she sent it over the ledge."

"Then how can you be sure it was Miss Wilson? Who identified the body?"

"Actually the body and vehicle were burned beyond the normal means for recognition. However, a hidden safe had been installed under the dashboard of her car. A steel safe that proved quite impervious to the fire. And one that the murderer apparently did not know about. We found some personal items in that safe, items that obviously belonged to the deceased, Miss Joni Wilson."

Walter Chapell didn't look too well all of a sudden. He stubbed out his cigar as though it was a stick of dynamite about to explode.

"What were those items? As her attorney and executor of the estate, I have a right to know."

Sam smiled her nice, police-officer smile. "I'm sorry, but I'm not at liberty to discuss the contents of that hidden safe until this investigation has taken its full course. As an attorney and officer of the court, I'm sure you understand the need for us to handle all such evidence confidentially." She hoped her sarcasm wasn't showing, but she needn't have worried about Chapell's noticing. At the moment, other things were obviously bothering him.

He was squirming in his chair, and his gaze darted around the corners of his office as though he had buried something there that was about to be dug up. Before the crafty woodchuck could think up a good retort, Sam decided to dig in.

"You could be a tremendous help to us in our investigation. As executor of her estate, you know who would benefit from Joni Wilson's death, don't you?"

Chapell almost seemed relieved at her question. It suddenly occurred to Sam that Chapell must really fear what Joni Wilson had kept in her safe. And Sam's seeking his help must have allayed some of his fear about what the police had found there.

"I'm afraid I won't be much help. Miss Wilson began squandering her assets soon after her father's death a couple of years ago. There's very little left and what little there is will go to her next of kin. The perfunctory will drawn on her twenty-first birthday leaves the estate to him."

The news shocked Sam. She couldn't help but show her surprise. Nor could she fail to notice the obvious nonchalant attitude with which Chapell related the news.

"There's nothing left of a twenty-million-dollar estate?"

"After the liabilities are seen to, I would say about half a million is all, which includes the sale of the house and furniture, of course."

Sitting back, Chapell was perfectly at ease now. He was well versed in the deceased's financial status, a financial status of which he obviously couldn't care less. And although Sam would hardly have described half a million dollars as nothing, she understood that compared with twenty million, it might be considered a pittance, especially by a Beverly Hills lawyer.

"Miss Wilson squandered her inheritance?"

Chapell was almost happy to share the news. "Yes. She threw money away. Just kept withdrawing enormous sums each month. Her father must have kept her in check while he was alive, but when he passed away, she went wild. The only thing that kept her from eventual bankruptcy was her death."

Sam didn't think the lawyer was lying. This kind of information could be easily checked, and check it she would.

"Who else knew of her financial status?"

"I have no idea."

The lawyer's look was almost a dare as he reached into his top drawer for another cigar.

"You told no one?"

Chapell's wiry eyebrows sat up in insult as he lit the new brown stick. "Sergeant Turner, I do not discuss my clients' financial affairs with unauthorized persons."

"No, naturally you wouldn't. You mentioned that her next of kin would receive what's left of the estate. Who would that be?"

Chapell seemed relieved to be getting something off his chest.

"Peter Taswell. A second cousin."

"Have you been in touch with Mr. Taswell?"

"Not really. He presented himself to my receptionist this morning without an appointment. I would have seen him, except that shortly after he arrived, I received your call. So my receptionist informed Mr. Taswell of my inability to meet with him at this time."

Sam got the impression that Chapell had been happy to disappoint Peter Taswell on any pretext. She wondered why.

"What do you think?" she asked. "Could this second cousin, this Peter Taswell, have killed Joni Wilson to inherit her estate?"

"Half a million dollars?"

Obviously Chapell thought the amount was hardly worth worrying about, and certainly not an inducement for murder.

"He may not have known about the depleted status of the estate. How close were they?" Sam persisted.

Chapell sat back and folded his arms at the back of his neck. The smoke from his cigar rose from behind his head like a leak.

"I have no idea."

"You never saw them together?"

"When I was a guest at the Wilson home during the time Greg Wilson was alive, Taswell was occasionally in attendance. He appeared to get along with his cousin."

"And since Greg Wilson's death?"

"I have not been to the Wilson home."

"What was your relationship with Joni Wilson?"

"I have already answered that. I was Miss Wilson's attorney. I dislike repeating myself."

Sam would have liked to snatch the cigar from the lawyer's hand and shove it down his throat. Again she instead forced herself to be pleasant.

"I didn't make my question clear. When Greg Wilson was alive, you were a guest in his home. Since his death, you have not been a guest there. How did your relationship with Greg Wilson differ from your relationship with his daughter?"

Sam watched the small man sitting in the large chair and thought she saw a quick flicker of anger cross the pinched, pointed face.

"I had a personal as well as a business relationship with Greg Wilson. No personal relationship existed between myself and his daughter."

"You didn't like Joni Wilson?"

"I had no feelings for her one way or the other."

Yet something was causing the pinched nose and mouth to quiver ever so slightly. Sam was sure Chapell was trying to hide something. She decided to keep pushing.

"You didn't think she was foolish to be spending her money the way she did?"

"Of course! I just told you so!"

Finally the anger had burst forth. But Sam sensed it was coming from something else. Maybe Chapell was not nearly as indifferent about Joni Wilson as he pretended.

"Did Miss Wilson have any life insurance?"

"No."

"To your knowledge, did Miss Wilson have any enemies? Anyone who might have wished her harm?"

"I have no idea."

Chapell was looking at a hangnail on the index finger of his right hand. He couldn't have broadcasted his indifference any clearer. Still, there was a certain tension in his posture.

"Who were her friends?"

"I don't really know."

"You never saw her with anyone when you visited her father's home?"

"Well, I understood she sometimes dined with a woman named Rebecca Myers and the woman's lover, Julian Harris. And sometimes an acquaintance from school, Claire Buford. No, it's Claire North—she married the hot-dog king."

"Hot-dog king?"

"Yes. Surely you've heard of Colin North? The baker who revolutionized the hot-dog bun industry four years ago? Developed a self-sealing bun that prevents the hot dog, mustard, ketchup and whatever else they put on them these days from dripping out. Became a wealthy man overnight, and married his socialite wife soon after."

"I see. And Joni's men friends? Romantic interests?"

"They came and went so frequently, no one could keep track."

"What about Monty Larkin? The society columnists have been linking him and the Wilson woman for months."

"Have they?"

Chapell didn't look up from his continuing examination of the hangnail. If anything, he appeared to be studying it more intensely.

Sam made her next approach carefully. "I hope you understand these questions I must ask you are only routine. Absolutely no suspicion is implied." She paused. "Where were you last evening and early this morning?"

Chapell looked up from the scrutiny of his finger, and his thin lips almost curled into a snarl. Yet for all his show of distaste, he was somewhat flustered. Sam had the impres-

sion he was making a quick mental journey of the verbal
road he was going to take.

"Last evening I attended a dinner at the Beverly Hilton.
It lasted until just before eleven. After that, I drove home
and went to bed. This morning I got up at eight. I've been
in my office since nine-fifteen."

"Is there anyone who can verify your whereabouts?"

"You can check with the other attorneys who attended the
dinner. My wife will verify when I arrived home, and my
secretary when I arrived at work."

"When was the last time you saw Miss Wilson?"

"Two years ago at her father's funeral."

"So you've only spoken to her on the phone to conduct
your various business matters?"

"No. There has been business correspondence, as well."

His tension had worked its way to the corners of his eyes,
which were squinted almost shut.

"Anything unusual in these business matters? Something that didn't strike you as reasonable?"

"Nothing Miss Wilson did in the last two years of her life
could be considered reasonable."

"Could you be more explicit?"

"I've already explained. She lost her fortune. There's
nothing else to say. Now, if you don't mind, I'm very busy."

She minded. However, from the tone of the attorney's last
words, she knew she would learn no more from him today,
even though she was sure there was a lot more he could say.
She made her polite goodbyes and left.

The intense heat outside the air-conditioned building hit
her like a slap in the face. As she walked toward her car, she
heard a wolf whistle.

Once it would have annoyed her. Now she found she
could just ignore it, as she ignored most men. They seemed
all alike. It was almost impossible to tell the good guys from
the bad.

Yes, men could certainly be deceptive. Take that private
eye from San Francisco. He had seemed so cooperative and

understanding when he had helped to disperse the crowd at the accident scene. But later in her office when she had tried to get him to tell her what he knew about Joni Wilson, he had made her feel like a kitten chasing a string. A string he controlled.

What a frustrating man! She'd have the report on him from the San Francisco Police Department probably by tomorrow, and she was interested in seeing what it said. She could still feel the vibration of his voice down her spine.

She shook her head trying to dispel her disturbing thoughts. She wasn't a kid. In a couple of months she'd be thirty. She'd had a love affair, and it was more than enough for one lifetime. She had no desire to repeat the experience.

She had her work, which was enough. She liked it and she was good at it. And Joni Wilson's murder might prove to be an interesting case, after all. Could it be true that the woman had spent close to twenty-million dollars in two years?

As Sam drove back to her office, she recalled the scared look on the lawyer's face when she'd mentioned the secret safe in the deceased's car. Walter Chapell was hiding something. Something big, which might even be a motive for murder.

CHAPELL DIDN'T WAIT LONG after Sam left to pick up the phone. His fingers dialed nervously. As he listened to the rings, he removed his suit jacket. Even in the air-conditioned office, his shirt was wet with perspiration.

He counted six rings before a deep voice answered.

"We've got a problem," said Chapell.

"What do you mean?"

"The police know it's murder."

There was silence on the other end of the line.

"Did you hear me? The police know it's murder!"

"Cool it, Walter. That won't stop us. Maybe delay us a bit, but that's it."

Chapell licked his dry lips. "She had a secret safe. They found it."

"What?"

"It was in the car."

"Dammit! What was in it?"

"I don't know! I don't know!"

Chapter Four

"Scotty, she wasn't Jane Williams. She was Joni Wilson. I was right!"

As he listened to Warren, Scotty sat down on the bed in his hotel room and put his feet up. He had called his partner back just as soon as he had seen the blinking red light on the phone.

"How can you be sure?"

"Because I talked with Jane Williams this morning. The real Jane Williams!"

"Back up. Tell me from the beginning," Scotty said.

"Right. Well, the airlines verified that neither a Jane Williams nor a Joni Wilson flew out of San Francisco. So I ran down the gas-company lead as you suggested and, sure enough, I found Jane Williams's father."

"He's alive?"

"And kicking. Retired from the gas company a couple of years ago. He took me to see his daughter. Her name's Jane Schneider now. And both of her kids have inherited her red hair and tendency toward plumpness. She even showed me a copy of her birth certificate. The same one I got for that damned heiress. What a chump I was."

"So we know she wasn't *that* Jane Williams, at least," Scotty said.

"She isn't *any* Jane Williams. She was Joni Wilson. The moment I saw her picture on TV, I was sure of it!"

Scotty was still unconvinced. "Any picture you saw on that old, nineteen-inch, fuzzy-screen black-and-white TV set of yours can't be considered conclusive."

"I tell you, it was the same woman!"

Warren was adamant. And the evidence he had uncovered made Scotty admit his partner might just be right.

"Okay. I'll stay down here a few more days. See what I can find out."

"How did it go with the police?" Warren asked.

Scotty smiled as he thought of Samantha Turner.

"About what you'd expect. They weren't interested in giving information, only in getting it. I'm not giving up, though. If anyone contacts you, you know what to do."

"Right. I know nothing about nothing."

"Should do it. I did learn that the case is considered a homicide," Scotty said.

"Murdered? Damn. She was so young and beautiful. I hate this business."

"The business didn't kill her, Warren."

"But it's going to kill me, Scotty. It's different for you, being an ex-cop and all. You're used to this blood-and-guts stuff. Hell, you carry metal in your chest and a scar around it that's enough to give a makeup artist the shakes. Me, though, I'm an actor. Almost twenty-eight. My agent tells me time's awasting. I should be getting exposure, doing some TV spots. He has one lined up for me in two weeks. It's for a men's deodorant. I've got to take it."

Scotty shook his head. "Sometimes I wonder why you ever asked to be my partner."

"Unemployed actors have got to eat. Anyway, it's just not really me. You know that."

"Okay. I should be finished with this case by next week. Tell your agent you'll be there."

"Thanks, Scotty."

"Just don't let them see you sweat, Warren."

"Very funny. What's next?"

"Do you still have your contact in the mayor's office down here?" Scotty asked.

"Yeah. I have a favor or two coming. What do you need?"

"Three symphony tickets for tonight. Two of the best seats in the house and a third as close as you can to a reserved seat I'm going to give you."

"I guess I can swing it. What's up?"

"Let's just say a little night work. Have the tickets waiting for me at the box office. You may not hear from me again until tomorrow. I've got to move out of this hotel after tonight. It's too expensive for our bank account," Scotty said.

"Have you learned anything else about the case?"

"I've done some research. The Heritage Insurance Company holds a life-insurance policy on the deceased. I thought I'd pay them a visit and see if I can work a new angle."

"I WAS AN INSURANCE INVESTIGATOR for several years, Ms. Grenville. I have a sixth sense about this case. Something is different about the death of Joni Wilson."

"I appreciate your interest. But we do have investigators of our own."

Her words didn't cause Scotty concern. He liked the large, gray-haired woman who ran the Southern California branch of the Heritage Insurance Company. She had a no-nonsense way about her, and a warm, firm handshake.

"Yes, I do realize you employ your own investigators. I've spoken with a couple and found out you basically insure property in amounts of millions of dollars. A life-insurance policy of one hundred and fifty thousand dollars is generally not even considered substantial enough for special investigation. Generally you would rely on the police reports for your findings."

Ms. Grenville's eyes sparkled in speculation.

"Your information is correct. But what makes you think that the death of Miss Wilson might not qualify the beneficiary to receive the insurance? No claim has been made on the policy. There isn't even a double-indemnity clause. I see no indication that we are dealing with a person who has murdered someone for the money of a small life-insurance policy."

Scotty was not at all surprised to learn that Ms. Grenville had already heard the afternoon news, which revealed that Joni Wilson had been murdered. His earlier assessment of the vice president was that she kept on top of everything and was nobody's fool.

Still, her comment that a payoff of one hundred and fifty thousand dollars was a "small" life-insurance policy made him smile. He knew a lot of people would kill for a lot less. But of course, everything is relative.

"I have only vague suspicions concerning this matter. What I would like to propose is that I investigate the circumstances surrounding the woman's death as your authorized agent. If your company ends up paying the beneficiary, then you owe me nothing. However, if evidence I uncover results in your company not having to make the payoff, then I will take thirty percent as my fee."

Ms. Grenville leaned forward in the large leather chair. Her hazel eyes opened wide and stared straight at Scotty.

"That would cost me forty-five thousand!"

"That would save you one hundred and five thousand," Scotty replied.

She smiled ever so slightly. Scotty could feel her assessing him intently. "I think ten percent would be more than fair," she said finally.

"Certainly it would be for a larger payoff. But as you pointed out earlier, this is a relatively small amount," Scotty said.

Ms. Grenville did not give in so easily. "I could put one of my own investigators on the case."

"Yes. You could take them off their investigations of the theft of a million dollars in paintings and a quarter-million dollars in rare coins." He was well schooled in the art of polite negotiation. And he always practiced its basic tenet: Be prepared.

Ms. Grenville's thick eyebrows lifted in appreciation. She almost smiled as she leaned back in her leather chair.

"You've done your homework. I'll give you twenty percent. That's thirty thousand dollars. But I'll have to have proof that whatever you uncover to substantiate nonpayment was obtained solely through your own efforts. If the police investigation removes my company's financial responsibility, you will receive nothing. Is that agreed?"

"Yes, that's agreed."

Since he knew he was going to investigate anyway, he would have settled for the ten percent. However, there was no reason to take the smaller amount if the larger one was possible, and he knew from the beginning it was. Of course, he had no real reason to suspect that the beneficiary to the small policy had killed the Wilson woman. Only an uneasiness about the murder.

"I'll have my secretary draw up a contract," Ms. Grenville said, reaching for the intercom button. "But I feel I need to warn you...."

"Warn me?" Scott asked, somewhat surprised.

"I know the sergeant—a detective—who has been assigned to this case. A good, tough, thorough investigator. I've worked with her before. She got my company off the hook and didn't give a second thought about anybody who got hurt in the process. And I mean anybody."

Scotty wondered if Ms. Grenville was referring to Detective Sergeant Samantha Turner. His interest was aroused.

"What was it all about?" he asked.

"Ask me another time. My next appointment is here. Just remember, I warned you. What else will you need?"

"An authorization from Heritage Insurance Company stating that I am your representative in this matter and a complete copy of the policy and file notes made by the underwriter.''

"I'll have the information for you within an hour. You may wait in the reception area.''

Scotty rose and walked toward the door of the office. Ms. Grenville's next words stopped him.

"Satisfy my curiosity. How did you find out about our life-insurance policy on the deceased?''

Scotty stopped in his process of opening the door and turned to face the scrutiny in her eyes.

"I didn't know whether there was one. So I just kept calling insurance companies and advising them I was the beneficiary on a policy for Joni Wilson until your company informed me my name was not on the policy. Which told me, of course, that you had a policy.''

Ms. Grenville shook her head. "A little logic and a little luck,'' she said.

"Most investigative work is, don't you think?''

She nodded.

"Now, satisfy my curiosity,'' Scotty said. "Why did you write a life-insurance policy for Joni Wilson when life insurance has never been considered a profitable line for your company?'' Scotty asked.

"Her jewelry was insured with us. So we wrote the other policy as a courtesy when she expressed the desire for one about a year and a half ago. That was before she decided to sell off her jewelry. Now all we have left is the life-insurance policy.''

"She sold off all her jewelry?''

"A few months ago.''

"I . . . see,'' Scotty said, not really seeing at all.

Chapter Five

"I've been trying to find you, Sarge."

"I've been working on getting the telephone company served with a subpoena, so that they'll have to give me the records of all the telephone calls of the Wilson woman during the past six months."

"Well, I've got some good news and lots of bad. Which do you want first?" the plainclothes officer asked Sam.

"The good news, please. Might help to ease me into the bad," Sam answered.

"Okay. Here goes. I've talked with the housekeeper, Isabel Kane. She's a live-in on the Wilson estate. She'll get you a key and be available whenever you are." The officer paused.

"That was short and sweet," Sam said. "Are you telling me that's the extent of the good news?"

"Afraid so. We're having trouble reaching any of the people on this list you gave us. It's tough to get their statements when we can't even get in contact with them."

Sam looked over the list and sighed. "Still no sign of this second cousin, Peter Taswell?"

"None. The Kane woman hasn't seen him. The airports, trains and bus stations are all covered. No sign of him yet."

"You've tried Colin North at his various hot-dog franchises?"

"No. We've only tried him at his regular office number. They just say he's not in and they don't know when he'll be back," the officer said.

"His home number?" Sam asked.

"It's been busy the two times I've called."

"I don't think his wife works, so there's no lead there. We've got to get hold of them both. All I can suggest is to keep trying his home and office and start trying at his other franchises."

"What about the others on the list?" the officer said.

"Joni Wilson's lover, Monty Larkin, was supposed to have a room at the Beverly Hilton. What did they say when you called?" Sam asked.

"They told me he wasn't registered."

"Maybe our information was wrong, or out-of-date. Try the other major hotels, and call the Hilton again to see if he was ever there. If so, see if he left a forwarding address."

"Right."

"This is Friday. We should be able to catch Julian Harris and Rebecca Myers at Hollywood Savings and Loan where they both work. What's been the hang-up there?" Sam asked.

"Rebecca Myers is in a meeting all day. I've left a message for her to call. But Julian Harris's secretary won't say where he is. She's real uncooperative and doesn't even seem to want to take a message."

Sam paused to consider. "It sounds like we're being given the runaround by these people. Sort of makes you wonder what they've got to hide, doesn't it?"

FOR THE FIRST TIME in the six years since he had given up the habit, Julian Harris wished he had a cigarette. He sat in his spacious office of elegant wood and glass, drumming his short fingers on the polished beauty of his mahogany desk and wearing a deep frown on his weathered face.

He was small in stature—only five foot five. And, at forty-four, he was having difficulty keeping his waistline

down. The desserts had gone first. Then the French bread
and butter. And now when he visited the L.A. Athletic Club
for a workout and lunch, his waiter automatically brought
him the American Heart Association's feature for the day.

His light brown hair had never been thick, and his hair
stylist had suggested on his last visit that he might like to
invest in a hairpiece before the baldness became too notice-
able.

These were his constant worries. The ones he woke up
with, carried around all day and took to bed at night. But
they all faded into the background when viewed in the light
of this morning's news.

The plan had appeared sound. Except it wasn't supposed
to have happened this way. Something had gone wrong. Seriously wrong.

Of course, there was no question of pulling out. He was
in deep. Two million deep. And it was safe, as long as he
kept his head.

But unfortunately, success depended on people other than
himself keeping cool. Doing and saying the right thing.
And, as soon as the news got out he knew—

His intercom buzzed.

"Yes?"

"Colin North is on line one, Mr. Harris. I know you
asked not to be disturbed, but he says it's urgent."

"Put him on."

He heard a click on the line and then Colin's excited voice
booming in his ear before he even had a chance to say hello.

"That radio news is saying it's murder!"

"Yes, I heard. A friend at the police station called me as
soon as the story was released to the press. This makes
things a little more complicated," Julian said.

"A little more complicated? Get real, man. They say it's
murder! Don't you realize what's happened?"

Julian moved the receiver farther away from his ear.

"Dammit, Colin. You don't have to shatter my eardrum.
I know this is serious. I've been sitting here for the past half

hour trying to understand what went wrong. The only thing that's clear is that we probably won't get an explanation right away. In the meantime, we've got to protect ourselves."

"Protect ourselves? What do you mean?"

"Well, think it through. A murder has been committed. The police are bound to suspect friends and relatives first. Do you have an alibi for last night?"

Colin paused only slightly before answering.

"Hell, I don't think so. Claire and I just spent the night at home. I had some stomach upset and didn't feel much like going out. We watched television until eleven, then went to bed."

"Both of you? You were together?" Julian asked.

"Yeah. We were together."

"Then you can alibi each other."

Julian was relieved. He didn't want the Norths suspected. Neither of them could hold their own under a solid questioning, particularly Claire.

"And you?" Colin asked.

"No problem. Rebecca and I had dinner and watched a show at a local comedy club. We were there from about eight-thirty until a little after ten. Then we drove to Rebecca's and I spent the night. Didn't leave until seven this morning."

"Then we just need to check with Monty," Colin said.

"It depends on when the murder happened. Monty came by Rebecca's last night and crashed on the couch. I'll call him now. Have the police tried to get in touch with you?"

"I'm not sure. I'm home with Claire. We were on the phone trying to reach Rebecca before I called you. Would they try so early? I mean it's only just been discovered Joni's been murdered."

"I would say they are past due. My secretary has already intercepted a call. Look, you and Claire get out of the house and go somewhere the police can't find you. We'll all meet tonight at my house in Malibu around eight to get our stories straight. It's important none of us talk with the police until then. Is that understood?'' Julian asked.

"Yeah. But until we're sure of when the police believe the murder happened, how can we be sure our alibis are for the right time?''

"Let Monty and me work on that. We both know enough people in the right places to keep this thing in hand. You and Claire just work on keeping out of sight.''

"Okay. But this all seems so wrong. How could it be murder, Julian?''

"Don't give me that innocent act. You know damn well how it could be murder!''

Chapter Six

Isabel Kane finished her vacuuming and dusting, and neatly put away the implements of her work. Then she laid her head on her arms on the kitchen table and burst into tears. Now that the shock had worn off, she could hold back no longer.

The doorbell rang. Maybe it had rung before. The other servants were gone now, for the mistress of the house had dismissed them all gradually, over the past year or so. Isabel and the weekly gardener were all who remained. Was that another bell? She had to get up. Life had to go on. Somehow. She went to the door.

"Hi, Isabel. It's just me. I thought I'd best come by to pick up some of my things I left in the guest room before the police start snooping around about Joni's accident."

He was in his middle thirties, six two, blond, broad shouldered, narrow hipped—a well-kept body with a curiously youthful, unlined face. Even the tiny frown now puckering his forehead would smooth out as soon as the emotions generating it dissipated. A mere ripple over a placid lake, as if nothing would ever make a lasting impression on its calm surface.

Isabel stepped aside to let Monty Larkin enter.

Monty had always liked the housekeeper who doted on Joni so much. He could see from her current appearance that he must have caught her crying. Poor thing. He knew she had taken care of Joni ever since Joni's mother had died.

Old servants devoted to a family were a dying breed. His mother still had one. The aging Carson, the butler. He'd give his life rather than let someone get past him who Monty's mother didn't want to see.

Monty made his way up the stairs to the second-floor guest bedroom where he had left a few of his things for the nights he had stayed over with Joni. Of course, they had shared her bed, but she was funny about anyone using her dresser or closet. Made him wonder what she kept there that was so secret. She always insisted he put his things in the adjoining room.

After carefully placing his cigar on the edge of the dresser, he took his overnight case from the bottom of the closet and began to remove his shirts from the hangers and stuff them into the bag. His maid would sort the things out later and iron what had gotten wrinkled.

He stopped packing for a minute when his eye caught Joni's framed picture on the bedside table. He reached over to pick it up.

It was a good likeness. The deep gold of her skin contrasting with the light blue of her eyes. He had taken the photo when they were at his small, rented beach house in Malibu. She had stepped onto the deck to breathe in the ocean air after one of their long nights of making love.

Monty frowned and put the picture facedown on the table. Really a shame what happened. He was sure he would have been the one to land the elusive Joni Wilson.

He and his mother had carefully studied her previous suitors, those who'd had any staying power. They had all been handsome and in good physical condition, like himself. But unlike him, they weren't from good families. And although Joni's mother's family was acceptable, she could hardly have expected much, considering her father's lineage. . . .

That would have made the difference. But obviously now, marriage was out. Which was okay, if the other went well. The odds were in his favor for after all, he had the knowledge....

When he looked up from his packing, Monty saw the figure leaning against the doorjamb. "Peter! Well, this is a nice surprise. I didn't know you'd be here," he said.

Peter Taswell's tanned, slim body was poised stiffly like a snake ready to strike.

"Is it a surprise, Monty? Why should you think that, you hypocrite?"

The smile vanished off Monty's face. The placid lake was back.

"Don't be a twit, Peter. We can behave in a civilized manner or not at all. Now which is it?"

Monty finished collecting his things as though he didn't care how Peter answered the question.

The hissing voice resumed, full of venom.

"It was you who tried to cut me out and get it all. Pretending to be my best friend when all the while you were waiting for an introduction to my wealthy cousin."

Monty's face started to turn a sickly white beneath the tan. His lips pressed into a straight line. He attempted to close the too-full suitcase with shaking hands. The shirtsleeves hanging over the edges impeded his hasty efforts.

"Well, it didn't work, you leech," Peter continued. "She's dead. I've made sure of that. And now it's all mine, including this house. So, get the hell out of here before I call the cops!"

Since Monty wasn't having any success closing the suitcase, he just pressed the two ends together and secured it underneath his left arm in frustration. He strode angrily toward the door and pushed aside the much smaller man with a powerful swing of his right arm.

Monty descended the stairs quickly, slamming his way to the front door, only then becoming aware of the man in gardening clothes who had probably heard some of his exchange with Taswell and was now witnessing his hasty retreat.

At the front door, he turned to face Peter, who was still standing on the landing, rubbing his shoulder where Monty had shoved him aside.

Monty's voice boomed like a rifle shot in the quiet house. "So you want to take credit for fixing it? So you've got it all, huh? What a laugh. Take inventory, you pathetic fool. What she left isn't worth my time."

Chapter Seven

A white Porsche was squealing toward the exit side of the circular drive when Sam started into the entrance to the Beverly Hills estate of the deceased Joni Wilson. She caught a glimpse of its license and quickly wrote down the plate number. She'd check it out later. Watching the Porsche's trail of exhaust made her feel even hotter, like being wrapped in a suffocating blanket. She felt glued to the cheap, vinyl seat.

A day that had started out badly seemed to be getting worse. She was particularly frustrated at not being able to locate Peter Taswell. That and the coincidental unavailability of all of the deceased's friends.

But it was Taswell's disappearance that really bothered her. Since his unannounced visit to Chapell that morning, the man seemed to have vanished. Still, Sam didn't think he had left L.A. yet.

A mildly attractive woman in her mid-forties with dark brown hair and blue eyes, quite red from recent tears, opened the door before Sam reached the top step. The clue to her identity was the white apron she wore. When Sam presented her badge, the woman said, "I'm Isabel Kane, the housekeeper. A man called to say you were coming. Please come in."

A blast of air-conditioning washed Sam's face as she crossed the threshold. She drank it in greedily. Momentarily blinded from the change in bright sunlight to the subtle glow of the entry, she immediately removed her sunglasses.

The large, marble-floored entry hall was backed with a sweep of stairs rising to the second story. Nearly every wall Sam could see was paneled in expensive, gleaming wood.

But she wasn't here to look at the premises. Police officers had already searched the home for clues to the death of its mistress. No items that surfaced had shed light on a suspect or motive for the murder.

Sam's mind quickly replayed the inventory.

A man had been occupying the guest bedroom next to the deceased's, or at least his clothing had been. He had probably been Joni Wilson's lover. His fingerprints were being checked, but Sam suspected they belonged to Monty Larkin.

She was still awaiting a complete report on Larkin. All she knew so far was that he was purported to be a blue blood from Boston.

Joni Wilson's closets were curiously sparse for a socialite, in Sam's estimation. No more than thirty outfits had been found, six pairs of high heels and one pair of slippers. It was possible that Miss Wilson's financial difficulties had caused her to cut down on spending, but one would think she would have collected more than thirty outfits in her twenty-four years as an heiress.

A crumpled dentist's receipt from a few months earlier was found in the back of a desk drawer in the library. Sam had noticed he was a different dentist than the one from the black address book, found in the secret car safe, who had verified the X rays taken of the deceased's mouth matched those of Joni Wilson. But since the dentist listed in the address book had made a positive identification, there was no reason to contact the second one.

The contents of a wall safe showed the charges for paste jewelry, copies of the fine pieces that used to be owned by the deceased, but that seemed to have been recently sold.

Receipts for the copying and selling of some fine paintings were also there.

But the bills for the paste jewelry were all dated within the past two years. As were the bills for copying some of the fine paintings. Had Joni Wilson sold off the original jewelry and paintings in her overspending?

The safe-deposit box key at the bank had yielded Joni Wilson's birth certificate and school records. The copies of the fine paintings had been accounted for on the walls of the deceased's home. But so far, the paste replicas of her jewelry were missing.

The telephone company hadn't gotten back yet with the records Sam had subpoenaed. Some plainclothes officers were checking on Chapell's alibi, and that information would be available later in the day. So, at the moment, only the housekeeper was on hand for an interview.

"Did my office explain about my needing a duplicate key to the house?"

Isabel Kane reached into her apron and handed Sam the key as her answer.

"May we talk for a few moments?" Sam asked.

The housekeeper looked a little surprised. "Yes, of course. But I assumed you came here to speak to Mr. Taswell?"

It was Sam's turn to look surprised. "He's here?"

"Oh, yes. Showed up right after I got the call from your office. I thought you knew. You'll find him in the library, Sergeant."

Sam hesitated a moment. She needed to talk with them both, but whereas she could probably count on Isabel Kane's staying put, she had no idea what Taswell's plans might be. It would be prudent to see him first.

"Thank you. I'll see Mr. Taswell now. But I want to speak with you, too. You'll be available later?"

"Yes, ma'am. I'll show you to the library."

Sam clenched her teeth. She hated being called ma'am. She couldn't say specifically why. But it always made her feel like an old Southern matriarch in a decrepit, crumbling plantation.

She found Peter Taswell going through Joni Wilson's desk.

Her first impression was that he was exceedingly thin and impeccably groomed. His meticulously styled, straight, dark brown hair was quite full and free of gray strands. His deeply tanned skin indicated a life of leisure. A thick gold chain, flashing beneath the open collar of his beige shirt, matched the gold watch and rings he wore.

He was frowning in obvious frustration, adding to an already well-lined face. His expression remained unchanged as Isabel announced Sam. When he spoke, it was after Isabel had left the room and apparently to himself.

"You realize all of the finer paintings are missing? They've been replaced with copies. The housekeeper says Joni removed them. I don't believe it. What reason would she have? Something's wrong—someone's been here before me. I've been robbed!"

Sam was surprised at Taswell's high voice. She also wondered whether the man had even heard Isabel announce her.

"Mr. Taswell, I would like to talk with you...."

"Police detective?" Taswell looked up, finally acknowledging her business.

"Yes. I'm investigating the death of Joni Wilson."

He immediately resumed his search through the deceased's desk.

"What's there to investigate? She drove off a cliff. She never could hold her liquor."

Sam realized that here was another person who would not mourn the death of the heiress. "Miss Wilson's death," Sam said, "was not accidental. It appears her car was pushed off the road into a ravine and deliberately set on fire."

Taswell looked up, and Sam saw the blood drain out of the tanned face. His expression had turned to stone. She watched, not sure whether the shock was real or rehearsed. Her gut feeling was that it was real. But if so, was it shock at his cousin's being murdered, or was it shock at the police's discovering it was murder and not an accident? She'd reserve judgment for the moment.

"I understand you are the sole heir to your cousin's estate?"

Peter Taswell came back to life. He stood and backed away from the desk, away from Sam. His expression was that of a cornered bird being stalked by a hungry cat.

"I want my lawyer."

Sam wasn't surprised. Whether he was innocent or guilty, Taswell's position was precarious.

"I assure you, these questions are only routine. You have not been charged with anything."

Taswell wasn't buying it. He could almost hear the word "yet" at the end of her sentence. His body went rigid and his hands balled into fists by his side. "I tell you I refuse to talk without my lawyer. I want my lawyer!"

Sam wished she had gotten a few questions in before Taswell had yelled for a lawyer. She had probably come on too strong. Her interview with Isabel Kane would have to wait. It was time again for the nice police-officer tone.

"Very well. Why don't you call your lawyer now? Then we'll go down to the station and wait until he arrives?"

"You'll get nothing out of me!" Taswell shrieked.

"IT HAPPENED about three years ago, Mr. Lawrence," Ms. Grenville was saying on the phone. "My company was paying off after investigating a fire that had destroyed a large warehouse complex on the fringes of the industrial section. All evidence pointed to carelessness as the cause—a lighted cigarette thrown away, which ignited some empty cardboard boxes and ended up burning down several structures."

"Did you have an idea who was responsible?" Scotty asked.

"No, not really. We thought maybe some loitering teenagers or even the night watchman. But we had no proof."

Scotty lay back on the pillow of the motel's bed considering Ms. Grenville's information. With the receiver of the telephone in one hand, he positioned his other hand behind his head. He could anticipate what she was going to say next.

"No proof, that is, until Detective Turner entered the case?" he asked.

"Right. She had evidence that the owner of the warehouse had paid off the night watchman. He was told to throw the cigarette and start the fire, then to delay reporting the blaze to the fire department until he knew the buildings would be a total loss. Detective Turner advised us to hold off payment until she could get an indictment against the owner and his accomplices for arson."

"And she did?" Scotty asked.

"Oh, yes. Both the owner and his son were in on that scam and several others. The night watchman turned state's evidence and the Grand Jury indicted them both. Unfortunately an expensive lawyer got them off with fairly light sentences. But at least Detective Turner saved my company a considerable amount of money."

"You said in your office earlier that Turner didn't care who got hurt? What did you mean?"

"She was engaged to the owner's son."

Ms. Grenville's information took Scotty by surprise. He tried to imagine what it had been like for Samantha Turner to turn in her fiancé. He suddenly had a vivid image of her look of determination when she refused to be blackmailed into giving him information. Ms. Grenville's words interrupted his thoughts.

"Yes, he was her fiancé. And don't think they didn't try to use that on her. Their expensive lawyer tried to break her down on the stand. The cross-examination dragged on for two days, but she held firm. Ms. Turner's a tough cookie, and an honest one. Frankly I was surprised to find someone her age with such a strong backbone. I thought that kind of character and guts went out with women of my generation."

"Why do you say that?"

"Well, when I was growing up, there were high moral standards being set. Theft was wrong no matter who was the thief or victim. But look at television and the movies today. They're making heroes and heroines out of the people who bilk insurance companies, banks, all institutions. Young people aren't learning to respect the property of others. A rip-off is being presented as smart, funny, acceptable. The only crime is being caught."

"There's truth in what you say. But do you really think this Samantha Turner is any different? Maybe she got a promotion out of the bust, or she just decided her career was more important than the guy," Scotty said.

"No. That reasoning doesn't make sense. Her fiancé's family was financially and politically strong. My guess is that her career could have been helped a lot more if she'd kept her mouth shut. Besides, her promotion didn't come till two years later. I doubt it was based on that case at all."

Scotty was silent for several moments as he digested the information.

"Your curiosity satisfied?" Ms. Grenville asked finally.

"Yes, thanks."

"Don't mention it. But remember, this lady has a strong sense of right and wrong. Violate it and you're dead meat as far as she is concerned."

Chapter Eight

She was bench pressing, exerting smooth, even pressure. A flawless form. The perspiration glowing on her golden skin.

But Scotty saw much more. The determined chin. The alert flash of the silvery eyes. Despite her obvious concentration, she kept aware of her surroundings. On guard.

There were other women in the gym wearing skimpy exercise outfits and flirting with the guys. But not Sam. She wore nondescript gray sweats and worked out over in a corner away from the mirrors. She wasn't there to watch her body or to show it off to others. She meant business.

As he stared at her from the shadows, Scotty felt both excited at seeing her again and uneasy at how she might respond to seeing him. She wasn't stupid and would know his showing up at her gym wasn't just coincidence. But she'd probably have no idea how much the top of her desk told him: the ticket to the symphony, her desk calendar marked with "gym." It hadn't been difficult to find the one the cops in the district frequented.

She was someone he wanted to get to know. Naturally it would be important to his investigation to have her cooperation, but he knew it was more than that.

"Really beautiful!" The words had come unchecked from his lips.

"Yes, she is. But if I were you, I'd forget it. That woman is here for the exercise only."

Scotty started, unaware that Phil, the gym manager, had been so close. Then he just looked at him and smiled. "I appreciate your bending the rules to let me in. Don't worry, I'm not here to make any trouble."

Phil took Scotty's assurance with a shrug and walked away. Finally Scotty got his chance. The bodybuilder to her right headed for the showers.

A minute later Sam became aware of the stranger moving beside her. Unlike most of the bodybuilders, he wore full sweats. Baggy ones at that. She found it hard to tell from her peripheral vision what the physique was like beneath the dark blue material.

His face was away from hers, but she could see his head over the curve of his back as he worked to adjust his weights. He had straight, sandy hair. A flash of sudden recognition brought her up to a sitting position.

"Scott Lawrence!"

He turned to her and smiled. "Hi. Glad you remembered my name. This bench press taken?"

Sam shook her head at the lightness in his tone, the flash of mischief in his eyes. She was both happy and annoyed at seeing him. He was obviously following her and trying to get her to collaborate on the case. She decided the best thing she could do was to ignore him, or at least try to. She lay down again.

From the corner of her eye, she watched him settle himself in preparation for a press. But she soon found she couldn't remain silent. He had overloaded his weights to the left and was about to be in a lot of trouble.

She leaned over. "Excuse me, but I think you might have a problem lifting your bar unless you rebalance your weight."

Scotty looked at the bar before him with mock seriousness. "I don't know, Sam. It looks okay to me. Of course, if you're sure I can't lift it, perhaps you'd be open to a small wager?"

He had called her by her first name, her nickname at that, and his manner was just as informal. His tone held a slight challenge. Sam tried to keep the smile off her face. "How small?"

"How about a walk on the beach. At midnight?"

It wasn't the bet Sam thought he was going to make. She had expected him to pursue the Wilson case. She wasn't disappointed, however.

"And if I win?"

"Then I owe you an ice cream after the workout."

The wager certainly seemed to be harmless. What could she lose? She got up and made a big show of examining the unbalanced weights, noticing as she did so the smile playing on his lips. It didn't look possible that he could lift the weights, but Sam wasn't going to underestimate this man. Still, even if she lost, his company on a moonlit walk along the beach wouldn't be hard to take.

"Okay. You're on."

Sam reached out her hand to shake on the bet. Scotty grasped it warmly and held it for a moment. Sam felt the warmth right down to her toes. She told herself it was just excitement over the bet.

Scotty abruptly became all business. His eyes closed in a moment of concentration. His hands addressed the bar. Then, to Sam's surprise and embarrassment, she watched him lift the unbalanced weight without the least bit of difficulty.

He was grinning at her shamelessly. She shook her head remorsefully. He had done it again—dangled a string in front of her and she had jumped at it. Why couldn't she be angry with him?

Then, as if to add insult to injury, he put more weight on the left and half as much on the right and lifted again. Next he turned completely around and began lifting with his feet the same bar he had been lifting with his hands.

For the fifteen minutes of workout she had left, Sam found herself absorbed and fascinated by the unusual and

somewhat absurd positioning of the man beside her. She
didn't even attempt any further bench pressing herself, so
totally entertained was she by his antics.

When he finally quit, he turned to her. His hair hung
damply about his face. Perspiration had seeped through his
warm-up suit. He was drying his forehead and neck with a
towel.

"Just to show you I'm a good winner, I'm still going to
buy you that ice-cream cone."

Sam looked purposefully at her watch. She really wasn't
sure it was such a good idea to get too friendly with this
tricky private eye. "No thanks. I didn't realize how late it
was getting. I have an appointment."

He got up leisurely and started to walk with her toward
the showers.

"I'll come with you on your appointment. We can go for
the ice cream afterward."

"No. Wouldn't work out. The appointment is police
business. I'm not sure how long it will take. And I have
plans for this evening."

"Are you sure I can't change your mind?"

His gray eyes caressed her face. She was tempted to say
yes. She was also a little surprised and disappointed he
hadn't mentioned the midnight walk on the beach again.
After all, she had lost the bet.

"No. Got to attend to business."

Sam wasn't concentrating on where she was going. She
was just walking alongside Scotty thinking about how nice
it would be to go get an ice cream with this attractive man.
To forget about her appointment with Isabel Kane. To forget about the Wilson murder.

"Sam? I think we should part company now. That is, if
we're to leave this club with a good name."

Sam looked up at Scotty's words and saw the laughter in
his eyes. Then she read the sign on the door in front of her:
Men's Showers.

He had done it to her again. He knew that she was going the wrong way, but he waited until the last possible minute to stop her. The last possible, embarrassing minute.

Yet, strangely, Sam didn't feel embarrassed. The laughter gurgled in her throat as she said, "So good of you to tell me before we started to dry off with the same towel!"

"I hope you would have noticed on your own by then!"

Scotty's smile was infectious. His laughter joined with hers. She decided she'd better retrace her steps and get away from this intriguing man while she still could. But as she turned the corner to the women's showers, she ran into the gym manager.

"You okay, Sam?" Phil said. "You look a little funny. Was Scotty bothering you?"

Sam was a little surprised. Since the private investigator was from out of town, she hadn't expected anyone to know him. "You know Scott Lawrence?"

"Scotty? Sure. It's been a while though. This isn't his turf. Come to think of it, I'm not even sure what he's doing in the neighborhood. But he's okay, Sam. Used to be a cop."

"A cop?"

"Yeah. Damn good one up in San Francisco five or six years ago. Till he got shot up. I mean really bad. Machine gunned by some heavy-duty drug pushers. Can't remember all the particulars, but the force gave him a medical discharge."

Sam thought she was beginning to understand the workout she had watched with such fascination.

"That might explain the odd balancing of his weights," she said aloud.

"I wasn't watching his workout. But from what I heard about his injuries, the guy shouldn't even be walking around, much less lifting weights. Why all the interest, Sammy? You want me to introduce you or something?"

"Not necessary, Phil. I know the man. At least, I think I'm getting to."

Sam said goodbye to Phil and went in to shower. So Scott Lawrence used to be a cop; now he was a private investigator. And he had something to do with Joni Wilson.

Damn. She was tempted to exchange information with him if only to hear what he had to say about the dead heiress. He wouldn't be down here on a whim and following her if it wasn't important. Unless his interest in her wasn't purely professional? She wanted to believe that might be true. But she knew better.

As the hot water beat against her skin, her thoughts were replaced with business as she once again felt the confusion of the Wilson case build up like the steam around her. She had been able to forget the murder for only a short while. Now it once again demanded her attention.

Peter Taswell was a good suspect. Maybe too good. If Joni's inheritance had still been intact, she might not feel so reticent about going after him. But since most of the money was gone, too many questions remained to make his arrest a simple move. At least as far as she was concerned.

She kept coming back to the money. How could an heiress squander twenty million dollars in less than two years?

Maybe if she could understand what Joni Wilson had been like—the type of family she came from, her strengths and weaknesses, whom she cared about and hated—she could find out who the murderer was. The person who had hated her enough to pour gasoline over her and light a match.

Despite the hot water beating down on her body, Sam shivered.

Chapter Nine

"I'm . . . sorry." That was Isabel's only response to every question Sam asked about Joni and the night of her death. The woman didn't seem to be able to control her grief.

Sam realized she would have to lead up more gently to the questions that had to be asked and answered. Perhaps a more general approach. "Tell me about the Wilson family."

Isabel fought to regain some composure. "There were just the three of them. Greg Wilson, his wife Debbie, and their daughter, Joni," she said, drying her eyes.

"Did you like working for the Wilsons?"

"Debbie Wilson was pregnant with Joni at the same time I was pregnant with Jessica, my daughter. I had just turned seventeen and Debbie was twenty. It helped so much to be able to share it all with someone who could understand! And Debbie was so sweet. In those nine months we became close. Very close."

"You came to work in the Wilson household when you were only seventeen?" Sam asked.

"I was sixteen. My family was dead. I had no relatives. Debbie took me in."

"You weren't married when you were expecting your daughter?"

"I've never been married."

Isabel held her head high with dignity. Sam found herself liking the housekeeper—and the rich, young woman who had taken her in. Apparently Debbie Wilson must have realized the young girl was in trouble and offered her a home and job so she could have her baby and take care of it. Not many people would have been so kind. No wonder Isabel Kane spoke of her with such genuine affection.

"What was Gregory Wilson like?"

Isabel's dignity became tinged suddenly with anger.

"He never understood. He'd yell at Debbie to stop spending so much time with me. Over and over he'd say things like: 'She's just a servant. An obstinate girl.' He was always so angry."

"How would Debbie respond?"

Isabel smiled.

"She never paid him any attention, never talked back. She'd just pretend she hadn't heard him. It was her way. She probably realized it infuriated him more."

"And, after your babies were born?" Sam asked.

"Jessica came first. I was so afraid, but Debbie was at my side every minute and helped me through. She was so good. Then two weeks later, it was Joni's time to be born."

Isabel sighed. For a moment Sam thought she would need more prompting. But then the housekeeper continued. "Debbie wasn't strong. Her labor went on for three days. I was afraid she'd die, but somehow she made it. And little Joni came yelling into the world, a healthy baby girl in contrast to her spent mother.

"I was the one to take care of the two babies. Debbie was too weak, and the doctors kept her in the hospital for a month. When she came home, she hardly even got out of bed. She was always so tired."

"What was Greg Wilson's reaction to the birth of his child?"

There was no mistaking the hatred in Isabel's face.

"Debbie had disappointed him. She'd had a girl, and she had proved to be a weakling. He didn't seem to care any longer that she spent time with me, didn't seem to care about Debbie at all. Didn't even want to see his child. But at least he left us alone and stopped talking about sending me and my daughter away. He only started to be civil to Joni when she grew up."

"Why the change?"

"Joni grew up clever and pretty. His friends admired her. So he decided to claim her after all."

"And Debbie?" Sam asked.

The hatred in Isabel's face melted into sadness.

"Her strength never came back. She was never able to resume a normal life. Debbie hung on only for Joni's sake for almost a year after she was born. In the last month, when she knew the end was near, her biggest concern was that Joni be protected from her father."

"Protected?"

"Yes. Debbie left all her money to her daughter. Debbie had most of it, you know. She told me that was the only reason Greg married her. She fixed it so he'd never get it. Her lawyers put it in trust for Joni when she became twenty-one. She provided for me and Jessica, but Greg Wilson got none of it. Not that he really needed it—he had quite a bit of money of his own—not her millions, but some."

Isabel looked almost defiant.

"So Debbie provided for you and your child?"

The housekeeper nodded.

"All she asked me to do was to promise to take care of Joni, and not to let any harm come to her."

Isabel's eyes began to silently fill again with tears. Her anguished face drew closer to Sam's. "You must understand. It was a deathbed pledge. I promised my dying friend. I promised! Oh, dear God, please forgive me!"

Chapter Ten

Colin North stretched his long legs out in front of him and began to sip his second drink. He had no tolerance for late people. He and Claire had had the courtesy to arrive on time. And now they and everyone else were being held up because Julian's girlfriend couldn't get it together.

Finally the doorbell rang, and she made her appearance.

"Aren't we going to wait for Chapell? Didn't you decide to invite him?" Rebecca Myers asked of their host, Julian Harris, as he led her to the others and motioned her to a seat.

"No. He said he'd already talked with the police. Besides he had some business to attend to and couldn't break away," Julian replied.

Monty Larkin was pacing in obvious agitation.

"So do I. This better not take long. Damn. I still don't believe it! How could it have been murder?"

"You rehearsing for the police, Monty dearest?"

Colin could tell Rebecca's question was playful, rather than sarcastic. She was looking at the tall blond man with pleasure and approval. And he knew Monty did not mistake the look.

Julian had just finished drawing the draperies for privacy. Colin saw him catch Monty smiling at Rebecca and noticed the instant frown that dressed his face. Monty looked over at Julian and began to pace again.

Tension was mounting. Colin watched in disgust as the pacing man flicked his cigar ashes on the white carpet of Julian's Malibu beach home.

"Use the ashtray, Monty. And sit down! We can get this over quickly if everybody just cooperates," Julian said.

The handsome blond man smiled good-naturedly. He bowed his head toward Julian and sat down in deference to the short man's demand, an act that made Julian look and feel even shorter. It wasn't the first time Colin had witnessed such a scene.

From the moment Joni had introduced Monty to the rest of them, Julian and he had disliked each other. At first Colin couldn't understand why such animosity had arisen between the two men. Monty had been helpful to them all, seemed more than willing to introduce them to the social circles and contacts he had in abundance. And he always displayed such cool, unruffled charm.

But it was apparently this easy charm that most grated on Julian's nerves. He considered himself a man of wit and intelligence. He had always seen Monty as an empty-headed, body-beautiful character who lacked brains, talent and drive, but one who seemed to be able to attract any woman he wanted without difficulty. Something the short, balding Julian felt ill-equipped for. Particularly now that Joni was missing from the picture. And Monty was smiling at Rebecca.

Colin, however, had a different impression of Monty. There was a cleverness in the way he handled Julian. Something that belied the lazy look in his eyes and the easy smile. Also, there was the fact that Joni had selected him and Joni didn't like stupid men. Of course, if she hadn't planned on keeping him around, she might have just been satisfying a physical desire.

It had always been so hard to tell with Joni. Out of all of Claire's friends, whom he had inherited with his marriage, Joni had been the biggest enigma of all. An extremely intelligent, beautiful woman who could be both incredibly charming and incredibly cruel. She was the most exciting woman Colin had ever met.

It was being caught up in that excitement that had caused him trouble, however. Big trouble. He should have said no. But he didn't. And now, he had to get the money back. No matter what it took. No matter who stood in the way.

Julian returned to the center of the room from the now darkened windows. Rebecca leaned over to turn on a lamp next to the sectional where they were all sitting.

"We're bound to be questioned by the police," said Julian. "I think we all need to be clear on what we are going to say."

"They already questioned Chapell and Peter," Claire said. "And they made Peter go downtown."

Colin heard the anxiety. It was riding her voice, whipping it into jumping imagined hurdles. Her face was becoming almost as red as her hair—partly from alcohol and partly from emotion. She was disarmingly fragile, a trait that had drawn him to Claire in the first place. It made him feel so strong. Little had he known what strength she could exert on him. He looked at the pale blue eyes now and smiled.

"Nothing to worry about, darling. All we have to do is plan our strategy," he said.

"Right," said Julian. "Continue to be a well-functioning team, just like we were when Joni was with us. That's why I insisted we get together tonight."

Claire leaned back in her chair and picked up her drink, quiet now, if not entirely at ease.

Julian kept his standing position to maintain his authority. Colin knew he probably enjoyed seeing the tops of people's heads for a change instead of the bottoms of their chins.

"When we're approached for questioning, we must not say anything unless our lawyers are present. Now, except for Colin and Claire, each of us has a different lawyer. That's good. Doesn't tie any of us together too closely."

Julian took a last swallow of his drink and headed toward the portable bar at the far corner of the room. His voice carried back to those on the sofa.

"Your lawyers will advise you not to volunteer any information. If you're unsure of what you should say to any question, just turn to your lawyer for confirmation that the question can be answered. Stick only to the facts we're about to discuss. Everything you say should be rehearsed. If we haven't rehearsed it, don't say it."

As Julian paused to fill his glass, Colin noticed the silence. Everyone was waiting patiently for him to continue, just like they did when Joni had the floor, when she would set out the ground rules for their next activity.

"Should we contact our lawyers and advise them to be ready?" Colin asked.

"Yes, good idea. Each of you try to reach your lawyer tonight as soon as you get home."

"But the drive back could take an hour or more, depending on traffic. Won't that be too late to call?"

"A lawyer gets a retainer just so you can call him anytime you want. Get him alerted. The last thing you want to happen is for the police to drop by your place and you're unprepared. Then you have to sit around for hours waiting for your lawyer while a fast-talking cop tries to trick you into incriminating yourself," Julian said.

"Hell, I would think we'd have more difficulty staying away from reporters," Monty said. "I've already had calls from the newspapers."

Colin watched Monty look around for someplace to throw his cigar butt. Before he could get any ideas about the fireplace, Julian placed a ceramic ashtray in front of him. Colin heard the condescending tone of Julian's next remarks.

"You can always refuse an interview with a reporter. You can't with the police. Remember, the police don't have to read you your rights until they charge you with something.

And by then, you could have talked yourself into the gas chamber.''

Monty ignored the ashtray and threw the butt in the fireplace. "My lawyer's back in Boston," he said.

Colin could tell Julian was fighting for control. The next words were spit through clenched teeth.

"Get him to recommend someone locally. Do you have to be told every little thing?''

Rebecca rose to stand beside Julian, almost as though she was acting as a barrier between the two men. Colin thought it was a good idea.

"Darling, I'm a bit worried. What if the police get to us before we have a chance to talk with our lawyers? You know they've already tried. More than once my secretary and servants have turned them away. What if they stop our cars on the way home?''

Julian took her hand. "You're right. What we need to do is go over what each of us is going to say, then call our lawyers from here. Get everything set up before we leave. And if we can't, we'll all spend the night here. There are plenty of extra bedrooms. This property is registered under the firm's name, and the police won't think of looking for us here. Then, if any of us are stopped on the way home, we'll be ready for them," Julian said.

"As I said before, I can't stay. I have an appointment. A very important one," Monty said.

Colin watched Julian's face begin to redden at Monty's words, as though they were a personal affront to Julian's authority. But before the short man could respond, Claire contributed her rebuff to the plan.

"Neither can we. Colin and I have an appointment with his franchise manager. We delayed him to meet here tonight, but he can only wait so long. We must see him later. It's urgent!''

Julian exhaled his frustration and threw his hands in the air.

"All right! All right! Let's get on with it. If we can get our stories ironed out, maybe we'll have time for the calls to the lawyers and all these important appointments everyone seems plagued with. After all, I'm just trying to keep us out of jail. Pity no one wants to make any effort to assist."

Rebecca put her hand on his arm. "We'll work it out. And maybe things aren't as bad as they seem. After all, they did take Peter unawares. And can you ever remember the man when he wasn't shoving both feet into his very large and obnoxious mouth?"

Chapter Eleven

Samantha closed her eyes and listened to the music as it washed away her thoughts and cares: the look of disgust on Chapell's face; Taswell's fear and suspicion; Isabel's tears and pain. She always forgot how absolutely renewed beautiful music made her feel—until she felt it again.

But it wasn't just the full-bodied Brahms's Symphony no. 1 that lifted her spirits. It was the whole ritual she went through to make herself a worthy listener: anointing her body with perfume, dressing in an evening gown; brushing out her hair and wearing it loose and flowing, like the music. She prepared her body as the reverent resting place for the world's greatest sounds. Then she relaxed in her seat at the symphony hall and let them pour over her, a mere mortal being touched by the gods.

That was why the sudden, discordant noise shook her being like an earthquake. Instantly her eyes came open and alert. There it was again. Dammit! A man had come in late to take the seat next to her, and he had a bad cold and was wheezing heavily. She tried to tune him out. But soon he began to cough. Then, out came the handkerchief and he blew his nose.

Sam found herself in agony for the final ten minutes before the intermission. She had handled sleepers who insisted on snoring through performances by unceremoniously waking them up. But she didn't have the heart to tell off the heavyset man next to her. He already seemed to be feeling pretty miserable. There was only one thing she could do. Talk to the management about getting a different seat. She felt confident as she walked to the office at intermission time. After all, she was a season-ticket holder. Surely, they would understand this request from one of their valued clientele.

"No, I'm sorry. We're sold out. I wish we could do something for you, but there simply isn't another seat to be had."

"Are you sure—" Sam began, but was interrupted by a familiar deep voice.

"There is, in fact, an empty seat next to mine, and the lady's welcome to it."

Sam turned to find Scott Lawrence holding out a front-row ticket to the manager. He smiled knowingly in her direction and added, "Hi. Remember me?" Then he simply turned and walked away.

She tried not to smile. She tried not to feel happy at seeing him again.

Sam accepted the ticket from the manager's hand with a mixture of pleasure and chagrin. He had done it again. Dangled a carrot in front of her, somehow knowing she would take it.

"This seat must belong to a season-ticket holder. Can you please tell me who?" Sam had the presence to ask the manager.

"I'm sorry, ma'am. We don't give out that kind of information."

Sam pulled out her badge. "It's not ma'am. It's Sergeant. Please look it up," she said pleasantly.

"Oh, excuse me. Yes, ma...I mean, Sergeant. Uh, I don't have to look it up. It's one of several seats reserved for the mayor's office."

Sam made her way to her new seat in the front section, full of questions for the irritating Scott Lawrence, but perfectly aware that he probably wouldn't give her an opportunity to ask them.

She got seated just in time for the next selection. Scotty was already leaning forward in apparent anticipation, completely ignoring her presence. She leaned back and tried to relax. For a moment, she thought the evening might have been entirely ruined, but then, magically the music began to wash over her.

This time she felt totally surrounded, immersed in the flowing waves of sound. It was all so much clearer, sweeter. Never before had she experienced such a fullness of flutes and oboes over a descending bass. . . .

Suddenly it was over. Sam was aware of people getting up and leaving around her, but she made no attempt to herself. Her eyes remained closed. She couldn't explain her lack of concern for things outside her being. She felt as though she had experienced—

"A full banquet for the spirit," a deep voice finished for her.

The words had been Scott Lawrence's, of course. Only now he was interrupting her thoughts. Still, he had expressed her feelings so perfectly. Only someone who really felt that way could describe it. Sam opened her eyes and turned to him.

His gray eyes seemed to be brimming with an inner melody. And he was smiling. Smiling at her with the knowledge of the joy they had shared in the performance. She found herself smiling back. Wanting to admit to the shared pleasure. Finding it both strange and wonderful that, for the first time, she felt she had lived the music with another human being.

His face came closer and his lips brushed hers ever so gently, like the first tentative notes of a melody. Then he got up abruptly and helped her to her feet. She was surprised at his sudden movement. She still felt the imprint of his kiss.

"You act like we're going somewhere," she said.

"Of course. We have a date for a midnight walk on the beach. You didn't think I'd let you welsh on your bet, did you? By my watch, we have just about an hour to get there."

So he had remembered, after all. Sam couldn't help but feel pleased, and somewhat off balance at the same time. She had to try to find firm footing again. "All right. But only if I pick the beach, we take my car and I drive."

He capitulated immediately.

"You'll make a lovely chauffeur. Lead the way."

"I LIKE YOUR CAR. A classic, isn't it?" he asked as they started out of the parking lot.

"Yes. It's a '55 T-bird. My pride and joy."

"Had it long?"

"Almost eight years. It was a wreck when I bought it, but I've been able to restore it by devoting a lot of weekends to it and enlisting the help of a good mechanic. Might be a foolish waste of time and money, but I love this car. The effort's been worth it."

Scotty could smell the new leather seats and could feel the plush carpeting beneath his feet. The ride was smooth. The time and effort spent on the car showed. And, the concern for a job well done. It told him something more about her.

"I think I know what you mean. I've been renovating an old Victorian house in San Francisco for almost a year now. It can really be back-breaking work. But when things come together, when I know they're just right, it's so satisfying. All the hard work, all the frustrations, are forgotten."

She smiled over at him, and suddenly he found himself wanting to share his home with her. To walk her through the newly painted rooms. To watch her face when she saw the leaded-glass windows filter and separate the afternoon light into prisms across the solid wood floors.

He looked at her profile. A beautiful face, but not a delicate one. Her nose was strong. Her jaw firm. A determined face. One that had glimpsed something of life and love. One that seemed to know where it was going. Maybe that's why he got such a kick out of being able to surprise her.

It was a long ride. The night air rushed in through the windows, cool and refreshing after the heat of the day. When they turned onto the Pacific Coast Highway, he detected the smell of the sea. He had always loved that smell. It was why he had bought a home on the San Francisco peninsula. He leaned back, just enjoying the ride and the company.

"We're here," she announced at last.

Sam had pulled off the highway onto a narrow soft shoulder. The spot she had selected was dark, despite the bright moonlight. He followed her lead and took off his shoes. They made their way carefully along the sand.

Scotty took her hand. She made no objection. It felt soft, like her lips had been when he brushed them with his. He still didn't know why he had done that. It certainly hadn't been planned. There was just something about the way she had looked at him that made it seem right somehow. But, it had still caught him as much off guard as it probably had her.

Well, he thought, maybe the reason he had kissed her wasn't such a mystery. He couldn't deny how attractive he found her. He watched her hair blowing about her shoulders, dark, swirling waves around the golden glow of her face. As she spoke, her voice rolled against his ears like the surf running up the shore.

"I like the beach at night," she said. "When the sand no longer feels like hot coals beneath your feet. When all the noises from the kids and dogs are back in the suburbs. When the cool breeze off the ocean tastes clean enough to drink. It's the only breathable air in Los Angeles anymore."

"Yes, this is nice. I can't tell you the last time I took a walk on a beach in the moonlight. Makes me wish we had more public beaches in San Francisco. Although I have to admit this doesn't look like a public beach to me."

He could detect the smile in her voice, as well as on her face.

"It's not."

Scotty reminded himself that the woman he was with was a cop, not a fool. She wouldn't deliberately go out and break a law. But no amount of self-reassurance could blot out the uniformed figure who had obviously spotted them and was now walking purposefully toward them. Despite the cool breeze, perspiration began to collect at the middle of his back.

"Sam, uh, if this is a private beach, perhaps we should cut our walk short? I mean there are a lot of things I'd like to do with you, but getting arrested for trespassing isn't one of them."

Her laughter washed over him. She was obviously enjoying his moment of discomfort. She disengaged her hand from his and called out to the policeman who was walking toward them. He hailed her in recognition.

"Larkin hasn't shown?"

"No, Sarge. But the neighbors have confirmed he's been staying here. He rented the place about four months ago. I think this is our best shot."

"Well, let's hope we catch him by morning. This cat-and-mouse game has gone on long enough."

Sam said goodbye to her stakeout and turned to walk back the way she and Scotty had come. He was smiling ruefully as he fell into step beside her.

"You set me up."

"It was my turn, don't you think?" she said with a smile.

He had the grace to laugh. "You're having trouble getting in touch with Joni Wilson's lover?"

"So you know who Monty Larkin is?"

"I spent an hour looking through newspaper microfilm this afternoon—the gossip columns. Thought I better start brushing up if I'm going to help you."

"Mr. Lawrence—"

"Call me Scotty."

"Scotty, I know you're an ex-cop. I shouldn't have to tell you that it's against all the rules to involve a civilian in a criminal investigation."

"I won't be involved. I'll be assisting you. Just think of me as your snitch. Pay me with information instead of money."

"Come on, come clean. What do you want from me, Scotty? I mean, really?"

He looked down at her silvery eyes, swimming in the soft moonlight, and realized he wasn't sure. Yes, he wanted her to work with him on the Wilson case. But he also wanted to go on seeing her regardless. "I want to take you home," he said.

She looked away from the message in his eyes. "You can't. I drove. Remember?"

"Okay. I want you to take me to your home," he compromised.

"No. The sensible thing is for me to drop you off where you parked your car at the symphony hall," she said.

"I didn't drive. I took a taxi there."

"All right. Then I'll drive you to wherever you're staying."

"You can't."

"Why not?"

"I don't remember where I'm staying."

Her laughter told him she wasn't fooled. Then she decided to give up the game.

"Okay. I'll take you to where I live. But from there we call a taxi and you are on your way. Agreed?"

"Agreed."

It was almost two in the morning by the time they walked up the stairs from the garage that led to her townhouse. Sam got up at six every day, and normally by this time would be dead on her feet. But she felt wide awake and even a little exuberant in the company of this man. The Joni Wilson murder case had completely left her mind. As had most of her thoughts. She was left with a warm, excited feeling.

But as she got out her key and approached the door to the house from the garage, she saw a sliver of light coming from behind what should have been a closed door. She stopped and felt Scotty stiffen next to her.

Her pulse quickened as she drew the gun from her purse. She felt the moisture collecting on her palms. Gently she pushed the open door wider with her foot. She was too late.

The loud noise to her right went through her like a shotgun blast.

Chapter Twelve

She hit the floor and rolled into the room, her gun aimed in front of her. But her assailant proved to be only the ironing board that had noisily fallen from its normally secure position in a wall cabinet. Her heightened senses had given it its shotgun quality.

Scotty had silently followed her in. His gun, too, was drawn. He pointed toward the other rooms wordlessly, and Sam nodded her understanding that he would take the position of first entry.

He burst through, and she came in afterward. One by one they cautiously checked each room and closet, working as a team, performing the well-established routine of seeking a hidden intruder. Papers were thrown everywhere, but no intruder was found.

"Do you have any friends in the burglary section? This lock's been jimmied," Scotty said after their search was concluded and he returned to the door leading to the garage.

"I know a few."

"How can I help?" Scotty asked.

"You can check on the front door. Make sure it's secure while I do a room-to-room inventory of what might be missing."

"Right, Sarge."

Sam knew he had called her that to make her smile. She wanted to oblige, but under the circumstances it was difficult. She had taken reports from the victims of a burglary many times. But until now she had never really understood what the total invasion of privacy felt like. The very real sense of violation and loss of personal security. She was angry. And more than a little shaken.

Sam tried to concentrate on making her search systematic. She took her time to make it thorough, careful not to touch anything that might later yield fingerprints. And she tried to forget that unknown hands had made free with her possessions.

At the conclusion of her search, she found Scotty in the study looking at her collection of books and records. At her approach, his head came up.

"Anything missing?"

"No, but something's peculiar."

"What's that?"

"Well, whoever it was, they turned this room over more thoroughly than the others. As though they were looking for something on paper. The only things in the bedroom that were disturbed were some bank receipts I had left out. My jewelry box hasn't even been touched, and it was in plain sight. Wait a minute..."

Sam reached across the desk and felt the top of her personal computer. It was warm.

"Information. The intruder had to be after information," she decided.

"But what information do you have that would cause someone to go to these lengths?" Scotty asked.

Sam shook her head. "Frankly I've no idea. All physical evidence for my cases is in the evidence room at headquarters. The only things I keep at home are my notes. And I'm confident my computer code can't be broken. Unless I'm dealing with a computer whiz...."

A frown crossed Sam's forehead. She quickly sat down at her computer, switched it on and hit a few keys, careful to touch only their edges and not the surfaces where finger-prints might lie.

"No. Guess I'm not. Whoever my intruder was, they lacked the sophistication. The password's secure. That's probably why the person ended up ransacking the place looking for something on paper," she said.

"But what?" he asked.

"I don't know. What do I have I don't know I have?"

Scotty watched the confusion cloud her eyes. "Maybe the question should be, what does the intruder think you have that you don't? And, how far will he or she go to get it?"

SCOTTY WATCHED HER move around her home directing the crew from burglary, her long dark hair shining as it bounced and caught the light. He knew he would never get tired of looking at her. And tonight, she looked so beautiful.

It had been a great evening before they'd discovered the break-in. She shared his interests in music. She was intelligent. She had a good sense of humor. He had enjoyed her company immensely, and had even been able to forget his primary objective for pursuing her—the Joni Wilson case.

The investigative crew was finally leaving. Scotty acknowledged their departure with a wave and left it to Sam to see them to the door.

He found her home so simple and neat. Even with the disarray from the intruder, he could still see the clean lines of her furniture. The soft muted colors of the fabric coverings and draperies. It was the home of a woman at home with herself.

As he waited for her to return, he felt a twinge of pain from the metal plate along his ribs and sought a more comfortable position on the couch. Then she walked into the room and came toward him, and for a moment he had a hard time thinking of anything except how lovely she was.

"They don't have much hope for the fingerprints they lifted. Too much smudging. Doubt if they can identify enough points for a computer match," she said as she sat across from him.

He tried to put aside thoughts of her physical attractions and asked the question that had been troubling him since they'd first found evidence of the intruder. "I have to know what you think. Could this break-in be connected with the Wilson case?"

She seemed to consider his question carefully. "Yes. I think it could. In fact, I think it probably is. But it also may have nothing to do with it. This isn't the first time someone has tried to get into my files."

"Someone's broken in here before?"

"Not my home, but my office files were compromised once. Tell me, Scotty. What is the extent of your involvement in the Wilson case? Are you working for a client?"

He looked at her for a moment in silence. What if the break-in did have to do with the Wilson case? What if the information he had to give could help her solve it? If he didn't give her the information she could get hurt because of it. He just couldn't take that chance. He had to tell her what he knew, even if it meant giving up *his* chance at thirty thousand dollars.

"My partner, Warren, had a visit on Thursday from a young woman. She told him she was trying to find her birth certificate. He supplied her with one that we know now to be false. This particular woman was the image of your murder victim."

"Joni Wilson was a client of yours?" Sam asked.

"Possibility exists. The woman called herself Jane Williams."

Sam shook her head as though the action could make these new pieces of this strange murder puzzle to fall into place. Scotty could see he had obviously supplied her with pieces that didn't fit.

"You said she called herself Jane Williams. What do you make of it?" she asked.

"I'm not sure. But it struck me that if this woman was Joni Wilson, she might have been looking for another identity. Rich people have been known to play such games. Assume another name and go somewhere their face isn't likely to be recognized to engage in whatever it is they don't want anyone to find out about."

"Sounds plausible. Have you found anything to tell you what the Wilson woman was up to?"

"No. But if it was her, she didn't go to all that trouble for nothing."

Sam seemed to consider for a minute.

"You don't have a client on this case. What are you hoping to get out of it?"

"My investigative firm has supplied an unknown woman with false identification. I have no idea whether it has been or is intended to be used illegally. If it is, I feel a responsibility. I can't just forget it and walk away. I have to at least try to find who the woman calling herself Jane Williams was."

"And if Jane Williams and Joni Wilson prove to be the same?"

"Then my case will be closed. Unless I uncover evidence to the contrary, I'd conclude that whatever use the woman was planning to make of the false birth certificate, she probably didn't get the chance."

Sam sat back in the soft-cushioned couch and considered his words for several minutes. Scotty watched her intently, trying to read her thoughts. When she looked up, he was a little surprised at her small smile.

"Thank you for telling me, Scotty. It means a lot. Particularly after the break-in. I know you didn't have to, and I promise I'll seriously think about your offer of collaboration. Frankly it's getting to sound better by the minute."

Scotty was elated. With nothing left to bargain with, he still had a chance of working with her. He didn't even care that her last few words were punctuated by a yawn. It was almost four in the morning and they were both tired. He didn't want to leave her, but he would. It would be inappropriate to ask her if he could stay or to keep her up any longer.

He stood and smiled down at her. "I'll call you around noon. Hope you manage to get some sleep."

She looked up at him, stretched and smiled again. Without conscious thought, he found himself leaning down to kiss that smile. Her breath was warm and sweet. She tasted like melting sunshine. He knew its warmth would stay with him throughout the night.

He sent her a muted goodbye as he found his way out, but he was worried as he walked down the steps to the garage. The intruder or intruders apparently hadn't found what they were looking for. What if they returned?

Chapter Thirteen

Sam woke up on the couch, her hand clutching the handle of her gun under one of the pillow cushions. The grandfather clock in the hallway chimed ten times.

The first thing that occurred to her was surprise for having slept at all. She remembered vividly the events of the night before: the symphony, the break-in, and the unsettling gray eyes of Scott Lawrence.

She stretched lazily and seemed to be aware of the movement in every cell of her body. She felt different this morning. A little excited and expectant.

Sam smiled as thoughts of Scotty filled her mind, interfering with what she knew she should be concentrating on. There was no doubt she was very attracted to him. She had sometimes wondered if she would ever feel this way again. And why did she have these feelings for Scotty? Why not for the half-dozen or so other men she had met since John?

It had to be chemistry. A mixture of mental, physical and emotional ingredients. All energizing into a potent biological magnetism. Nothing mysterious. Probably quite scientifically explainable.

She leaned back and laughed at her own mental explanations. And remembered again the gentleness of his kiss.

At last, pleasurable thoughts of him began fading. The realization of what she had to do got her off the couch and on her way to the shower. She made it hot and quick and put on slacks and a T-shirt, twisting her hair into one large, loose braid that fell over her left shoulder.

The first thing she did on Saturday mornings was the wash. Mundane, but necessary. And after she got some of the household chores completed, she could go down to the office and see what, if anything, had turned up on the Wilson murder. Then get the witnesses in for questioning and try to find a connection to the break-in—if there was one. She collected her laundry basket and headed for the washing machine in the garage.

As soon as she opened the door, she remembered it was the one that had been jimmied the night before. It swung away from the lock loosely, giving her an eerie feeling, as though a multitentacled, invisible bug had begun to crawl up her back, bringing every small hair follicle to attention. She walked down the stairs to the garage level slowly, still feeling the creeping sensation.

Daylight was pressing through the one window on the outside door, but the room still seemed dark. And maybe a little too quiet. She probably should have turned on the light at the top of the stairs. Briefly she thought about putting the laundry basket down on the step and going back. But it would mean turning her back on the blackness below, re-climbing the thirteen or more steps to the top. She only had a couple more steps to the bottom.

Her bare foot slowly descended onto the next step. The squeak of the board sounded like the death throes of a falling redwood. The nerves tightened up her back. Her goose bumps had started to sprout goose bumps.

Then she heard the sound. She turned quickly toward it, her temple throbbing in response to its vibration. Her heart raced madly as her mind brought forth the image of her gun far away under the cushion of the couch.

The shape was in shadow. Hiding, awaiting her approach. A flicker of light gleamed off the barrel of the gun he held. It was pointed unerringly at her heart. She wanted to run. But stark terror had turned her to stone.

"Sorry. Didn't mean to frighten you," Scotty said, putting away his weapon, his lips forming a smile.

Sam put her laundry basket down and sat next to it on the first step. Her legs would hold her no longer. The sudden adrenaline that had rushed into her bloodstream was making her shake uncontrollably.

"Where did you come from? What are you doing here?" she asked. Her voice didn't sound familiar even to her ears.

Scotty sat next to her and put an arm around her shoulders. Its immediate warmth eased her shakes a little.

"I spent the night here. I thought that maybe whoever it was might come back and try to get what information they wanted from you personally since they apparently couldn't find it in the computer or on paper."

"Is that who you thought I was just now?"

"I wasn't sure. The door opened without a sound. The light didn't get turned on. Your bare feet on the steps sounded muffled, as though on purpose. I thought for a minute someone had gotten through the other way, and that I might be too late...."

He had stayed close by because he had worried about her safety. She had never been told more eloquently that someone cared.

Sam looked at his face, the sandy stubble on his chin, disheveled hair and slightly bloodshot eyes. He looked wonderful.

On a sudden impulse, she kissed his cheek.

"Just one thing I want to know. How much did you pay that guy with the cold to sit next to me last night?"

"YOU'RE SURE SHE KNOWS?" the deep voice asked.

Transmission interference crackled over the phone line.

"No, I'm not sure. I'm not sure of anything. I told you. Joni kept something in a secret safe in her car. And that cop has it. That's the only thing I know," the nervous voice replied.

"All right. But nothing is in the official report, and I didn't find anything at her place. I might have applied some of my persuasive techniques later on the lady herself, but you didn't tell me she had a date."

"She didn't have a date when I followed her to the Music Center!" the nervous voice said.

"Must have arranged to meet him there. Anyway, he ended up spending the night. Maybe it's just as well. Maybe there's another angle here."

"What do you mean?" the nervous voice asked.

The deep voice laughed.

"Hasn't it occurred to you that this cop may not have reported the location of the money because she plans on keeping it for herself?"

The nervous voice went up an octave higher. "What are we going to do?"

"Since we don't know what she's found or what she knows, let's just watch her a day or so. It will be interesting to see what turns up and who she ends up arresting for Joni's murder. That should tell us if we've got a problem."

"And if we do?"

"If Samantha Turner proves to be a problem, I assure you she won't be one for long."

Chapter Fourteen

Despite the fact she had finally managed to pull all of Joni Wilson's friends in for questioning, Sam didn't kid herself for a minute that she'd gained the upper hand. She'd found them because they'd allowed themselves to be found.

As soon as they left, she reviewed the taped interviews of the group: Rebecca Myers, Julian Harris, Monty Larkin, Colin and Claire North. Then she busied herself typing in the important points of each to update her file on the Wilson case.

All suspects had been well counseled. Their statements were concise and all questions were fielded by the attorneys representing them. Not one iota of information more than they wanted to give was forthcoming.

It was late in the afternoon when she finally closed up shop and went home. A security van was sitting in front of her house, recommended by a colleague from burglary. Sam had almost forgotten it was to arrive that afternoon.

She listened to the instructions given by the security company's system representative, impressed with the movement and pressure sensors beneath windows and the alarm's tie-in with her smoke detectors.

"And if either the security or fire alarm goes off, what happens then?" she asked.

"Our twenty-four-hour monitoring center receives the signal and we call the proper authorities—either police or fire department. An emergency vehicle gets sent to your place right away.''

When the security van left, Sam went over to the control panel to set the system on. As soon as she pressed the activation switch, the telephone rang, causing her to jump a foot. It finally got through to her numbed brain that the ringing was coincidental and she had not inadvertently activated the alarm. She reached to answer the phone, and smiled when she heard Scotty's voice.

"I've got some information on the background of Joni Wilson you might be interested in. I can be there in twenty minutes. Forty-five if I bring pizza."

"With pizza, by all means. But let's leave the background on Joni until another time. Tonight, I want to go over the military records I got from the various armed services. I need some help in deciphering the coding."

THEY WERE THROUGH three-fourths of the extralarge pizza and most of the coding by nine o'clock.

"What's all this information told us, Sam?"

"I don't know. I wasn't really looking for anything specific. But military records can be helpful. They sometimes reveal antisocial behavior that has spilled over into a person's civilian life. If you don't look at the records, you can miss an obvious problem. Besides, they're always good for filling in background information like obscure medical data. And look at all this weaponry experience these men have."

"Too bad whoever killed Joni didn't shoot her before they pushed her off the cliff. Then maybe we could figure out who did it."

Scotty's voice was teasing. Sam smiled.

"It was good of you to decipher this stuff for me. Your hitch in the Air Force has come in handy. I appreciate your coming."

"It was good of you to agree on this collaboration. Besides, we're partners now. What I do for you I do for myself."

He leaned over to take her hand. She was no longer surprised at her body's sensitivity to his touch, how even the slightest contact with him quickened her senses. But his next question threw her off balance.

"You've told me that the various financial institutions have confirmed the withdrawal of her funds. That the woman was approaching bankruptcy. Have you considered the possibility of suicide?"

Sam decided it was time to take Scotty to the scene of the crime. It would help him to put some facts into perspective.

"Come on. Let's take a ride."

The moon was full. It was the only object in the night sky that could compete with the lights glaring up at them from one of the largest cities in the world. Sam parked the car and then used a flashlight to lead the way to the edge of the cliff.

"Tire tracks were found here. The car's trajectory confirms this is the spot where she went over. The transmission was in neutral. You don't commit suicide by coasting off a cliff. You put your foot on the gas and go like hell. And then there's the gasoline."

"Its significance?" Scotty asked.

"It's a painful death. Generally chosen by those who wish to make some social statement to the world or who are so ridden with guilt they feel they must do penance for their sins. I've never heard of it being combined with another form of suicide."

"Yes, I see. If Joni Wilson was going to kill herself by dousing herself with gasoline and lighting a match, she wouldn't combine the deed with coasting off a cliff in her car. Even in suicide there is *some* sense."

"My thoughts exactly," she said.

"Okay, suicide is out. But how did you decide it wasn't an accident?"

"The lab determined that gasoline had been poured over the seats and the body. The trail of gas was made to look as though it had leaked from the gas tank. However, the murderer missed the fact that when the car fell, the gas tank was punctured on a rock and all the gas had already leaked out by the time the fire took hold."

Scotty borrowed the flashlight and moved closer to the ledge. He was trying to get a sense of the steepness. Sam came to stand by his side.

"The angle of descent is eighty degrees at this point. The drop is close to one hundred and fifty feet through heavy brush."

Sam felt a little nervous standing so close to the edge. Her fear of heights was beginning to act up. Being aware of how treacherous the terrain was didn't help, either. She finally decided if Scotty wanted to do any more peering over the side of this cliff, he was going to have to do it alone.

But just as she turned to step back, she lost her footing. For one horrible moment, she thought she was going to fall. Her hands fought to hold on to the empty air. Then miraculously, Scotty's strong hands reached out and found her.

At first they held her steady, until her feet were once again firmly planted on the ground. But then they drew her slowly to him, his arms folding around her gently.

His embrace was comforting, and she quickly regained her composure. Scotty seemed in no hurry to release her, and Sam found she was in no hurry to be released.

His body was hard, muscular. She remembered the ease with which he had lifted the heavy weights. Yet his touch was gentle and caressing as his hands found the bare skin of her back and neck.

She could feel his breath on her cheek. Hear his sigh at her ear. Then his mouth found hers, pressing and exploring. His arms drew her closer. It was the tenderness that reached her, caused her defenses to fade away. Her arms circled his back.

Only once before had a man shown her such a gentle approach. John. His had been the subtle charm that cloaked her gently and tangled her up before she could pull away, embedding her in a quagmire of deceit and emotional betrayal.

Memories of John caused Sam to stiffen, then pull away. Scotty felt it immediately, his hands moving to her shoulders.

"What is it? Sam?"

"We . . . I need to make a stop at the Wilson estate. Before it's too late. We should leave now."

His arms dropped back to his sides as she turned toward the car. He stayed back to pick up the flashlight he'd dropped when he had reached for her. She felt his eyes on her back as though they were trying to see through her for the answer to a silent question.

They made their stop at the Wilson place brief. Sam used the key she had obtained, not wanting to disturb the housekeeper. She showed Scotty the layout of the house, Joni's personal effects. But mostly she had gone there to satisfy her own curiosity. She wanted to see the clothing that was in the deceased's closets.

After close scrutiny, she stood before the closet, shaking her head. "Something's wrong. These outfits are older. Out of fashion. This woman had twenty million dollars. She had to have dressed better than this."

"Money can't buy everything. Maybe she didn't have your good taste."

The unexpected compliment warmed the skin on the back of Sam's neck just as though it had been kissed. She turned her head to find him smiling at her.

"Compliments will not turn my head."

"Careful, Sarge. Your head just turned."

His literal translation of her comment made her laugh. As they walked out to the car, he took her hand again. It seemed so natural. She felt good being with him.

"Are you free for tomorrow?" she asked. "We could go over that background information on Joni you've gathered. There's a restaurant down the street from me that specializes in Sunday brunch. I could meet you there, at, say, eleven-thirty?"

"Eleven-thirty it is. Unless you'd like a watchdog in the garage again tonight. I'm housebroken and only bite prowlers."

Sam was tempted. He was nice to have around. But if she was honest with herself, she felt perfectly safe with her new alarm system.

"No. But thanks. I have everything under control."

The quickening of her pulse at his smile belied her words. Around this man she found herself less and less in control.

Chapter Fifteen

"Greg Wilson wasn't a self-made man. He inherited most of his money from his parents at the age of seventeen—when his father killed his mother, her lover and then himself."

Sam put down her fork, no longer interested in the food. Scotty's opening statement had eclipsed her appetite.

He paused to refer to his notes. She caught a glimpse of the meticulous entries that spanned several pages. He'd put a lot of time and effort into getting the data for her. And she hadn't even asked, just commented she wished she could learn more about the deceased and her family.

"He found them in bed together," Scotty went on. "His brother and his wife. He reached into the nightstand, removed the gun he kept there and shot them both through the heart. Then turned the gun on himself.

"They were found later that evening. Two naked bodies, draped over the bed. A third body, in a business suit, crumpled next to the nightstand. You can imagine what the papers did with that story," Scotty said.

"Oh, yes. A story of lust, betrayal, murder and suicide. They must have loved it. But where was the boy, Greg, during all this?" Sam asked.

"He was away at school, but he came back for the funerals. The reporters hounded him, twisting anything he said about his dead family to sensationalize it more. So, at seventeen he apparently learned a lesson: avoid the press.

Nothing specific about Greg Wilson ever appeared in the newspapers again until his death two years ago. For nearly thirty-three years, his personal life was totally private,'' Scotty said.

"Except for the fact of his daughter, Joni. As I recall, she cropped up in the society columns when she turned twenty-one and inherited her mother's money," Sam said.

"Right. Her mother was Deborah Vine Wilson. The only child of Martha and Fred Vine of Philadelphia, an established family with old money. They died when Deborah was sixteen.

"Story goes that Greg Wilson was a wild young man. Showgirls, waitresses, any woman was fair game. Properly managed, his inheritance should have grown at least with inflation. But he lived pretty high, traveled in the fast lane, vacationed in the more exclusive spots. Most society parents knew his reputation and made him unwelcome, but Debbie wasn't well chaperoned. They say he seduced her. Hard to tell now.

"Anyway, their daughter, Joni, welcomed the press. When they mentioned her grandparents, she just laughed. Her favorite quote went to a well-known gossip columnist who asked her if the thirty-five-year-old scandal didn't cause her shame. She looked him straight in the eye and said, 'No, I'd only be ashamed if my grandfather hadn't shot them.' "

Sam was beginning to get an impression of the deceased. She sounded strong, sure. And clever.

"She turned a past scandal into an almost enviable family history. Good twist," Sam said. "She gauged the spirit of her times accurately. Since twenty million isn't considered much these days by the society columnists, I presume their perpetuation of Joni's notoriety stemmed from her grandparents' scandal and the 'old' family tie—her mother's line—right?"

"Yes, primarily. Rich old families are often treated like royalty. But I think she was also popular in the press because she was young and pretty. And although real money, the kind that can move mountains, is considered to be in the hundred millions, twenty million can still move a little hill or two."

Scotty watched Sam sip her ice tea as she reflected on Joni Wilson. He found himself staring at the light shining on her skin, at her lips, soft and wet. He imagined what it would be like tasting those lips again.

"Anything else?" Sam asked.

"Uh . . . yes. Ready to hear about her lovers?" he asked.

"By all means."

"Ever since Joni emerged into society, her love affairs were the hottest news around. Just about the time one society columnist put her together with someone, she would be seen with someone else. And the descriptions of her men were all the same—young, tall, handsome and aspiring," he said.

"Aspiring?"

"Yes. Aspiring for her money through marriage. Actors mostly. Two of whom sued for palimony when Joni called it quits. Both cases were thrown out of court. And Joni would hit the papers again. Happy. Smiling. Victorious. And still single. With quotes about how she would never let a man marry her who didn't have at least as much money as she did. Otherwise she could never be sure he loved her."

"I wonder if there might be a motive there. A jilted suitor?" Sam spoke her thought aloud.

"No. Normally a crime of passion takes place right away. When the passion is high. It's been almost a year since Joni was involved with the last of those suitors."

"Hmm. Good point. What about this Monty Larkin, her current interest?" Sam asked.

"He doesn't quite fit the pattern. Oh, he looks the part, but he's from an old Boston family and apparently wealthy in his own right. A departure from Joni's normal aspiring choices. The columnists had begun to wonder if Joni was about to succumb. Never know now. Have you had him in for questioning?" Scotty asked.

"Oh, yes, for all the good it did. He brought his lawyer along and gave me just the information he wanted to. Boston police provided me with some information about some radical right-wing associations he made when he was younger. He may still be involved with one particular fanatical group, but one of its members I spoke to didn't say anything that seems to relate to this case. All I'm really sure of is that he was ready for us. All of Joni's friends were.

"I had them picked up. Separate officers questioned each one, simultaneously, in separate rooms. Didn't do any good. They had ironed their story all out beforehand. Only one I surprised was Peter Taswell," Sam confided.

"The beneficiary?"

"Yes. But as I told you yesterday, most of the money is gone. And the only thing I can get out of Joni's inner circle of friends is that she gambled it away. But there's something strange about that bunch. I feel it," Sam said.

"What did you learn from Taswell? By the way, he's a second cousin isn't he?" Scotty asked.

"Yes. The only living relative. On her mother's side. Frankly we have some strong evidence against him. He's up to his ears in Vegas gambling debts. He admitted to knowing he was Joni's beneficiary. And he made it obvious to me he was unaware of his cousin's recent spending. As far as he was concerned, the estate was still worth millions."

"Giving him a strong motive for murder," Scotty commented.

"Right."

"Why didn't he know what her lawyer and apparently her friends knew—that she was going broke?" Scotty asked.

"Apparently he and Joni had a falling-out a couple of years back. Around the time of her father's death. All he'll say is that they disagreed about something."

"So they haven't been in contact for a while?"

Sam smiled. "This is where he tripped himself up. I have proof of a series of recent telephone calls between the deceased and Peter Taswell during the three days before her death. In his statement to us, Taswell claimed he hadn't talked with his cousin since the disagreement almost two years ago."

"Interesting."

"Not only that, but Taswell claimed he was in Las Vegas at the time of the car crash and fire. Said he didn't come to L.A. until a 9 a.m. flight on Friday. However, I have a Las Vegas airline ticket agent who identified Taswell in a lineup as the man who purchased a ticket from him for an afternoon flight from Vegas to Los Angeles on Thursday. He bought it under an assumed name. The agent couldn't remember what."

Scotty looked at Sam's small smirk. He was beginning to be able to anticipate her thoughts by watching her facial expressions. "But you found out the assumed name?" he said.

"Right. A Leonard Mifflin took that flight and sat in seat 12B. The passenger in 12C also picked Taswell out of a lineup, as the man in the seat next to him calling himself Lenny," Sam said.

"So Taswell was in Los Angeles on the night of the murder?"

"No doubt in my mind," she said.

"Have you been able to connect him with a rented car?" Scotty asked.

"No, but a Leonard Mifflin flew back to Vegas from Los Angeles at 4:45 a.m. Friday."

"When was the car set on fire?"

"Somewhere between ten and midnight. A homeowner noticed the brush fire around midnight and called the fire department. We were on the scene almost immediately, found the secret safe and little black book, woke up Joni's dentist, and got a positive ID in time for the morning news."

"So Taswell had motive and was around at the time of the murder. What about means?" Scotty asked.

"Nothing conclusive. All he really needed was a filled gas can. None of the officers I sent out could locate a garage in

a ten-mile radius that remembered anybody buying a gas can
Thursday afternoon or evening, but there's a lot of ground
and a lot of gas stations between the airport and the scene
of the murder. Besides, there could have been a gas can in
Joni's car he used and then carried away. He could have
gotten rid of it anywhere.''

"I can't wait to hear what he said when you questioned
him about the discrepancies in his statement regarding the
telephone calls. And the little trip he took under an assumed name, which put him in L.A. at the time of the murder," Scotty said.

"Sorry to disappoint you, but no explanations were
forthcoming. His lawyer informed me Mr. Taswell would
answer no further questions unless he was formally
charged.''

Scotty paused to shove a cracker and dip into his mouth.
He studied her face and found doubt and concern.

"What does your lieutenant think of the evidence against
this second cousin? Does he want him charged?''

Sam rubbed her temples as though she was trying to get
rid of a headache. "Oh, yes. He's pressuring me to get together with the D.A. to charge Taswell with Murder One.
He's satisfied with the evidence gathered so far.''

"But you're not?''

Sam shook her head. "No. Things don't fit. This woman,
from all reports, squandered a fortune. But I'm having difficulty believing she gambled it all away.''

"Why?" Scotty asked.

Sam looked at him, trying to assess the spirit in which his
question was being asked. She detected interest and concern only. A genuine curiosity for a possible explanation.
No challenge to her thought processes.

"You gave me Joni's history," Sam said. "I think it
shows she had emotional strength, as well as mental capa-
bility. A strength I don't believe someone with the gambling fever possesses. She may have been a gambler, but I

don't think it controlled her. But of course I'm no psychologist.''

"Psychologist or not, your reasoning is sound. Do you have any other thoughts?''

"Well, I'm back to her clothing again. Remember, she only had about thirty outfits left in her closets. All faddish and now out of style.''

"Actually, Sam, I think I only have about five suits, outside of a couple of pairs of jeans and sweaters. Thirty outfits sounds like a lot to me.''

Sam shook her head again. "Not really. We all have more than we think—especially women. I went through my closet last night and counted. I have thirty-two outfits, and I wouldn't say I'm clothes conscious. But the point is, I don't believe an heiress would have only thirty. You saw her room. She had enough closet space for three hundred. But she only had thirty.''

Scotty took a strip of roast beef, wrapped it around an olive and popped the unusual sandwich into his mouth.

"Do you have any idea what this clothing deficit means?'' he asked between swallows of several more.

"Not really. But I do think Joni Wilson had more clothing. I think someone removed her clothing before we arrived for some reason. I also can't find any of the paste jewelry she had made to replace the expensive stuff she sold. It's gone. And just like her clothing, there doesn't seem to be any reason for its disappearance.''

"So someone stole some clothes and some worthless paste jewelry. How does that affect your investigation?''

"I don't believe that someone was Peter Taswell. I think it was one or more of Joni Wilson's so-called friends, who all refused to talk to me or my staff without a lawyer present. There's more to this. Much more. They're lying through their lawyers' teeth.''

Scotty watched Sam using her fork to play with the food on her plate. She stabbed a raisin in her carrot salad and broke it apart. The anger she was feeling was obvious.

"Okay, let's say they are hiding something," he said calmly. "Were any of them unaccounted for on the night of the murder?"

"Their alibis check out only because Chapell's wife is backing up his story and the rest are providing alibis for each other. They're definitely hiding something, and I know we're missing another angle here. I guess what I'm saying is that I don't believe Taswell killed his cousin."

Scotty knew that Sam was in a precarious position. The amount of evidence she had gathered against the likely suspect would not be dismissed by her superiors because of a hunch she had that more could be learned. More could always be learned. But realistically, bosses never afforded enough time.

He knew her suspicions might be right. He'd had the same kind of gut reactions to cases himself. And when he followed them, he had never been disappointed. In hot water with his superiors initially maybe, but never disappointed.

"What you need are some straight answers from these tight-lipped friends. The funeral is tomorrow. Why don't you get me in and let me take an unobtrusive look at the bunch. Then I'll see what I can find out."

Sam looked at her companion, unable to deny the strong attraction she had for him, hoping it was not clouding her vision. She knew she was breaking a lot of rules, both professionally and personally, by collaborating with him on the case.

Only one other time had she shared department business with an outsider. John. And it had seemed so inconsequential. So innocent. Just a passing remark concerning information she had uncovered on corruption in the building of a major shopping mall. She had wanted to assure him that the reason for breaking their date was important.

Sam hadn't been aware that it was his father who had bribed a city planning-department employee into releasing information regarding the site. A site the senior John Bateman bought up immediately at a dirt-cheap price, and then torched the buildings for the insurance money. He then turned around and sold back the land to the city at an inflated rate, combining two of the oldest con games around.

She'd had no idea about the Batemans' involvement until the break-in at her office. John had waited until she left that evening to break the lock on her desk and take her file on the case. His intention was to delay her progress and give his father time to bury the incriminating evidence before Sam had an opportunity to trace the transactions to his family, or destroy the records entirely. She never found out which.

What John hadn't realized was that Sam had a copy of the file at home. His break-in only resulted in his own arrest. An arrest he was sure Sam would never go through with. Because of her love for him.

She remembered the scene at the Bateman home. Some nights she was afraid she would never be able to forget. She had confronted John with what she knew. And he had tried to convince her that his father had hurt no one. The city had the money to pay. So did the insurance company. It was no big deal. People did things like this all the time.

Of course, he had been sorry about having to break into her office. But couldn't she see he was just trying to keep her out of it? Protect her?

He talked of their future. Their marriage. How fond his parents were of her. The lovely home his father would give them as a wedding present. The family they would have in their turn. And Sam had walked out and gone directly to the D.A.

But Scotty wasn't John. She had checked him out with the San Francisco Police Department. His record was excellent. Spotless. He had opposed corruption just as strongly as she. And his medical report described a man who had paid dearly for upholding his principles.

He proved to be a real fighter, too. Found himself a new profession as an insurance investigator for several years. Uncovered a lot of deception. Then started his own investigative firm. Modest, but honest. A sound reputation throughout.

Of course, John and his father had been upstanding members of the community, too. Belonged to all the major social clubs. Headed the fight for urban renewal. Supported programs for the disadvantaged. Given regularly to charity. Had a reputation for honesty. Until their indictment.

Which all went to prove that what you see isn't always what you get. With a sudden pang, she hoped she was not being a fool.

Chapter Sixteen

Monday morning was sunny and bright. Flowers lifted multicolored faces toward the light. Birds raised their voices in lush treetops. Green lawns shook in their bath of sprinklers. And the casket was rolled into the still chapel.

Personally Sam thought funerals were a waste of time. A celebration of death. A formal bowing to its ultimate victory over life. Then she reminded herself everyone needed an appropriate time and place to unload their sorrow, to come to terms with their loss so they could go on living. That was supposed to be the purpose of the ceremony.

But Joni Wilson's funeral was missing something. All the trappings were present: everyone dressed in black for the occasion; long, solemn limousines; an abundance of flowers. But it was missing a vital ingredient, one that would infuse it with humanity. Grief.

During the impersonal ceremony around the closed, simple casket and the eulogy delivered in a monotone by the clergyman hired by the mortuary, Sam wondered why none of the people present stood up to protest. The unfeeling procedure sickened her.

Yet these people, who were supposed to be the deceased's only relative and friends, sat like dummies, utterly dry-eyed, devoid of any emotion. Except boredom. She watched them yawn. She watched them whisper to one another and suppress laughter when something funny occurred to them. She even saw one man take out his nail clippers and give himself a manicure.

Could any of this group really have cared about the dead woman?

It was the same story at the grave site. It was a procession of zombies who watched the casket being lowered. And then Sam finally saw the glistening of a tear behind a woman's black veil.

It was a quiet tear. No sobs punctuated its flow. But it was soon joined by others, marching in unison down the barricaded face. Isabel Kane's face.

"You did a good job of keeping the press away."

Scotty's voice interrupted her thoughts. They had stood in the shadows together, remaining out of sight, as unobtrusive as possible.

"Thanks, but right now I almost wish a few would show up," Sam commented.

"To find out if we've got any actors or actresses in the bunch?"

So Scotty had seen it, too.

"Who's the one who cried?" he asked.

"The housekeeper. You missed her last night at the estate."

"That's Isabel Kane?" he asked.

Sam was a little surprised that Scotty knew the housekeeper's name. She decided she must have mentioned it to him at some time. His next words interrupted her attempt to remember when.

"I trust you've questioned her. What do you think? Are those real tears?" Scotty asked.

"Yes. Of this entire bunch, I think she's the only one who really cared for Joni Wilson. She raised her, you see. Just like a daughter," Sam said.

Scotty seemed to consider for a moment. "Do you think there's any possibility that she had a part in the woman's murder?"

Sam shook her head. "No, Scotty, I don't. I won't rule anyone out totally, of course, but I would think her the least likely suspect. I believe her grief is genuine."

"I'll take your word. Where's the cousin?" he asked.

Sam put a name to each of the other faces in the funeral crowd. Peter Taswell, the second cousin. Walter Chapell, the attorney. Monty Larkin, the lover. Rebecca Myers, the friend. Julian Harris, Rebecca's lover. Claire North, a college acquaintance, and her husband, Colin.

"Have you noticed the way Taswell sits apart from the others? Almost as though he didn't belong?" Scotty asked.

"Yes. He's an outsider, all right. Not part of Joni's group. Have you decided who you'd like to follow up on?"

"Well, you've been able to talk at length with Taswell and Chapell. I've got an appointment with Rebecca Myers this afternoon. Thought I'd try her boyfriend, Julian, next. What do you think?" Scotty asked.

Sam was surprised. "How are you going to arrange to see Julian Harris?"

Scotty couldn't answer Sam's question, because getting to see Julian involved his connection with the Heritage Insurance Company. Telling her about his arrangement with Ms. Grenville would mean he would have to explain relinquishing his claim on the money for her sake.

And he had relinquished his claim. He no longer cared about the money. He cared about Samantha. But that fact and its admission could make her uncomfortable, because she might feel a responsibility and under some obligation. Independent people fought unsolicited obligations. She might push him away.

He couldn't take the chance. Their relationship was still too new and fragile. They were building a friendship, and trust. He wanted that...and much more. He wanted his relationship with Samantha Turner to grow beyond their collaboration. He would do nothing to jeopardize his chances.

"How about lunch? What do you feel in the mood for?" he asked.

"Oh, just some yogurt. And maybe an apple." She recognized his look. "No. There's no restaurant I know that serves just that sort of thing alone. I'm in the habit of grabbing a couple of items from a grocery store and then getting back to what I really want to do."

Scotty nodded in understanding. "I know what you mean. The going-out-to-eat process is sometimes too much. First you wait to be seated. Then you wait for someone to take your order. Then you wait for the food to be served. And finally you wait for someone to bring your bill. A lot of time wasted if there are important things to do."

They had begun walking back toward the cars and Scotty had stopped to write something in the notebook he was carrying with him. Sam took the minute to think about his words. She hadn't thought about eating in those terms before, but now she found she agreed with him.

"You must not like dating," she said to Scotty, "since it always entails the going-out-to-eat syndrome."

Scotty continued to jot something down as he spoke. "I've never felt comfortable dating. Haven't done it much. Though lately it's seemed much more appealing, considering the company I've been keeping. I think I'm revising my opinion."

He looked up from his notebook to smile at her. Sam didn't mistake the message in the comment or the smile. She felt as though she had just been hugged.

"How do you feel about fixing dinner at home?" she asked.

"Now that I can get into. Especially when I'm doing it with a friend. I think sharing an everyday task brings people closer. Lets them really get to know each other, naturally."

Scotty's arm brushed against Sam's as they continued toward the cars. His next statement sounded as though it was just a continuation of the same topic.

"After lunch, I'd like to go over the information on the Wilson woman's finances with you."

"Sorry, Scotty, but I've got to get back to the office. I have a meeting with my boss to update him on the case, and to convince him I need more time. Maybe we could meet later?"

"Tonight?"

Sam hesitated only briefly. "Sure. Why not? How about my place? Around eight?"

His hand was lightly rubbing her elbow through her sleeve.

"Is it safe?" Scotty asked.

There was an underlying innuendo in his words, which Sam appreciated. But she had no intention of letting him know she noticed the double meaning.

"Remember? I have a new security system. Doors and windows are wired. Feel better?"

"I think your crime rate here in Los Angeles must be worse than ours in San Francisco. Even the car I'm leasing has a burglar-alarm system. If someone tries to get into it by means other than the key, it triggers the most awful sound. Wakes up the pigeons for miles."

"Yes, well, there's a bright side to everything. The worse the crime rate, the less likely I'll be laid off."

His hand continued to hold her arm lightly as they walked to their cars. Somehow he knew she didn't mind. She seemed very socially balanced, able to accept simple courtesy and affection for what it was without looking for sexual or chauvinistic underpinnings. She was a real pleasure to be with. Not to mention lovely.

"I'll have the financial reports for you tonight," she said. "I'll bring home a copy you can keep, and go over if necessary. I find that one reading doesn't quite do it for me. Rereading always seems to bring out new information I missed the first time. That's why I go to such lengths to record everything and organize it so that I have it later to peruse. Give it time to sink in."

"Yeah. Me, too. I fight information overload all the time. So much interesting stimuli being presented to me, I can only fully appreciate a little at a time."

From the smile on Scotty's lips as he watched her face, Sam knew they had changed subjects somewhere along the line. Still, she found his way of expressing his physical attraction to her subtle and inoffensive. In fact, quite enjoyable. In his presence, Sam felt more like a woman than she ever had with anyone else. What was it about him that brought it out?

They reached her car. As their eyes met she smiled. He opened the door for her, but for some reason she hesitated, as though she had forgotten something. Before she could think what was delaying her, he put his arms around her and gently pulled her to him.

She felt the instant heat of his body. The gentle kiss on her hair. His breath escaping in a sigh. She was in contact with him only a moment before he let her go and turned away toward his car. She stood there a little breathless, before she slid into the seat of her own vehicle.

She looked up, just as she started the car engine, and caught a glimpse of two figures standing beneath the shade of some nearby trees. Watching her. The engine died. She glanced back at the ignition to switch it on again, and by the time she looked up once more, the two figures were gone. She might have thought she had imagined them—except for the tingling of the tiny hairs at the back of her neck.

Chapter Seventeen

Rebecca Myers was gracious and charming. She even disarmed Scotty for the first few moments of his visit to her home. It was located off Topanga Canyon Boulevard in the Santa Monica Mountains, not far from Mulholland Drive—where Joni Wilson had met with her fate.

She greeted Scotty at the door in a flowing, gold-colored gown, which accentuated the rich chestnut of her hair and eyes. He remembered her vividly from the funeral. Thirtyish, about five four, with a rounded figure and deeply tanned skin. The skin of a true Southern Californian.

He saw only the living room of her house. Very modern in both furniture and architecture. A spacious room in wood and glass with a magnificent view of the Los Angeles basin, on the one or two days each year it wasn't obliterated by smog. Unfortunately today wasn't one of those days.

She was no doubt well off and must have had servants. But she alone showed him into her home, asked him to make himself comfortable on a black, satin-covered sectional sofa, which sunk into the deep, light silver carpet, and asked what he preferred to drink. And it was Rebecca who disappeared into the kitchen to get his glass of cola and one for herself.

She gave him every indication that he was a valued guest, to be shown every courtesy and not rushed into pursuing the business he had come to discuss. Scotty was a little surprised at the treatment. It wasn't what was typically afforded insurance investigators.

"When we spoke on the phone, you said you were from the Heritage Insurance Company? Something about an insurance policy Joni Wilson had taken out?" Rebecca asked.

"Yes. Miss Wilson took out a policy with the company more than a year ago. Before we can issue payment to the beneficiary, we must assure ourselves of the extent of our legal obligation. Do you know why Miss Wilson would leave you money?"

Rebecca blinked and returned her drink to the top of the glass coffee table.

"Money? To me?"

"Yes. Do you know why Miss Wilson wanted to do that?"

Rebecca stood and moved toward the window to stare out into the smog. Scotty didn't feel guilty about misleading her into thinking Joni Wilson had left her some money. It was always the way he had operated in insurance investigations. It was amazing how much people were willing to tell you when they thought they might be getting some money. Especially the ones who didn't need the money.

He rose from the couch, too, giving the appearance of being ready to leave.

"I know this is a difficult time for you," he said. "If you'd like me to come back later, I'd be happy to. I understand you and Joni Wilson were best friends?"

She turned to face him but remained standing near the window. All the softness had gone from her voice and suspicion wove webs into her previously unlined face.

"Yes. The very best of friends. Now what is this latest joke? What was she trying to pull?"

"Miss Wilson took out a legitimate life-insurance policy, and I am representing the company that will be settling the claim. If you wish to check on my credentials, I encourage you to do so. I'm not a joker, but my presence has obviously distressed you. So I'll leave."

The webs almost instantly disappeared from the corners of her eyes and mouth.

"No, don't go. Forgive my outburst. It's just that this is so...unexpected."

Scotty sat down again. Rebecca remained standing. Ill at ease, like a spider was about to alight on her shoulder.

"I suppose the reason Joni would make me her beneficiary is because of our friendship. Still, quite a surprise for me."

She didn't believe it any more than Scotty did.

"But," he said, "since Miss Wilson was an heiress, I assume she would show you her friendship by mentioning you in her will—as a person with money might well do, wouldn't they?"

Rebecca seemed ready, even glad to answer that one.

"If she had the money. But Joni, uh, lost hers recently. There really wasn't any money to leave. So you see, she must have bought the life-insurance policy only in case anything happened to her."

It was just as Sam had said. Rebecca knew that Joni wasn't the heiress everyone thought. And her evasiveness told Scotty she knew precisely how Joni had "lost" her money. He would have to play this carefully.

He leaned forward to give the impression of idle gossiper. "She lost her money? She gambled?"

"She gambled. Quite a lot."

Rebecca was still standing, still uncomfortable. She still seemed to be waiting for the lurking spider. He wondered if he could push her off balance.

"Do you think the gamblers might have killed her? If she couldn't pay her debts?"

"Oh, no! I mean, I don't think so. Wouldn't they rather try to collect than kill?" Rebecca offered.

So, she could slip. But she was also quick to right herself afterward. She wouldn't stay down. He'd best try to continue to be the gossiping neighbor.

"Hmm. Good point. I trust your judgment. Were you aware of anyone who might wish to do her harm?"

"No. Everybody loved Joni. She didn't make enemies," Rebecca said. Now she seemed to believe herself on firm ground.

"Then you don't think that whoever killed her was someone she knew?"

"Of course not. It had to be some maniac. Some robber maybe."

"Sad commentary on our society that produces so many of these maniacs. By the way, when was the last time you saw Joni?"

"About a week ago. Sunday before last I think. Yes, Sunday. We had lunch. At Perrino's," Rebecca replied. Her slight hesitations were intentional. She knew exactly what information she was going to give.

"Oh, yes. I ate there once a long time ago. Great steak tartare. And was there anything unusual about Joni's behavior at lunch? Any worries or concerns she shared with you?"

Rebecca crossed from the window to sit opposite Scotty on the couch. She leaned back, getting comfortable. Scotty guessed she decided the spider wasn't going to show after all.

"No. She was in good spirits. Talked about taking a short trip somewhere. I didn't pay too much attention. She hadn't suggested I come along."

Scotty tried to control his excitement. "Was there a purpose to this trip?"

"Um, nothing serious. Just a change of scenery, I gathered."

"I can understand that. We all need to get away once in a while. Was anyone else going with her?"

"She didn't say, but I don't think so. She said she thought she would get away for a day or so, before the pool party we were going to have on Saturday."

"She was going to drive?"

"I'm not sure. Joni didn't like driving long distances. I guess it would depend on where she finally decided to go."

Rebecca was talking as easily to him now as she might to a familiar neighbor. He leaned forward as though hanging on her every word, displaying an interest few talkers ever received. She wasn't even wondering about the appropriateness of his questions. She was just responding.

"Is there anyone likely to know whether she decided to drive?"

"Maybe her maid, Isabel. You could ask her."

"I will, thank you. What can you tell me about this pool party?"

"It was just going to be the normal crowd. Myself, Julian, Monty, Claire and Colin. Nobody special."

"Who are all these people?"

"Sorry. Should have realized you wouldn't know. Julian Harris is a . . . friend of mine. He and I always attended Joni's get-togethers. Julian is president of Hollywood Savings and Loan.

"Monty Larkin is a special friend of Joni's. Her latest special friend. His mother is *the* Catherine Larkin. You know, from Boston. He's clever, charming and quite rich. He and Joni had been dating for about six months.

"Claire Buford, I mean North, is a friend of Joni's from college. She comes from a good family with good connections. She can be fun, but only when she's plastered.

"Colin North is Claire's husband. Colin made his money in hot-dog buns. They're exactly suited to each other physically. Sometimes it's hard to tell who's who from the back. Shaped the same," Rebecca said.

Scotty gave the little, gossipy chuckle Rebecca expected. "Did Joni have any other friends?" he asked.

"Of her class, no."

"Her class?" Scotty repeated.

"I mean of her same . . . interests."

"Was there someone not of her, uh, same interests?"

"Well, there's Isabel. You remember, the maid. She has a child, Jessica, who's Joni's age. They grew up together. Isabel cared for them both and was the only mother Joni ever knew. Joni always fussed about Isabel's daughter. She insisted she be kept in the house, takén care of."

"Taken care of?"

"Yes. You see, Jessica was born mentally retarded. Birth defect, or hereditary, or something."

"I didn't know. A shame," Scotty said.

"Yes. Well, I remember that several years ago when Joni's father wanted the girl sent away, Isabel fought him. She appealed to Joni, and Joni told her old man the girl was staying. They had one hell of a fight, I can tell you. And Joni won. I was flabbergasted. So was everyone else. Greg Wilson always won, except on that occasion. Joni really took care of Jessica."

"What was Greg Wilson like?"

"Well, not very likable. Strong, gruff man. Ruled everybody in his circle—except Joni. Particularly after that fight over Jessica. Joni was different from that moment on. She seemed to grow up somehow. She was no longer afraid of her father. I think her winning over the Jessica question matured her. Because from then on she marched to nobody's tune. Not even her own, sometimes."

From the sudden expression on Rebecca's face, Scotty realized the spider was never too far away.

"I don't understand . . ." he said.

"An idle comment. Doesn't mean anything," Rebecca said, though her expression told Scotty something had disturbed her.

"Does Jessica live at the Wilson mansion?" he asked.

"No, not now. She's in a special school or institution, I think. Joni told me she was taking her there a few months ago. I really don't know much about her."

"What about her second cousin, Peter Taswell? Were he and Joni very close?"

"You must be kidding. All he wanted was access to Joni's money and her rich friends. He thought nothing of making a play for any woman in the room. The man was a real embarrassment to Joni and us all."

"Yes, I can understand why Joni wouldn't include him in her circle of friends. But what about her attorney, Walter Chapell?"

Rebecca laughed. "Strictly business, I assure you. I remember vividly a juicy little story Joni told me about him when her father was being laid to rest. They were in the mortuary together checking to see if the arrangements were being taken care of, and Chapell started to come on to Joni."

"At the mortuary?" Scotty asked.

"Yes. In a viewing room next to her father's dead body! Chapell must have gone mad. Joni was livid."

Scotty shook his head. "Sick."

"I quite agree. She told him to get lost, of course. Threatened to tell his wife if he ever tried anything funny again. Walter was scared to death, I'm sure. He knows what a divorce would cost him."

"What would that be?"

"Money. Mrs. Chapell is the one with it," Rebecca said.

"What about the men in Joni's life?"

"Oh, she had a few flings. But, don't believe everything the society columnists say. She never really lived with any of them. Or promised to marry any of them, even though a couple tried to take her on palimony suits. Both suits were dismissed."

"Did her lack of desire for marriage hold true for Montgomery Larkin?"

"Yes. She was fond of Monty, but Joni liked being single. They never would have made it to the altar. I'm sure that's how Monty felt about it, too. He can have whom he pleases. No reason to restrict himself to one."

For a moment, Rebecca's expression reminded Scotty of a predatory hawk's. A hawk that constantly soars over the earth for food. Her eyes shone as if they'd spotted a juicy morsel that just couldn't be passed up.

"Don't you think that the men who tried to marry Joni and failed might be bitter?" he asked.

"Bitter? No. Their palimony suits were manufactured and Joni's lawyer proved it. Joni could have prosecuted, but instead she let them both go. Believe me, they were grateful. Joni didn't make enemies. She always looked for an easy way out of difficulties."

"Do you know what easy way she was planning to use to get out of her financial difficulties?" Scotty asked.

Rebecca looked startled. Then Scotty heard movement in a room behind him.

"Easy way?" Rebecca said. Her voice had become slightly higher.

Scotty rose before his seated hostess.

"It doesn't matter. I can certainly see why Miss Wilson would consider a good friend like you the appropriate beneficiary of her insurance. Thank you so much for your help."

His intent to leave was unmistakable. He knew the friendly chatter he had lured Rebecca into had been shattered by another presence. A presence that was just emerging from a back bedroom.

She rose quickly to escort him to the door. She seemed eager for his departure. Apparently she didn't want him to meet the other person in her home.

Scotty said goodbye again as he walked out into the bright sunlight. But he put his ear to the door as soon as Rebecca closed it behind him. He heard a few sentences before the couple moved into the living room.

"Who was that?" a male voice asked.

"An insurance man. I forgot I had made an appointment with him yesterday," Rebecca said.

"Insurance? What insurance? And why was he asking about Joni's finances? What was this 'easy way' business?"

"I . . . guess we got off the subject a bit. It was the strangest thing. Joni had a life-insurance policy that made me the beneficiary. Do you suppose she was . . . ?"

Scotty heard no more as the couple moved out of the entryway. He stopped to check the license-plate number of the white Porsche parked around the house out of view from the driveway. It matched the one he had recorded at the funeral.

Monty Larkin. Joni Wilson's latest lover. And now he and Rebecca were obviously having a fling. Why else park around the house out of view and give the maid the day off?

Julian Harris was supposed to be Rebecca's "friend." No wonder Rebecca had been so gracious to Scotty. Since she had forgotten their appointment, she was probably very relieved to find he wasn't Julian.

So the golden hawk had her juicy mouse. Well, it proved Monty couldn't be too broken up over Joni if he was sleeping with Rebecca. Joni hadn't exactly surrounded herself with the best of friends and lovers.

If you lie down with dogs, you'll get up with fleas.

Funny that particular thought should come to mind just now. Was Joni like the friends she chose?

"SHE'S BEGINNING to dig up things. Her companion turned out to be an insurance investigator. Something about a life-insurance policy. I don't believe a word he said. She knows something and is using him to pump us. She's got to be stopped."

The voice sounded irritated over the telephone. It had lost some of its deep quality. The other end of the line was quiet for a moment, as though the person was in thought.

"But her place? She's taken precautions. I saw the security van."

The irritated voice seemed to regain its confidence. More in control now that the decision had been made.

"Don't worry. There's always a way to get in. Always."

Chapter Eighteen

Samantha was distracted when she parked her car in her garage. She had to think of a way around this new obstacle.

She automatically went to her mailbox and pulled out the bills and her half-pound quota of junk mail. Normally she sifted through it right away. But tonight she just carried it inside and dropped it in her bedroom. She'd attend to it later. Later, when she got the taste of anger out of her mouth. Out of her mind.

That damn fruitless session with Lieutenant Mansfield had caused her to miss her workout at the gym. She wouldn't have minded so much if the meeting with her boss had served a purpose. But it hadn't.

Using her muscles always gave her a feeling of relaxation. She missed it. Maybe a few stretching exercises now would help. She glanced at her watch. No time. Ten minutes before Scotty was due. She could just have a quick shower and change.

At least she would be seeing him tonight, be able to talk it over with him. She felt strongly that he was on her side. And what a great feeling that was! To have someone there, someone who would listen and understand.

FROM THE MOMENT he walked into Sam's place that night, Scotty knew he was in trouble. She was wearing a pair of tight jeans and a white sweater, which didn't leave a whole lot to the imagination. If she had been another woman, he would have read the attire as a come-on.

But unless she was acting subconsciously, Sam wasn't the type to dress provocatively, Scotty knew. Such behavior just wasn't an ingredient of her classy style. No, it was probably an oversight on her part. She had come home, taken a shower and dressed hurriedly because she had stayed late at the office. Probably hadn't even looked in the mirror.

His guess was confirmed by her state of mind. She was noticeably upset. After letting him in, she paced the living room for several minutes while he tried to read the reports she had immediately handed him along with a soft drink. Hardly the props for a seduction scene.

After trying to concentrate with the minor distraction of her pacing and the major distraction of her attire, he finally gave up.

"What's wrong?" he asked.

She stopped pacing and came to stand before him. A light, clean soap scent reached his nostrils. "They want the case closed. They're satisfied with Taswell."

From his sitting position, his line of sight was level with her breasts. He decided he'd better stand.

"You've only had a few days. And two of them have been the weekend. I haven't heard the media clamoring for her killer to be found. Are your caseloads that heavy?"

"No. I've been looking 'too closely,' Mansfield says, into the financial backgrounds of Joni's acquaintances. There was a complaint. Someone who has a politically strong friend."

Sam's look told Scotty that they both were thinking the same thought. The somebody who complained might be their killer.

"Did you find out who?"

"No. I've been trying to for the last couple of hours. But the rich have power far beyond us mortal folk. And all of Joni's friends have moved in circles that could give them access to an ear or two in high places. Monty Larkin, Julian Harris, Claire North. Even Walter Chapell might have pulled it off."

For the first time Scotty heard frustration in her voice. He wasn't surprised. He had been on the carpet with his superiors many times, told to keep hands off, and he knew it was because strings were being pulled.

"Is it in the request stage or the demand stage?" he asked.

"Strong request."

"And you've refused?"

"Yes."

She was back to pacing again, and Scotty found his eyes following her. As he watched her thick, dangling braids sway with her movement, Scotty felt a growing wave of concern. She was right. Secrets were being kept. Her persistence in uncovering them could make her job more and more difficult, and even dangerous. He had a sudden strong urge to take her in his arms. Try to convince her to leave the case alone. Walk away with him now.

He sighed. No, he couldn't try to make her less than what she was any more than he could be less than what he was. But he could stay close. Be there when she needed him, and try to protect her.

"How much time do you think you have?"

Sam stopped to pick up her glass of diet cola and take a drink. "I'm not sure. I tried a compromise and asked for two more days before I go to the D.A. and pull Taswell in. I gave my boss the impression I was onto something, but that I didn't want to reveal anything until I had my facts straight."

"And?"

"Well, he didn't exactly back off, but at least he didn't demand I approach the D.A. tonight and make the arrest. I think he might go back to whoever is putting the squeeze on him and explain I'm uncovering new evidence. I think."

Scotty was considering the ramifications of her words when he was taken off guard by the subject change of her next question.

"You hungry?"

He thought about the last time he had eaten. He'd had a sandwich at noon when Sam hadn't been able to make lunch, but nothing since. Yeah, he was hungry.

"Now that you mention it, I think they can hear my stomach growling in the next town."

She laughed. "Me, too. Lunch was a long time ago. If you'd care to join me in the kitchen, I'll see what I have."

He got up and followed her, feeling a growing excitement as they walked into the kitchen. Each time he was with this woman, he found his reactions heightened. He was beginning to think an intimate dinner at home might not be such a good idea after all.

The day before when he had caught her from falling off the cliff, he had not wanted to let her go. He'd just wanted to continue holding her, luxuriating in the feel of her smooth skin beneath his hands, the sweet taste of her mouth.

And that morning at the cemetery he had almost gotten carried away. All it took was for her to stand beside him for a moment and let him catch the scent of her perfume, and he had been overcome with the desire to hold her again. To feel her soft, giving body next to his.

This was not like him. He had always been able to control himself before. But his deepening attraction to Samantha Turner and his feeling that she could be in danger were potent forces working against his control.

"I can heat up some canned clam chowder," she was saying, "bake some corn-bread muffins and make a salad. All in twenty minutes. What do you say? Want to help?"

"I think we should go out to eat."

Sam looked at Scotty in amazement. "After our conversation of this morning? I could have sworn you told me you hated going out to eat. Thought it was a waste of time."

"I'm in the mood for some Chinese food. Just got to have some lemon chicken. Do you have a light jacket you can put on? It's cooled off quite a bit from the heat of the day. You might even call it a little chilly."

He helped her on with a light nylon jacket she got from the hall closet, and for just a moment Sam felt his hands linger on her shoulders. Then they dropped to his sides.

"All set?" he said.

"I really should go into the bedroom to get my purse and brush out my hair."

"Your hair looks great. I like it braided. Get your purse and let's go."

Sam paused only long enough to set the automatic alarm. They had just stepped through the door when the bomb went off. Neither Sam nor Scotty knew what hit them.

Chapter Nineteen

Sam opened her eyes to find herself cradled in Scotty's arms. She felt as though she had been kicked hard in the back. With every breath she took, her lungs hurt. Her ears were filled with a loud swooshing sound.

"Sam? Thank God. I could hear your heartbeat, but it's taken you a while to come to. Sam?"

"What's that awful sound?"

"It's water pumping through the hose of the fire engine. I know, it's a dreadful racket. I couldn't imagine how you were able to sleep through it."

"Fire engine?" Sam sat up straight to find herself on the lawn in front of her house. Or what was once her house. Right now it was a mass of flames. She looked at it. Ashes like black ink scribbled their destruction across the moonlit sky.

Her hands reached out toward the raging torrent, as though she might be able to stop it. She felt Scotty's hands circle hers and gently bring them back to her side.

Her face was illuminated by the flames, and her look of pain hurt Scotty intensely. Anger began to replace his initial fear for her. Silently he pledged to get revenge on whoever had put that look on her face. And more importantly, on whoever had tried to take her life.

Sam knew she had to pull herself out of this terrible feeling of sinking despair at having lost all her worldly possessions. She must regain her perspective. She and Scotty were alive. That was all that really mattered.

She had a choice. She could sit on this wet grass and fall apart, give in to the black misery that threatened to engulf her, or she could get up and try to understand and do something about what had happened. Dispassionately now, she rose to her feet. "Whoever did it meant that for me. Maybe you, too. Are you all right?"

Scotty stood beside her. "Yes. Fine."

"I have to check on my neighbors. Be sure they're okay."

"Your house alarm brought the fire fighters. They got out everyone on the entire block. Your neighbors are taken care of."

"They're okay?"

Scotty noticed her repetition. "They're fine. No one was hurt."

Her eyes seemed to focus on him for the first time, and Scotty looked at her worriedly. He heard the siren come closer and then turn off. "The ambulance has just pulled up," he said. "Sit here so the paramedics can take a look at you."

Sam didn't even consider arguing with him. She just sat there dully while the emergency crew checked her vital signs.

Suddenly there was a new explosion. The garage. Now an angry torrent of flames and billowing smoke.

"The gas tank on the T-bird," Sam said as she got up to come stand next to Scotty. "Could we get out of here?"

Scotty opened the passenger door of his rental car. He marveled at her calm. Although what that discipline was costing her he had no idea.

They rode around for several minutes without speaking. The paramedics had indicated that she was fine, but Scotty was uncomfortable with her silence. She looked pale. He wondered if he should take her to the hospital. He was about to head in that direction when she spoke.

"Fortunately I keep my credit cards and checkbook in my purse. I need to rent a car. I've got to have something to get around in. If you're getting tired of being my taxi, I can get a regular one."

Scotty reached over and placed his hand on hers. "I'm happy to do anything for you. But before we get you a car, maybe we should go get a bite to eat somewhere."

Dinner. Sam had forgotten completely about it. Scotty had wanted to go out for Chinese food. Had to have lemon chicken. His insistence had saved their lives. Dear God. Was that how the fate of human beings was decided? Whether or not they went out to get Chinese food?

The landscape was fading around Sam. She looked out of the car window, but the images were misty. As though just beyond her vision. "I . . . I'm not sure I can face a restaurant right now. I'll wait for you in the car."

Scotty didn't answer. He just kept driving. Sam sat there, trying to keep her mind on the logical sequence of things she should do. She should have already called the arson squad, and her boss.

She was vaguely aware of Scotty's stopping and getting out. She was still going over in her mind things she had to do. The insurance company would have to be called. She had a homeowner's policy, but she couldn't remember exactly what it covered. No matter, she could look it up later in the file in her study. No. There was no file in her study anymore. There was no study.

Scotty returned, and Sam reacted to the odor of the food he carried the way a fainting person might to smelling salts.

"That isn't Chinese food. What do you have there?"

Scotty was already pulling the car out of the parking space.

"Chinese food takes too long to prepare. These are two chicken dinners. And a couple of fish-and-chips, just in case. Thought they might just resurrect your appetite."

Sam realized she had been moving and thinking in a daze. For the first time in many years, she had not even watched where she was going. She looked around for something familiar. "Where are we?"

"About a block from my motel. We'll be there in a minute."

They sat at the small table in his room and ate in silence. The warm food began to make Sam feel alive again. With some surprise, she realized she had been in a state of shock.

She sat back and looked at Scotty. He was finishing some hot chocolate, staring into the cup, apparently deep in thought. He had been so supportive. She had no idea what she would have done without him. "Thanks," she said. "I didn't realize how hungry I was."

Scotty looked up at her comment and gave her a smile that radiated across the table. Making even the bottom of her feet feel warm and happy. She smiled back.

"There's a lot I have to do," she said.

"It's after eleven. Let it wait until morning."

Sam thought about Scotty's suggestion. She did feel tired. And with her full tummy came a lassitude. The thought of leaving again to try to obtain a car and a . . .

She stood up. "I don't have a place to sleep," she heard herself say, as though the thought had just struck her, which it just had.

"There's an extra queen-size bed here. You can have my pajama top." Without waiting for her reply, Scotty walked over to the dresser and pulled out the light blue shirt. He put it on the second bed, retaining the bottoms over his arm.

Sam realized he wasn't asking her to stay. It was just the logical thing to do under the circumstances. "Can I use your phone? I've got to call in what happened. And let my office know where I am."

"Sure. I'll get rid of the remains of our meal down the hall. I noticed a trash bin there earlier. Give you some privacy."

Sam took off her nylon jacket, sweater and bra, somewhat surprised she was still wearing them, and then put on Scotty's pajama top. The room was warm enough. Not overly air-conditioned like many were. As she read the motel phone's dialing instructions, she was thankful at least her wits seemed to be returning. She was just finishing her report to the night desk when Scotty returned.

"Everything okay?" he asked.

"Fine. The arson squad will be there at first light. The fire's out."

Her voice was even, natural. But as she stood up beside the bed, she noticed the rip at the back of her jacket, the little holes burned by airborne ashes. She picked up the garment as though it was some strange object she had never seen before. Her fingers explored the rip, then circled the black holes in the fabric. Tears began to stream unchecked down her face.

Scotty saw the look on her face. He instantly realized what was happening, what she must be feeling. He felt as though he had just been punched in the stomach. He rushed over to take her in his arms. She buried her head in his chest.

"Everything's gone, Scotty. Everything."

The hurt in her voice cut him like a knife. He wrapped his arms more tightly around her and rocked her gently.

"I know, I know."

"The computer. My records. Such senseless destruction."

"Yes, it was. Senseless. Criminal." He stroked her hair, trying to calm her. Hoping to calm his own anger in the process.

"The T-bird. I . . . worked so hard for it. I . . ."

Her voice broke, and he thought his heart might, too. "Sam, Sam. Please don't cry. It's going to be all right. I'm here. I'll get the creep. I promise you, even if it's the last thing I ever do."

The fierceness in his voice got through to her. The tears subsided. She looked up at his face. His gray eyes were stormy, his lips set in a hard line. His look was almost frightening. She had never seen him like this. "You seem so sure," she said.

He smiled down at her, a tenderness once again in his eyes.

"Why not? I'm partnered with the best."

His words were so soothing, gentle. She smiled ruefully. "The best? How can you say that when I've just ruined your shirt? And besides, I need to blow my nose and I don't even have any tissues any more."

"Easily remedied. Use my shirt. It's pretty moist already," Scotty said taking it off and handing it to her.

It was when she looked down at the shirt in his hand that she saw his chest. The shock caused a sudden intake of her breath.

There was a snakelike scar, digging deep and winding across his waist and the right side of his rib cage. It seemed to get fatter along its twisting route, swallowing up the flesh and leaving the contour of the body thinner and less muscular than its corresponding left side.

She knew what had caused it. She had read the full report from the San Francisco Police Department. Because of him, a ring of drug smugglers had been stopped. But it had cost him his friend's life. It had cost him his job. What had Phil at the gym said? He wasn't even supposed to be walking. Yet he was. He had faced and conquered it all. Emerged strong and straight. He was a man like no other she had known.

She moved closer. Her hand reached out to touch the scar. Feel the reality of its existence. There was no ugliness to it. There could never be ugliness associated with this kind of courage. She could feel the skin quiver beneath her touch and heard Scotty exhale deeply.

"Sam."

His voice was husky. She looked up into his eyes and found herself momentarily shocked at the openness of his desire. She suddenly realized she was standing close to him, intimately caressing his bare chest.

His arms came around her, urging her closer. She felt the increased heat of her blood. The sudden racing of her pulse. She told herself she could stop this now. She should stop this now. But his nearness was sending incredible waves of pleasure through her.

Her arms encircled his sides to touch the bare skin of his back. Her hands played across the hard muscles of his shoulders. She was amazed at his sighs of pleasure from her smallest touch. He seemed so sensitive, so aware. It made her want to give him more pleasure. Her hands began to follow the line of his spine.

But somewhere along the route, she got sidetracked. For his hands had found their way underneath her shirt and had begun to stroke the bare skin of her shoulders. She felt as though her backbone was melting. Soon he had lifted the pajama top above her breasts, gently pressing her bareness to his.

Her senses felt overloaded. And somewhere within her, a circuit breaker was tripped. In a sudden, cold, lucid moment, she realized what she was doing. She was being carried away with sexual desire. A desire so strong and forceful, she couldn't even believe it was hers. Panicked, she pushed Scotty away.

"No. I can't . . ."

She pulled the shirt back down over her body and turned to get in the second bed, stopping briefly to yank off her jeans. She could still feel her increased heartbeat and the excited state of her body, but she began to put up mental shields against the physical insistence. She was a disciplined, thinking human being. Raw emotions did not rule her.

A few minutes passed. With each one her breath came easier. From underneath the cool sheets, she looked over at Scotty and saw him sitting on the edge of the other bed. A wave of utter despair gripped at her heart.

"Scotty?"

"It's all right, Sam. I understand. I'll get the light. Try to get some sleep."

She lay wide awake in the dark for a long time. Understand? How could he understand? How could he know she just couldn't make love for physical gratification? It was a part of her makeup. Just as real and tangible as her arms and legs. And she wasn't going to apologize for it.

But she did feel she should try to explain it to him. Only what could she say? That she didn't care enough? That she didn't love him? What was the truth? Suddenly she was confused.

She sighed. Could she be falling in love? She had known Scotty what? Four days? She hadn't even dated John until she had known him a month. And sex had followed much later.

This was futile. She had no time for emotional turmoil. Tomorrow was an important day. Important things had to be done. Like catching a murderer who had sent a woman off a cliff into a fiery grave. Someone who had meant a second fiery grave for Sam.

When she finally dozed off, it was with flames flickering before her eyes. But her dreams were a crazy mix. In one, a powerful unseen hand was pushing her toward external flames. In the next, Scotty's powerful arms were around her pulling her into an internal fire. And on the fringes of consciousness, she knew they were both still out there. Waiting.

Chapter Twenty

"Where were you this morning? It's almost eleven."

Lieutenant Mansfield leaned back and rocked his squeaky chair, a habit that drove Sam crazy.

"Well? I'm waiting, Turner."

"My clothes, along with all my other worldly possessions, literally went up in smoke last night. I had to wait until the stores opened today so that I could buy something to wear."

She could see her answer disturbed him. He had wanted to find fault, but she left him with no room. He knew she had just been through hell. Probably wanted her to break down in front of him. She wouldn't give him the satisfaction.

"How did it happen?"

His voice was unmistakably cross. But then, Sam couldn't remember any time it wasn't. Even on the numerous occasions he had asked her out.

"I stopped by arson on my way in here. They found the remains of a letter bomb."

"All right, I'll bite. Who would be sending you a letter bomb?"

"It didn't have a return address."

As soon as the words were out, Sam knew they had been the wrong ones. But she hadn't slept too well last night and this morning she almost didn't care what she said.

Mansfield's chair squeaked forward in a sudden lunge.

"Okay. Very funny. See my laugh. But will you be laughing if the next letter bomb succeeds?"

Feeling somewhat contrite, Sam considered his words. Obnoxious or not, he was her boss. And now she owed him the truth. After all, this was his job. A murder attempt had been made.

"I think this ties in with the break-in at my home. Someone is afraid of information I have or may uncover. So afraid, they are willing to kill to bury it. And the only major case I've got right now is the Wilson murder. It has to be one of the suspects."

"One of the suspects? There is only one suspect in the Wilson case I'm aware of."

Sam maintained her patience. "As I've told you before, other things don't add up. I'm not saying Taswell isn't our man. But I think it's too soon to make an arrest."

"You prefer he blows you up first?"

Sam had a sudden sinking feeling. Of course the lieutenant already knew all about the arson report and would have checked on the suspects' backgrounds just as she had. But she took solace in the fact that she knew she was more thorough. The military records might pay off yet.

"Taswell isn't the only one with a munitions background from the service. Julian Harris was a weapons-control expert. Colin North was in charge of plastic explosives. And Monty Larkin belongs to a fanatical right-wing arms club. A club even suspected of sending a few letter bombs to politicians. No doubt he's picked up a few pointers from them."

"And no doubt you know where all these people were last evening?"

Sam wasn't sure now whether her boss was baiting her or whether he hadn't thought the question through.

"Not worth checking. The letter bomb could have been put in my mailbox at any time during the day or even the night before. The lab tells me it was a big manila envelope."

The heavy man in the squeaky chair was studying her carefully. She didn't flinch.

"Why couldn't I get ahold of you last night?" he asked. "Why weren't you at that motel whose number you left?"

"I didn't register under my name. It wouldn't have been a prudent move after an attempt on my life."

"Funny you didn't mention it to the night desk when you phoned in your report," he said.

"Didn't I? Must have been distracted."

Her answer didn't seem to satisfy him. His voice became even more harsh. "Where does the Wilson case stand now?"

"Not much different from what we discussed yesterday. I haven't had a whole lot of time to work on it today."

"You weren't exactly clear yesterday on what new evidence you were hoping to uncover. Give me the specifics now."

Sam couldn't miss the growing anger in Mansfield's demand. She had a feeling that no matter what she said, it wouldn't satisfy him.

"I'm searching for a lead to the whereabouts of the Wilson-estate money. I'm convinced Joni Wilson did not gamble away twenty million. Her personality just doesn't support such behavior."

"Which means that you don't have a damn thing and you're just stalling me for time, doesn't it?"

Sam could see the blood rising in Mansfield's pudgy face. Her feeling had been right. He wasn't interested in hearing the facts, only in baiting her. He was easy to anger. She was not. Her voice was steady. Unemotional.

"Actually I believe I will discover the truth concerning the estate of Joni Wilson. I have an abiding conviction in my experience and judgment." She knew it was her calm and composure that always seemed to make him lose his.

"I'm damn sick and tired of you and your abiding convictions, Turner. Get out of here and go arrest Taswell. And that's an order!"

Chapter Twenty-one

While Sam waited for Taswell to be processed, she looked out the barred windows of the city jail, trying to escape from the confining atmosphere. But the view didn't help.

Cars with idling engines were packed into the streets below. They reminded her of stacked coffins waiting for burial. Their exhaust vapors trailed into the sky almost as though the inhabitants of those coffins were discontented spirits attempting to rise from the dead. Attempting anything to get out of the traffic jam they were trapped in.

Her eyes followed the vapor trails. The only relief to the gray skyline were a few scantily clad palm trees, standing as stiff and still as crosses over graves.

Sam closed her eyes and willed away the ugly images. There was another way to negate her discordant surroundings. Another much more pleasant way. She was once again with Scotty. Feeling his caresses . . .

"Sergeant Turner?"

She opened her eyes and turned around. "Yes?"

"Your prisoner is waiting."

Taswell paced back and forth in front of Sam's critical eye, a cigarette smoking between his fingers.

"I'm being framed, I tell you!"

"Then you didn't take this trip to Los Angeles from Las Vegas on the afternoon of the murder under an assumed name? And you didn't make these calls to Joni Wilson after you told me earlier you hadn't spoken to her in months?''

Sam's words were designed to put pressure on Taswell. To cause him to spew forth, preferably with the truth. His face reddened. "Dammit! I thought you said you'd listen to me with an open mind. Without that stupid lawyer of mine who wants me to plea bargain. And without using what I say against me!''

Sam leaned forward in the straight-back chair of the interrogation room, matching the intensity of the man standing before her. "Look, Taswell. You've just been booked for Murder One. The D.A. and my lieutenant wouldn't have it any other way. And I'm not so sure they aren't right. But I'm here to give you a chance to explain. To answer the questions you've refused to do so before. And what you say will determine whether I keep looking into this murder or whether I walk away and leave you to the courts. Which is it?''

Somehow her words, purposely loud and direct, had their desired effect. Taswell stopped pacing and sat down to light up another cigarette. Then he noticed he had two going and savagely crushed one out.

"What do you want to know?" he asked.

"Did you take that trip to L.A.?''

"Yes. But not to kill Joni. I went to borrow money. I had to. The casinos were after me for their dough.''

"Why the fictitious name?''

"I didn't want the casino collectors to think I was skipping town, or find out who I was going to see. If you pay off with borrowed money, they figure you're a bad risk. You get a stinking reputation that never washes off, and they won't give you any more credit. That's why I went out of Vegas to get the money. Any deal made there gets right back to the casinos.''

"Who did you borrow money from?" Sam asked.

"A guy here named Luis.''

"I'll need his full name and address.''

Taswell dragged hard on his cigarette. He ran a well-manicured hand through his perfectly styled hair. When the hand fell back to his side, it was trembling.

"It's no use. He'll never admit to lending me money. Being a loan shark he's not exactly legal, you know. Hell, you'd close him down."

"All right. Tell me about the telephone calls," Sam said. "Did you make them?"

"Yes, I made them. I just wanted to borrow some money. To avoid having to go to Luis. It'd been a while since Joni and I had quarreled. I thought she might have forgotten she was mad at me."

"Had she?"

"No."

"I have the telephone records. The week before her death you placed five calls to Joni's house. The first two lasted about five minutes each. The last three, only a minute. What exactly did you say to each other on those calls?" Sam asked.

Taswell paused to take another deep drag on his cigarette.

"She spoke to me the first time and asked me what I wanted. I told her I just called to apologize for our misunderstanding two years ago. She said she accepted my apology."

Her prisoner stopped as though he was finished. But Sam knew there had to be more. "Go on," she said.

"I asked if that meant I was welcome in her home again. She told me she would have to think about it. I told her I was sorry it had taken me so long to get around to calling her. Told her I was ashamed, that I had been drunk. She told me she had to hang up, but that we could talk again."

"Okay, Taswell. What happened almost two years ago? What was this rift all about?"

"She caught me in her library...with some of her checks."

"You were going to forge her signature?" Sam asked.

"The thought had crossed my mind. But like I said, I was drunk. There was a party going on. I mean, I never did sign her signature. She came in and took the checks and kicked me out. Like I was a dismissed servant or something."

"She kicked you out. Then almost two years later you call for forgiveness because you want to borrow some money. Now tell me about the second telephone call."

Taswell waved his cigarette before his eyes as though erasing his previous thoughts. Some smoke curled under his left eyelid, causing his eye to water. He blinked out a tear before he continued.

"It was later Wednesday night. I was worried. I decided to try her again, and she took the call. She seemed friendlier and we chatted about inconsequential things like the weather. I asked her if she had thought about our getting together, becoming closer like we were when her old man was alive."

"And?"

Taswell paused. "She said it was too soon, that she was going away and would think about it while she was gone. Let me know later."

"And that was it?" Sam asked. She was getting tired of dragging the story out of the man.

"No. I panicked. I didn't know how long she planned to be away. I needed the money then. So I broke down and told her I was in trouble. That I had to have over one hundred thousand dollars right away because there were thugs after me."

"And she said no?"

"She hung up on me."

"And she wouldn't take the rest of your calls?" Sam asked.

"That's why I finally booked the flight out to see Luis. I knew Joni wouldn't come through."

"How long did it take with Luis?" Sam asked.

"A couple of hours. He knew I was coming because I called ahead."

"No other calls appear on your telephone record to Los Angeles. Just the ones to your cousin's number."

Taswell put out his cigarette only to immediately light another.

"I know, I know. I used a pay phone. I thought maybe the casinos were bugging my hotel phone," he said.

Sam shook her head in disbelief. "Are you telling me you didn't care whether the casino collectors heard you begging your cousin for funds but didn't want them to know about a two-bit loan shark you contacted?"

Taswell's fist slammed down suddenly on the table. "I didn't plan to ask Joni for the money over the phone! I planned to go see her. Present the problem to her in person. But she said she was going on a trip and didn't say for how long. I panicked! I had to ask for the money then."

Sam's voice was icy enough to deep-freeze Taswell's hot temper. "If you pound this table again, you're going to find yourself alone in this room and in a cell doing life for the murder of your cousin."

She looked at Taswell briefly before continuing in her normal calm tone. "So you were with the loan shark for a couple of hours. What did you do for the rest of the time?" she asked.

Taswell seemed a little shocked and wide-eyed for a moment, possibly still reacting from her threat.

"What?" he said.

"Your flight from Vegas got you in after six-thirty Thursday evening. Allowing for car rental and drive, that should have put you at Luis's place at eight or eight-fifteen at the latest. If you were there even until nine-fifteen, which I doubt, what did you do from then until four forty-five the next morning when you caught your flight back to Vegas?"

Sam could always tell when someone was about to tell her a whopper. And at the moment, Peter Taswell was conjuring up a big one. His eyes were blinking and his head was turning nervously trying to find a plausible explanation to account for his time. She decided not to wait. "Don't do it,

Peter. At the moment, you've got one person in this world willing to listen to you. If you don't give it to me straight, then you've got no one."

Taswell licked his dry, cracked lips and dragged on his cigarette.

"I went to see Joni," he said.

"Did you see her?"

"No. When I drove up to her place, Chapell was there. His Mercedes was right next to her Rolls in front of the house. I waited a few minutes hoping he'd leave. But he didn't. And I didn't want to see Chapell. Then I decided trying to see Joni wasn't going to do any good anyway. I had the money in my pocket. I could go back and pay the collectors without her help."

"Why didn't you want to see Chapell?" Sam asked.

"The guy hates me."

"Why?"

Taswell sighed as he exhaled the smoke from his nostrils and mouth. "I caught him in an embarrassing act a couple of years ago."

"What was it?" Sam asked.

"It was when I went to the mortuary to view Greg Wilson's body. I walked in on him and Joni just as she was telling him the last thing in the world she would do was go to bed with him. And she warned him if he ever laid a hand on her again, she'd tell his wife. Then she walked out."

"He knew you were there?" Sam asked.

"Yeah. Turned around as soon as she left. Found me grinning at him. Got real ticked off and threatened to kill me if I ever told. It was so ludicrous, I laughed. He's hated me ever since. Like you always hate the person who knows the worst about you."

"All right. Let's get back to Thursday night. Did anybody see you while you waited to talk to Joni?" Sam asked.

"No, I don't think so. I parked in some hedges on the right side of the house. Nobody came out. There was another car in the back. But I couldn't tell whose."

"What time was this?" Sam asked.

"A little after eleven when I got there. I waited probably about fifteen minutes before I took off."

"Where did you go?"

"To Hollywood Boulevard. I picked up this girl."

"Does this girl have a name?" Sam asked.

"She said her name was Tracy. No last name."

"Description?" Sam asked.

"Brown curly hair, about eighteen—charged fifty dollars."

Sam swallowed her disgust. "And you were with her from . . . ?"

"About eleven forty-five until two."

"In a motel?"

"In the car. There are . . . places," Taswell said.

"Is this everything?" Sam asked.

"Yes."

Sam leaned forward menacingly. "Then what about the screaming conversation where you said, 'She's dead. I've made sure of that,' to Monty Larkin on the following day in Joni Wilson's Beverly Hills home?"

Taswell's Adam's apple bounced from his chin to his chest several times. It seemed to inhibit his ability to speak for several moments.

"That. What I said . . . I didn't mean anything by that. I thought she had been killed in an accident. I didn't know she was murdered! I was just playing the big man for Monty. After all, I was the one who brought him to Joni's party and introduced them. That's all he wanted from me. He was happy enough to sponge off me when I was flush. But when I hit a losing streak, he turned to Joni and her millions."

Sam sat in thought for a few minutes. Taswell looked cooked from his own internal fires.

"You've got to believe me! I swear I didn't kill her!"

Chapter Twenty-two

As Sam was about to leave the jail, she was approached by a guard.

"You've got a call, Sarge. You can take it over here."

Sam was expecting to hear Mansfield's voice. She was delighted when she found it was Scotty's. And even happier when she detected his tone was as light and easygoing as ever.

"Boy, you've been hard to track down. How about lunch?"

"Lunch?" she said.

"Yes. You know. The meal that falls halfway between breakfast and dinner?"

"You weren't there when I got up this morning. I wondered..." she began.

"I had some errands to run. And I wanted to give you some privacy. You found the key and my note describing the car I rented for you?"

"Yes, thank you. Saved me a lot of time. I appreciate it more than I can tell you."

"Don't mention it. Just part of my deluxe service. Now, where shall we meet?"

"Do you think you could find a hamburger place called Tommy's a few blocks from the station?"

"Sure. See you there in twenty minutes."

Sam hung up the phone, but held onto the receiver for several moments, as though she might still be able to stay in touch with the caller that way. She was smiling.

"SO YOU PULLED TASWELL IN but you're still investigating? And what does your lieutenant think about that?" Scotty asked.

"Obviously he doesn't know I haven't closed the case. Or my head would be on the block along with several other parts of my anatomy," Sam answered.

Scotty leaned back against the booth and watched her fiddle with the small gold earring that pierced her right ear. He had the sudden urge to rub that ear with his fingers, to feel its softness. He tried to return his mind to the business at hand. "After those answers he gave you, you still believe the cousin's innocent?"

"I don't believe the man has ever cared for anyone but himself. He's a selfish user of people. And I got a dreadful headache from being locked up with his chain-smoking for over an hour. But yes, I believe him. I don't think he killed his cousin."

"Did he give you any leads?"

"A couple. For one thing, he claims Chapell was at the Wilson mansion on the night of the murder. Or at least his car was. If he's telling the truth, then Chapell isn't."

"Which means Chapell might be the murderer. What else did Taswell say?" Scotty asked.

"Well, I got a new impression of Monty Larkin, Joni's lover. His image has changed from wealthy blue blood to a slightly impoverished blue blood from Boston. Someone who used his social position to sponge off the really rich. I'm going to make some telephone inquiries to see if I can substantiate Taswell's insinuations. If I can prove it, we may have found a motive for murder."

"I don't know. Seems strange if this Larkin guy wanted to marry Joni Wilson for her money that he would kill her. How was he going to get her money that way?"

Scotty's comment gave Sam pause. "Good question. But you have to remember she wasn't rich. Not any more. And Larkin knew it. By the way, I never got around to asking you. Did you find out anything from Rebecca Myers?"

"Yes, as a matter of fact. She's having an affair with this Monty Larkin. And if he's a pauper, I don't think she knows it. At least, that's not how she described him to me."

"But she's supposed to be Julian Harris's lover."

"Yes, I'm sure she still is. The affair between her and Larkin is a secret one. I wasn't supposed to know," Scotty said.

"Hmm. Wonder when this affair started? Could Rebecca have seen Joni as being in the way? Or perhaps Monty wanted Joni out of the way? Opens up a lot of possibilities. What else?"

"Well, if you're keeping score against possible suspects, put another mark against Chapell's name," Scotty said.

"Really? What did you find out?"

"He apparently made a play for Joni at her father's funeral. The lady told him to flake off and even threatened to tell his wife," Scotty said.

"That fits in with what Taswell said. He claims to have walked in on the last part of that attempted seduction. Said Chapell got so angry he threatened him."

"Lots of threats being thrown around that day. But I understand Chapell would end up penniless if his wife found out. Story is she's the one with the money," Scotty said.

"Maybe, but how could that have anything to do with Joni Wilson's murder? It happened almost two years ago. Plenty of time for tempers to cool. And Chapell's marriage appears intact, from all reports. Anything else?" Sam asked.

"Yes. A point for the tie-in of Joni Wilson with Jane Williams. It seems Joni Wilson took a trip on Thursday and was gone all day. Could have been San Francisco. Told Rebecca she was planning it, but not exactly where she was going. Said the housekeeper might know. Have you had a chance to ask?''

"Yes. It fits. Isabel Kane said Joni left early in the morning and if she got back, it was after the housekeeper had gone to bed. And she doesn't know where she went. The car was gone, but it could have been parked at the airport all day. She could have made the trip to San Francisco and met with Warren," Sam confirmed.

"There's something else," Scotty said. "It might have nothing to do with the murder, but there is a mentally-retarded girl named Jessica—she's Isabel's daughter and apparently in some special school somewhere. Rebecca spoke of her uneasily. Very strange."

"Hmm. Isabel told me about her daughter. I didn't realize she was mentally retarded. I'll check it out."

As Scotty watched her make a note about the housekeeper's daughter, he was really seeing her as she was the night before in his arms. He tried to put the image aside.

"How about a non-fat blueberry yogurt or a crisp Washington State apple for dessert?" Scotty asked.

"You know the way to this woman's heart, but no. I have to get back soon. I got lucky and managed to get an appointment with Claire North this afternoon. What's on your agenda?"

"Julian Harris."

"How did you do it? He's one of the most inaccessible guys in Hollywood. Elusive as an eel."

"I have to keep some secrets from you. Otherwise, you might decide you don't need me," Scotty said, only half in jest.

There was a pause before Sam answered.

"No, you've really been wonderful. And the information you've been able to uncover has been most valuable. I...I want to explain about last night, Scotty."

Ever since he called to ask her to lunch, Sam had wanted to broach the subject. But she hadn't known how to begin. Now she saw her opening and decided to take it. "I...care for you, Scotty. But I want you to understand how it is with me. I expect a lot of myself, of other people. I haven't dated much. I . . . Things matter to me. I don't fall into bed easily.'' It had been a struggle, but she had finally gotten the words out. He reached over and took her hand. His voice was incredibly tender.

"I know that, Sam. But I think what you may not know is that I don't fall into bed easily, either. What's been happening to us, these feelings that have been building each time we meet, are very real for me. Last night was . . .''

Scotty looked away. He was staring out the window. Sam followed his look, but there was nothing out there to see.

"Scotty?''

When he turned back to her, she saw the moisture that had collected in his eyes.

"When you touched me, Sam. You didn't turn away from the scar. I . . . you'll never known how much that meant to me.''

His smile seemed to light up the room. She basked in its warmth. He was happy with who she was. He seemed to understand and accept everything about her. As she understood and accepted him. She squeezed his hand from the pure pleasure she felt.

"Tonight? Could we meet to discuss this afternoon's interviews?'' he asked.

"Absolutely. But I'm not sure what time. I could be at the office until late waiting for a couple of reports to come in.''

"Okay. Call me when you're on your way. I'll get you a room at the motel where I'm staying. We can eat at their restaurant.''

When Sam said goodbye to her partner, she felt light and happy. She would see him again soon. Once again they would discuss the case. And if anything else came up? Well, this time she would be prepared. She would be in control. She hoped.

"THE COP ISN'T DEAD!" the nervous voice said.

"Doesn't matter now. We've got it made," the deep voice returned.

"What do you mean?" the nervous one asked.

"Taswell's been arrested. Formally charged with Joni's murder. Get your passport ready. In a couple more days, we can leave for Europe."

"What about the cop?"

"I'll keep an eye on her, and the boyfriend. Until we leave."

"Couldn't she come after us?" the nervous voice asked.

"Not without blowing the whistle on herself. Don't worry. She's in my sights at all times."

Chapter Twenty-three

"I wasted time, and now doth time waste me."

Scotty's pun was not lost on the balding, frog-shaped man who stepped on the scales in front of him.

"*Richard the Second*, Act V, Scene V," the shorter man said.

He hopped off the scales and turned around to face Scotty.

"But I don't think Shakespeare meant it in quite the same way as we do here at the Los Angeles Athletic Club."

"Ah, a literate man. A revered, but dying breed. I'm Scott Lawrence," Scotty said, extending his hand and a smile,

"Julian Harris," his companion answered, shaking Scotty's hand. "Can't remember seeing you here before. Are you a new member?"

Julian had wrapped his towel around his shoulders and was headed toward the showers.

"Actually no. I'm in town for a short stay. A member invited me to be his guest today."

Conversation ceased for the next few minutes as both men stepped under their respective water sprays. As he toweled off, Scotty was wondering how best to approach Julian Harris.

The man had refused to see him as an insurance investigator. His secretary had informed Scotty that her boss wasn't interested. So, arranging a run-in with him at the health club was the only way Scotty could think of to talk with the elusive man.

"Apparently your member friend didn't join you today. Would you care to have lunch with me?" Julian asked.

Scotty's concern on how to continue their conversation was eliminated. "Nice of you. Hate to eat alone." He turned to his assigned locker to dress.

"I notice you're using Jack English's locker. Is he your friend?" Julian asked.

"He's the member who invited me."

"As I recall, Jack is on the board of some insurance company," Julian said.

It was a gentle probe but Scotty was on guard. "Yeah. That's how we were introduced."

Scotty was hedging of course. What he wasn't saying was that Ms. Grenville of Heritage Insurance had given him Jack English's membership card to use and he had only met the man for two minutes—long enough to get the card and some instructions on guest procedure.

He knew Julian was smart, as well as cagey. He obviously wanted to know whom he was talking to. He was not one to easily volunteer information about himself.

Scotty wasn't good at lying. If he could keep things as close to the truth as possible, he'd be better off. Since direct questioning would be considered suspicious, he would have to go easy. Just let the conversation drift until it settled into the areas he was concerned with.

The men soon headed for the dining room, which impressed Scotty with its white tablecloths and finely dressed waiters. He knew he had to let Julian begin the conversation. He could tell that the man wanted the upper hand—had to feel in command. Scotty had no problem in letting Julian have the illusion he controlled the situation.

"So what brings you to L.A.?" Julian asked between bites.

"I'm happy to say I'm on vacation from my San Francisco office—although I'm sure you don't know too many people who come to crowded L.A. to vacation."

"You read my thoughts. Only the Japanese vacation in Los Angeles these days. There must be a woman in your picture?"

Julian would never know how astute his guess was. "Isn't there always?" Scotty asked.

His companion laughed. "Well, life would be pretty dull without them. Who else could we blame for all the mistakes we make?"

"Mistakes like vacationing in L.A.," Scotty said with a grin. "Where do you prefer?"

"To vacation? That's easy. I go to Europe. The casinos," Julian said.

"So you're a gambler? That's where the men get separated from the boys. What's your game?" Scotty asked.

"Baccarat. Matter of fact, I think the other games are for suckers. Do you gamble?"

Scotty hung his head ever so slightly. "Not anymore. I had to quit cold turkey a few years back."

It was as good a dodge as any, decided Scotty. People always liked to hear about the weaknesses in others. Made them feel a lot stronger, superior. And when people felt superior to others, they started to think they were above mistakes, which was naturally when they made them.

"You were hooked?" Julian asked.

"Yes. Couldn't say no. But, it's under control now. Tell me about baccarat. Why do you prefer it?" Scotty asked. If there was one thing he was proud of, it was his ability to listen. And what was of particular importance in this situation, to show what appeared to be genuine interest in whatever his companion said.

Julian was caught in that interest. His eyes lit up with enthusiasm. His tone became reverent.

"It's the buildup. The players. The quiet that makes them feel like worshipers in church. And, of course, the excitement of thousands of dollars being won or lost with the turn of a card.''

Scotty knew the game well. The player or bank holding two or three cards totaling closest to nine won, along with those betting on him or the house. It was an ideal game for system players because the bank always won more often than it lost. However, it was best right now for him to sound naive. ''It sounds like the game to play, all right. But if the stakes are in the thousands, wouldn't it be easy to drop a bundle?''

Julian moved aside for the waiter to place the main course in front of him. He seemed irritated by the interruption, so eager was he to answer Scotty's question.

''Yes, but that's the real draw. At the special tables in the European casinos, it's played only by people who can lose one hundred thousand and not be bothered too much by it. And those are the kind of people to watch and to be.''

Scotty recognized Julian's soft underbelly, since he obviously considered himself one of those people. ''How much have you personally ever seen lost in one game?''

Julian leaned forward in his chair and pointed his fork for emphasis.

''Well, I saw this young guy from Kuwait drop a quarter-million dollars once at a Monte Carlo baccarat table.''

Scotty donned the appropriate facial expression. Julian smiled, obviously enjoying the storytelling and the effect it seemed to have on his rapt listener. ''What did he do?''

''That was the damndest part. He got up from the table, cool as you please, and just walked away like it was lunch money. I tell you, it's the best game. It has its share of winners, too.''

''Are you very lucky at it?'' Scotty asked.

''Oh, I've won more than I've lost. Runs in streaks, though. If I lose twenty-five thousand, I stop and come back another day. That's my break-off point. Never fails. Next time I'm back, I win.''

It was time for Scotty to dish out some approbation. "Have to hand it to you. You've got the smarts to know when to quit. Have you ever been a big winner?" he asked.

"Not really. Most I've won is one hundred and fifty thousand," Julian said. His accompanying shrug indicated it was no big deal.

"Sounds like a lot to me."

"Peanuts. Let me tell you. I have this friend, Joni, who is a whiz. Now, she can make a living at the game. She has everything it takes. The big stakes. The cool nerves. And an affinity for when the number nine will show up. I swear I never saw that woman lose. And we've gone on many a gambling trip together."

Scotty's pulse had quickened. "She wins large amounts?" he asked.

Julian chewed a bit more before he answered.

"Only a month ago I watched her turn fifty thousand into almost a half a million dollars within just an hour or two at baccarat. Needless to say, it's the only game she'll play."

"Fifty thousand. Half a million. Well, it's a good thing I gave up gambling. Sounds like an exciting game. I'm sure I would have lost my shirt at it."

Julian gave a superior little laugh.

"Life is full of games. You just need to find the one that's right for you. Cheer up," he said, conveying the impression that if Scotty did cheer up, Julian would feel cheated.

Lunch was over. Scotty and Julian parted seemingly as casually as they had met. It was two o'clock when Scotty pulled his rental car out of the club's parking lot and joined the stream of cars crawling along the one-way streets to the freeway entrances.

It wasn't a pretty city. Too much smog and heat. Too much concrete and congestion. But, Sam was here. And he was having trouble thinking about what would happen when this case was over. When she no longer needed him. When he would go back to San Francisco without her.

Their relationship wasn't exactly a practical one over the long run. Her work was here. His was there. He tried to face these facts, but his feelings for her kept getting in the way.

He wished he could see her now. He had learned more than he had hoped from Julian. Things he wanted to share. Joni Wilson didn't lose at gambling. And only a month before, she had won close to half a million dollars. Where had that money gone?

A red light brought his slow progress to a complete stop. He looked over at an ice-cream shop to see a man in a business suit come out licking a large vanilla cone with a dripping chocolate top. How had Warren described Jane Williams? A vanilla ice-cream cone dipped in chocolate. Something bothered him about that description. What was it?

He shook his head. Not many answers to his questions today. He hoped Sam would have better luck in her interview with Claire North.

Chapter Twenty-four

A maid showed Sam into the Norths' home, a place of antiques and Oriental rugs. She waited in the living room for approximately five minutes nosing among hundreds of figurines precariously perched on spotlessly clean, glass display cases. She knew only an avid devotee could appreciate the art before her. She saw the tiny, intricate objects as interesting items of one-time study, after which they were relegated to the status of dust collectors.

She heard the noise behind her and turned to watch Claire North enter the room. Her height was the first thing anyone noticed. She had to be at least six foot two, with the shoulders of a fullback, muscular arms and large, prominent breasts. Her gait was slightly swaying.

As she came closer, Sam could see the deep red of her hair, almost a blood-red. It framed her pear-shaped face in fiery waves, stopping about the middle of her neck. Her deeply tanned skin set off the pale blue of her round eyes. Her nose was short and straight above full lips painted the same blood-red color as her hair.

When Sam had seen her at the funeral, she had stopped and stared. Not because the woman was that beautiful, but because her looks were so strikingly different. And because her husband, Colin North, was shaped almost exactly the same except, of course, in the chest. Even seemed to move the same way. His facial features and hair color were dif-

ferent, though. Dark, curly hair and tanned skin. Hooked
nose with glasses. A solid, scraggly tree on which the exotic
flower leaned. That's what Sam had thought when she'd
seen them together.

"Miss Turner?" the exotic flower asked.

Her voice was high, quavering, belying the large form
from which it emanated. She motioned for Sam to sit down
on a delicate two-seater couch, which looked very old, very
frail and very expensive. Then she sat on a similar one opposite.

"I appreciate your seeing me on such short notice and at
such an unhappy time," Sam said.

"Oh...yes. My husband said you wanted to talk with him
about Joni's things?"

Sam did not miss the slight slurring of her words.

"Actually, the matter concerns you most directly. Can
you think of why Joni Wilson's clothes are missing from her
closet?"

"Clothes? Missing? What are you saying?"

Claire North was a surprising dichotomy. Physically she
was built as though she had the strength of cast iron, but
emotionally she was proving as delicate as the fine china and
other ornaments of her vast collection.

Sam watched her get up and go over to a portable bar to
pour herself a drink. Her already high voice had risen two
octaves. If she got any more excited, vibration of her voice
might break the delicate crystal and glass objects around
her.

Sam was glad she had lied to Colin North about the purpose of her visit and had not identified herself as police.
She'd just said she was an employee of the city of Los Angeles, deliberately making it seem as though she just needed
some statistical information concerning the late Joni Wilson's estate.

For that information, Colin North had referred Sam to
his wife, whom he described as a closer friend of the de-

ceased. She knew now she was talking with the weaker half of the couple. At least, emotionally.

"You know nothing about her missing clothes?" Sam asked.

"Of course not! I have no knowledge of any missing clothes. You can't be accusing me!"

Sam felt as though any attempt to challenge the exotic flower in front of her was going to cause Claire North to wilt. The woman had obviously consumed a few too many drinks and was reacting strongly to everything. She decided to take a different tack.

"Naturally you would never be suspected. Not a woman of your standing. That's precisely why I've come to you—because you are above reproach. Because you were Joni's good friend. Because you might know who removed her clothing," Sam said.

Claire seemed relieved. "I don't know. Does it really matter?"

Sam smiled reassuringly. "No, Claire. I guess it doesn't."

Claire downed her drink and poured another. Only then did she seem to realize she had not offered her guest a drink.

"Care for one?"

"I'd love one," Sam said, automatically getting up to fix her own. Claire brought her own drink back to the antique chair and sat down again, slowly and gently. She seemed perfectly happy for her guest to wait on herself. Sam put some plain soda in a glass and once again sat opposite the fragile Amazon.

"Tell me about her, Claire." Sam made every effort to keep her voice light, her manner gentle, encouraging.

"You want to know about Joni? Why?"

Sam shrugged. "Just curious, like everybody. One hears so many stories, but I know you'd tell me the truth. After all, you were the only one who really knew her well." Sam's words brought a smile to Claire's face. The woman obviously liked being considered an authority on Joni.

"She's very pretty, of course. Long hair. Good tan. That's what everyone notices first. Most men take to her right away. And she can talk to them as their equal."

"Did she love Monty Larkin?"

"Monty? Sure, in her way. Physically he's what Joni likes. A hunk. But not mentally. Joni likes mental challenges."

"What about Julian Harris?"

"For Joni? Never. Oh, he's smart. But not nearly as smart as Joni. And Joni likes a beautiful body on a man. If you've ever seen Julian Harris, the one thing you realize is that there is nothing beautiful about his body."

Claire made her statement as a matter of fact, but then she giggled.

"Did Julian ever want Joni?"

"Hell, no. Julian could never get together with a woman like Joni—too much mental competition. Besides, he's head over heels in love with Rebecca."

"And Rebecca? How does she feel?"

"Oh, she loves Julian in her own way. But she needs excitement. Something different now and then. Harmless, of course, just a fling here and there."

"Did she ever have a fling with Monty?"

Claire smiled again. "Oh, she'd probably be willing. I've seen her flirt a couple of times with him. But I don't think Monty encourages it. Monty wants Joni. He seems oblivious to other women."

"I understand Isabel, the maid, was close to Joni?" Sam asked.

"Oh, yes. Joni thinks the world of her."

"And, Isabel's daughter, Jessica?" Sam had pressed a button. The color began rising again in Claire's cheeks. A frown puckered her forehead.

"I never . . . really knew her," she said.

"What about Peter Taswell?" Sam asked.

Surprisingly Claire seemed to regain her composure. For some reason, discussing the accused murderer of Joni was easier than discussing Jessica, someone who was supposed to be Joni's childhood friend.

"I like Peter. He's uptight, but can be funny when he relaxes, although he has this obnoxious streak. I remember a couple of months after Greg Wilson died, Joni threw a party. She'd been feeling really down. I'd never seen her that way before. Withdrawn. Moody. She took her daddy's death hard."

"She loved her father?"

"Never showed it while he was alive. He liked yelling at people. And although it wasn't much fun for her, I think he liked it when she yelled back. I remember him telling one of his friends once that he was glad he had a daughter who was as strong as he was. And pretty, too. Then he laughed. You know, proud like."

"So they had a relationship that included a lot of yelling?"

"Seemed that's all they did. She stormed out many times. So angry. But as I said before, it was different after he died. She got so depressed. She really must have cared for him."

"What was her depression like?"

"I don't know. Like any depression, I guess. She didn't want to be around anyone she knew. It lasted maybe a month or two. Well, anyway, one day she just seemed to snap out of it. Called me up and said the mourning was over. Colin and I were invited to a party. Right then. Come as we were... Now why was I telling you this?"

"Something about Peter Taswell. An obnoxious streak. Was he at the party?"

"I remember now. Yes, he was there. Everybody was there. Even Monty, although he and Joni weren't an item yet. She was going with a guy named Steve. And that's where the problem started."

"Problem?" Sam asked.

"You see, Joni was having an argument with Steve about where some little country was. They had opened the library door to get an atlas to settle who was right. That's when Joni found Peter with some of her checks."

Claire squirmed in her chair as though she was avoiding sitting on a pin.

"What happened?"

"She called him a few uncomplimentary names. Most uncomplimentary. He left immediately after."

"And Joni didn't see him again?" Sam asked.

"I don't think so. She never talked about him afterward. And that happened almost two years ago."

"Did she ever talk to you about Walter Chapell?"

"Her attorney? Yes. Last month, as a matter of fact. We were supposed to be going somewhere together. Where was it now? Oh, Monte Carlo. Yes, that's right. She postponed the trip by a day because she said she had to see Chapell on business...."

Sam could tell Claire had just realized she'd made a mistake. The red crept up from her neck and started to spread beneath the tan of her face. She gulped as if to swallow the words she had just spoken.

"She was good at business?" Sam asked.

Claire took another drink before she answered.

"Oh, yes. Joni's very smart. She can figure anything out. We used to play games and Joni would always win."

Claire was obviously relieved that Sam didn't seem to notice the mistake she had made. Actually Sam had. Walter Chapell had told her he hadn't met with Joni in person. That all of their transactions were done by mail or telephone. Claire North had just put a lie to his words.

Maybe even more importantly, Claire knew she wasn't supposed to have mentioned the meeting with Chapell. It could mean only one thing. The real relationship between the deceased and the attorney was important enough to be kept secret. Even lied about. But Sam knew better than to call the fragile woman on it. Better to make her feel comfortable so that she would talk some more.

"You say Joni was good at games?" she asked. "What kind of games?"

"Oh, all kinds. Most of them silly. Julian started us out one day. Scrabble, I think. Then we tried Trivial Pursuit. Charades. No one, not even Julian, gave her any competition. She has a sociology degree. Graduated top of our class. She knows so much about so many different things."

Claire was only sipping her drink now, a great deal more at ease. Her admiration for Joni was also apparent. Neither her tone nor body language held the slightest bit of animosity toward the woman who must have bested her many times.

Sam had also noticed that Claire's descriptions of Joni were in the present tense. It was common for someone recently dead to still be referred to in present tense by force of habit, but Sam sensed Claire's use was because of something else. "You speak of Joni as though she were still alive. It's not possible to think of her as dead, is it?"

The large woman took a big gulp of the small drink.

"No. She's..."

Claire bit her blood-red lips. The lipstick was staining the whiteness of her teeth. She seemed to have no defenses. She also had no response to Sam's question.

"Do you think she's dead, Claire?" Sam asked. She watched the pale blue eyes begin to water. The woman's hands began to shake as she quickly downed the rest of her drink.

"Why are you asking such a question? I can't imagine why you would want to say such a thing. You must leave now. I'm tired."

Sam didn't attempt to fight the dismissal. She doubted she could learn any more. Not from a woman who couldn't even accept the death of the heiress.

But why couldn't she accept it? What was there about Joni Wilson's death that made it seem unreal to her college friend?

Chapter Twenty-five

Scotty sipped on his third cup of hot, bitter coffee, wishing he hadn't ordered it but reluctant to throw it out. It was only nine o'clock and already he was tired. Must be his lack of real sleep the past couple of nights.

He watched Sam's face. In the two hours they had just spent exchanging information each had gathered on the case, not once had the frown lifted from her forehead. She took her work very seriously.

She reminded him of himself. The years on the force. His constant search for more evidence. Needing to know he hadn't overlooked anything. Bucking authority when necessary. Not always following the rules, but rather doing what was reasonable. Driven by a strong sense of justice that was somehow a part of his being, as it obviously was of hers.

"So you don't think Chapell's and Joni's relationship was simply that of client and attorney. Yet they don't seem to have been friends. And you get the feeling Chapell didn't even like her. What else could it be? Did she have a financial manager?" he asked.

"No. At least not during the last two years. When she inherited her mother's money, she also inherited a finance-management company, which continued investments on her behalf until her father's death. Then Chapell oversaw her investments. Or as he puts it, her constant withdrawal of all her funds so she could lose at the gambling tables."

"But according to Julian Harris she didn't lose. Who's telling the truth?" Scotty asked.

Sam sighed in frustration. "I know we've got a lot of information. My real concern is that there's still so much we don't know. And before I can get the right questions answered, I have to have it clear in my own mind what the right questions are." She smiled for the first time in two hours as she listened to her own words. "Did that make any sense?"

Scotty grinned. "It made perfect sense. Before we start off for somewhere, we have to be sure of where we are, where we're going, and what we hope to find when we get there," he rephrased.

"Wish I had said that." She smiled again. It occurred to her she had been doing a lot of smiling lately. Usually at the man sitting across from her.

Most of the time she was able to lose herself in the business they talked about. He was a partner then. The best she had known: intelligent, perceptive, responsive and resourceful. It was a pleasure to work with him—that's what it felt like most often. But not now. Now she was too aware of the broadness in his shoulders, the strong line of his cheek, the sensuous turn of his mouth. Now it felt . . .

"What are you thinking?" Scotty asked Sam, as her silvery eyes began to gently glisten.

"Uh, nothing. Where were we?" She sat up straighter in her restaurant chair and attempted to again put her mind on business.

"Trying to make the information we've got into some kind of sense," he answered. "While we were standing on the ledge on Mulholland Drive the other night, I got the impression that pushing a car over wouldn't have taken much strength."

"Yes. Same conclusion I reached, which means the murderer could have been a man or woman," Sam said.

"Maybe we should look again at the statements made by Joni's friends and associates. Their alibis for the night of the murder."

Sam nodded. "Three other attorneys verified Chapell was at a dinner at the Beverly Hilton until about eleven. His wife said he was home by eleven-thirty. But Taswell claims Chapell was at Joni's place in Beverly Hills until eleven-fifteen," Sam said.

Scotty checked the map he had gotten from the automobile club that afternoon. He had marked the Wilson home, the Mulholland Drive location where the body was found and the respective houses of the suspects. All were in close proximity.

"It's possible Chapell left soon after Peter did and arrived home at eleven-thirty or shortly after. Their homes are not that far away," he said.

"Or he may have driven up to the Mulholland Drive location with Joni in her car and ended up pushing her and her car over the edge. It wouldn't be the first time a wife lied to protect her husband," Sam said.

Scotty spoke his questions aloud. "But how did he get back home? How did whoever it was leave the scene of the murder? Did he walk? Hitchhike? No, too risky. Two cars had to be involved. But if two cars had to be driven to the point where one went off, then two people had to be involved in driving the cars. Two murderers or one murderer and an accomplice?"

Sam took a sip of cold coffee. Either its taste, her thoughts, or both, made her frown.

"I suppose it would be unlikely for Joni to have driven her own car. Unless she had gone there for some reason, such as to meet someone?"

"But who? Rebecca Myers and Julian Harris alibi each other out at a comedy show. Then at Rebecca's house after ten, Monty Larkin joined them, and all three alibi one another. Both men spent the night at Rebecca's, Monty sleeping on the sofa because he'd had a little too much to drink. Except there are no live-in servants for verification," Scotty said.

"Yes, and the Norths alibi each other. Home all night. Colin claimed illness. But the servants went to bed before eleven. They can't verify one or both of the Norths' story that they remained home all evening," Sam added.

"What about the Wilson housekeeper?" Scotty asked.

"Isabel Kane said she went to bed in her quarters at the Wilson home at eleven-thirty. Saw nothing, heard nothing. No one was there to verify her story, either," Sam answered.

"So we're back where we started," Scotty said. "Everyone but Taswell and the housekeeper has an airtight alibi. Unless it is true that the murder needed two people or more. In that case, two or more people who alibied one another could have been working as a team...."

The idea had obviously piqued his interest. Sam picked up on his thoughts.

"And if it did take two to commit this murder, then Taswell and Isabel Kane were the only two people connected with it who could be eliminated as suspects because neither had an accomplice. Because if they had been working together, surely they would have arranged to alibi each other," she said.

Scotty rubbed his temples. "Too many possibilities. Is this getting us anywhere?" he asked.

"Probably not. Let's approach it from another direction. I'm partial to formulating a hypothesis and then testing what is known and what would have to be known to prove it."

"Yes. The 'what if' game. I know it well. Shall I begin?" he offered.

"Shoot."

"Let's start with what brought me into this case. What if Jane Williams and Joni Wilson were the same person? Now, assuming they were, why would an heiress want someone else's birth certificate?"

"She needed another identity," Sam said. "Now, let me take it from here. What if she needed another identity to commit a crime? If that's our hypothesis, what was the crime she intended to commit?''

The waiter who had served them dinner and numerous cups of coffee in the past few hours was at the next table noisily cleaning up. Neither could mistake his displeasure at their continued dalliance.

"I think we've overstayed our welcome," Sam said.

"Just as well. I need to go check at the motel office and make sure they got that room next to mine ready for you. It was still in the 'I'll try' stage when I called this afternoon," Scotty said.

Sam was thankful to be moving. She felt stiff and sore from the knockout blast of the night before, even worse now than she had then. Scotty didn't miss the careful way she walked.

"Sitting still for so long has allowed your muscles to tense up," he said. "I feel the same way. What we both need is a hot bath."

In less than thirty minutes, Sam was lying back in the lukewarm water of the motel's small tub. She tried to relax, but it was no use. The water wasn't hot enough and her long legs just didn't fit. She gave up and stood under the shower to wash her hair, feeling the ache in her shoulders and neck as she raised her arms.

It wasn't until she was towel-drying her hair that she remembered she didn't have a blow dryer to finish the job. She sat down on the bed feeling suddenly exhausted. Amazing how the little things in life could get her down.

She tried to give herself the big picture. Remind herself she was lucky to be alive. But the aches and pains were sapping her strength and making her irritable.

At least she had remembered to buy a robe that morning on her quick shopping trip. She put it on. But great. It didn't fit right. Hung open in the front almost down to her navel.

She looked in her shopping bags. She had forgotten to get a nightgown and slippers. She threw the shopping bags across the floor and sat down heavily on the bed, only to realize she couldn't find a comfortable position. For the first time in years, she felt totally defeated.

When Scotty knocked on their adjoining door, she didn't answer. The last thing in the world she wanted at that moment was company. Even Scotty's. Maybe he would go away.

"Sam? Everything okay?"

He wasn't going away. The door opened. He stood there looking at her sitting on the bed with her partially dry hair dragging despondently around her bent head. She tried to turn to look at him, but her neck didn't want to cooperate.

The next moment he was sitting next to her, his warm hand beginning to massage the back of her neck. A gentle, rolling motion. Easing away the tension, the pain. Working its way up into her scalp. Bringing back warmth and circulation.

"Oh, that feels wonderful."

"Lie on your tummy. Let me work on your back."

The last thing in the world Sam would have dreamed of doing was arguing with him. She obediently lay down and gave herself over to the fantastic feel of his fingers through her robe. They worked their way down her neck almost to her tailbone, then back again and again, leaving her muscles with the consistency of jelly.

"How did you know?" she asked in a voice muffled somewhat by a pillow. Once more she was feeling happily human.

"I was a recipient of that blast, too, remember."

Her head came up from the pillow. Her eyes twinkled at him.

"If that's a hint, forget it."

He took up the challenge.

"So you don't want to give me a massage, huh?" he said, then he picked up the other pillow and bopped her on the head with it. She exclaimed loudly and immediately attacked him with the pillow she'd been lying on. Lots of screeching and howling followed each subsequent bop.

It was an inspired fight, but short on effectiveness. For the most part, neither party seemed able to stop laughing long enough to take aim properly. It was all over by the second round when Sam's pillow disintegrated into clumps of foam rubber.

"I should have you arrested for assaulting an officer," Sam finally managed to say.

She was lying on her back trying to catch her breath when she looked up to see Scotty leaning above her. He, too, was flushed and breathing hard, but Sam also saw something more. Unmasked desire. It was then she realized her robe was lying partly open, exposing the cleavage of her breasts to his scrutiny.

She made a movement to try to bring the robe around her. He immediately sensed her discomfort and got up.

Scotty knew better than to press the issue. He wanted her, but she had explained to him how she felt. The attraction was there, but she would have to decide when the timing was right. He'd wait. She was worth waiting for.

"No, I won't do it. No matter how much you flaunt your body, I won't be seduced."

He turned his back to her and firmly planted his hands on his hips. His stance uncompromising. His face a determined mask.

She laughed at his teasing. The moment of embarrassment had quickly passed. She wrapped the robe around her and came over to stand next to him. A new game was afoot.

"You won't be seduced? You're sure?"

"Positive."

His hair was still a little damp from his shower. She reached up to run her fingers through it, luxuriating in its thickness and his clean scent. The parts of his arms and legs that extended from the confines of his robe were well developed and muscular. Her eyes drank him in.

She ran her hands lightly along the length of both his arms, then gradually circled his shoulders to the back of his neck. She didn't know what their contact was doing to him, but it was sending chills through her. By the time she reached up to gently nibble at his right ear, she could see the throbbing pulse in his neck. She smiled inwardly.

"You did say you were positive, didn't you?"

He saw the laughter in her eyes and was almost certain of what was to follow. He kept on talking, but his eyes were following her movements and he wore an expression that became more and more painful.

"Absolutely. I am a pillar of strength. I..."

She laid her hands on his chest and began to explore the mass of hair there. Then she slowly made her way to the hard muscles of his waist and circled around to his back. She felt his skin quiver beneath her touch. The feel of him was so wonderful, so exciting.

"A pillar of strength, is it?"

"Yes. Im... movable."

She noted with satisfaction the strain in his voice.

She moved her body close to his, brushing him tantalizingly. Her hands massaged his outer thighs, using the friction of his robe to emphasize their touch. Then she began to plant warm kisses all along his throat and chin. She heard him groan and looked up into his tortured eyes.

"Hmm. Now what was that about immovable?"

"I'm still holding... steadfast."

Sam could see his hands shaking on his hips. She reached down and took the right one in hers. Then she directed his hand to the neck of her robe where, at her direction, his fingers slipped it off her right shoulder until her right breast was exposed. The nipple was taunt and erect. She brushed his imprisoned hand against it.

The sound of his breathing was now audible. Her own had quickened substantially.

"I think that last word was steadfast?"

He had no breath left for speech. She was bringing his hand to her left shoulder where the remaining fabric covered her other breast. Slowly, as the perspiration popped out on his skin, she directed his hand through the folds of the material until that, too, slipped away and the robe dropped heavily to the floor. She stood before him naked, beautiful and triumphant.

His eyes were like fire as he reached for her. He crushed her to him, no longer interested in playing games. As he picked her up and carried her to the bed, her arms clung to his neck, her lips seeking his. There was no gentleness in his kiss now. It was fierce, demanding and full of pent-up desire. She responded eagerly.

His hands began to explore her entire body with a new kind of massage. His movements were achingly slow, the most sensuous she had ever felt. They awoke receptors in her which she'd never dreamed existed. His touch filled her senses, blocking out everything else. Her eyes were closed, but she knew if she opened them, she wouldn't be able to see a thing. The only reality was the feel of this man.

"I want you, Scotty!"

He pulled her on top of him on the bed. She reached for him. She felt the giving of her body to him. The giving of his body to her. And when the lovemaking was over, she had experienced a closeness to Scotty that couldn't be explained.

They were quiet for a long while. When he finally moved his head to look at her, the expression in his eyes was one of warmth and contentment.

"It's never been like this before, Sam. Never this exciting. Never this fulfilling. I feel like thanking you, somehow. Does that sound strange?"

She reached up to touch his cheek.

"No, Scotty. Not strange. I'm feeling...rather grateful myself."

He smiled down on her glowing face, full of life and joy.

"You're unbelievably beautiful, Sam. Inside and out. You realize you've got me? For as long as you'll have me?"

Sam thrilled at the pledge in his words. The depth of his feeling. Her hands encircled his neck, bringing him closer.

"Well, you do make the perfect partner," she said.

His lips once again met hers. It was a long, tender kiss, the seal to a night of love.

Chapter Twenty-six

Scotty lay on his side watching her sleeping and found he couldn't stop smiling. His night with her had far surpassed any fantasy he'd ever had. She had indeed seduced him. And how much he had wanted to be seduced!

Her life hadn't been a continuing series of one-night stands. Like him, she didn't take sex lightly. And although she might not know it yet, Scotty knew she loved him. Just as he loved her. Last night left no doubt in his mind.

He looked at his watch. Six-thirty. Maybe she'd had enough rest? He kissed her cheek, and by the time he had gotten to her lips, her eyes had opened and her arms had stretched wide.

"Good morning. What time is it?" She smiled lazily at Scotty.

"Early."

"How early?"

"Six-thirty."

She sat up suddenly and the sheet fell, exposing her bare body to his waiting eyes.

"I've got to get up. I'm due at work in an hour."

It was too late. His arms were around her. His fingers caressing the sensuous places with which her body seemed riddled. His breath felt hot and exciting in her ear.

"So you're late. I'll write you a note."

"And what's this note going to say?"

His breathy answer came somewhere from the back of her neck as he turned her over on her tummy.

"That you have a fever and have to stay in bed."

Her laughter quickly turned into moans of exquisite pleasure.

"WHERE WERE YOU EARLIER? The lieutenant was calling everywhere trying to get hold of you."

The impeccably dressed, black-haired man in the light blue suit seemed to be scolding her as if he thought she was a naughty child. Sam ignored him and his comments as she unlocked her office and he followed her in.

It had been a wonderful night and a wonderful morning, and nothing was going to spoil her good mood. Gone were all the terrible muscle aches that had all but incapacitated her before Scotty's massage. She felt more alive than at any other time she could remember.

Sam took off her suit jacket and hung it up while securing her purse in her desk drawer. She looked up at the insistent man before her.

Manny Gonzales was a likeable-enough colleague. But he was a yes-man to the boss, and Sam didn't like having to work with people who were just appendages of others. And she didn't like being questioned by a peer, someone she owed no answers to.

"Mansfield wants to see me?"

Manny sat down without an invitation.

"Yeah. And I think before you see him you should know he was very upset at your report to the D.A.'s office on the Wilson case."

"So he discussed it with you?"

Manny's antenna picked up the quick blink of Sam's eyes. He began to look worried.

"Uh . . . don't get upset. It's just his way of blowing off steam. Better for him to tell me than to write it down on your record."

Sam came to her feet. The intensity of her look belied the coolness of her tone. "There's nothing he can write down on my record, and he knows it. I'm entitled to a dissenting opinion as long as I make it in the proper way. And I did."

Manny threw up his hands in frustration. "The right way? Since when do I have to remind you that being right doesn't count for anything around here? Hell, you sound like a rookie. Are you forgetting the speech we always get about how we are evidence-gatherers only? That it's the D.A. who decides who gets arrested? That it's the court who decides who's guilty? And you know perfectly well that if Mansfield wants to put the screws to you, he can. And, make it look just as proper and procedural as writing a traffic ticket."

Sam sat down. Manny was right, of course. But he was overreacting. She wasn't stupid. She knew how far she could go with Mansfield. She could make her point and still keep her job.

Of course, Manny meant well and was trying to keep her out of trouble. But what he didn't understand was that, unless she made her point, she might as well not even have the job. If she didn't live up to her own standards, there was no satisfaction to be gained by meeting someone else's.

But she also knew that Manny, the future police chief sitting before her now, wouldn't understand that. His world was made up of soothing ruffled emotions. Knowing when things were politically right.

"Thanks for the message," she said. "I'll go see Mansfield now."

But just as she was about to leave the office, the phone rang. Manny waved farewell as she answered it.

"Hi. I've missed you."

Sam's grin was from ear to ear.

"I only left you thirty-five minutes ago, Scotty."

"Thirty-seven, but who's counting? When are you coming back?"

"Mr. Lawrence, have you forgotten we've got a murder to solve?"

"So, you're going to pull one of those business-before-pleasure things on me, huh?"

"Absolutely. I'm going to get another copy of the files I brought over for you to read the other night. The ones that got destroyed in the fire. I'll send them by special messenger. We can go over them tonight," Sam said.

"You want to go over *files* with me? *Tonight?*"

Sam heard the purposely overdramatic emphasis and disappointment in his voice. She laughed.

"What did you expect, partner?" Sam asked.

"Well, I was sort of hoping for a replay of last night."

"Oh, no. No more pillow fights. That last casualty is going to end up on my motel bill."

Scotty's voice was getting impatient. "Sam, I wasn't talking about the pillow fight."

"I know, Scotty. I know. But have you forgotten this murderer blew up my place and tried to kill us?"

She could hear his descending sigh. "No, Sam, I haven't forgotten. I was just trying to for a little while. I'd like to pack us both up right now and fly to San Francisco. Forget about the heiress and the Los Angeles Police Department!"

Scotty paused. Sam held on tightly to the phone. She had a sudden urge to take him up on his thinly veiled offer. But it was only a fleeting urge. She knew what she had to do. Her place was here trying to catch a murderer. But before she could say anything, her silence had given him her message.

"I guess it's a no-go? You're right, of course. You've brought me back down to earth. I'll wait for the arrival of your file," he said. His voice sounded sad.

Sam felt rotten as she hung up the phone. How nice it would have been to forget duty for once. To just follow her feelings for Scotty and let him take her away. She felt she had disappointed him.

Well, there was no use in delaying. She had to go see Mansfield and get chewed out for doing her job. She reached for her suit jacket, thinking how happy she had felt only a short while before when she had hung it up. The light seemed to have gone out of her day. But before she could leave the office, the phone rang again. She answered it.

"How about tonight *after* we go over the files?" Scotty asked without so much as a hello.

Sam laughed. He had let her release a building tension. Reminded her to look forward to the good things.

"I love you, Scotty." The words had just fallen out. She hadn't even thought them beforehand. But now that she heard them, she knew they were true. The other end of the phone line had become silent. She held on and waited.

"Tell me again, Sam. Come home right now and tell me again. We've got things to discuss."

She sighed. "I can't. I'm already late for a meeting with my boss. I have a million things to do here. I shouldn't have said it. This is no time to—"

"Sam, go talk to your boss. Just remember we have a date tonight—after the files."

"After the files," Sam repeated as she hung up the phone. It was a much lighter heart she carried to her meeting with Mansfield.

"WHAT'S WRONG? You look bushed!" Scotty said as he met her at the motel's restaurant for dinner.

He kissed her lightly on the cheek as he took her jacket, and Sam felt a rush of pleasure at his gentle touch. She had looked forward to seeing him all day.

"Here are the files I promised. I'm sorry they're late. Mansfield has given me two new cases, and I've been up to my earlobes all day trying to get them started. I just never had a chance to send the files over."

"It doesn't matter. I'll get through them quickly enough. Sit down. Dinner is on its way."

Sam and Scotty ate while Scotty read. He went through the material almost as fast as he did the food. By the time they were on their coffees, he was ready to discuss the contents with her.

"Okay. Time for your test. What did you learn?" she asked.

"That Joni Wilson inherited close to eighteen million dollars from her mother when she reached twenty-one. That any interest the money earned over the years went to cover taxes, money-management fees, a monthly bequest payment to Isabel Kane and the remainder was the property of Greg Wilson. That the principal was tied to her daughter with strict provisions that if Joni died before her father, the money was to go to charity."

"Yes." Sam nodded her approval of his recitation of the facts. "Obviously, Debbie and Greg Wilson's marriage was not a happy one. And it also seems obvious that Debbie felt a need to protect her daughter's financial interests, and maybe even her physical well-being, from her father. Greg Wilson would profit by receiving the interest on the money as long as his daughter lived to her twenty-first birthday. He would not have been able to financially benefit by her death."

"Well—" Scotty shrugged "—whatever doubts Joni's mother may have had concerning Greg Wilson and her daughter, he seemed to have cared enough to have passed on his earthly goods to his offspring. Three million in stocks and securities and his custom Rolls-Royce."

"Yes, but you have to realize that he really didn't have anyone else to leave it to. Discounting Taswell, of course."

Scotty didn't comment. He was finding it interesting that the car had been built for Greg Wilson. He must have been the one to have seen to the installation of the secret safe. Sam's report showed Chapell didn't know about it. Did Joni?

"Sam, how many fathers would tell their daughter about a secret safe? One that contained only an item of purely personal interest?"

"You mean the address book?"

"Exactly. An address book of personal numbers: a doctor, dentist and women who do not appear on the social register. Considering the profile we have of the man, I have a pretty good idea who these women were."

"Certainly not acquaintances he brought to his home. More likely ones he met in motel rooms. But what are you getting at?" Sam asked.

"Just this. The old address book found in the secret car safe after the fire had to have been Greg Wilson's address book, not his daughter's. Something she probably didn't even know existed. Something that took a fire to reveal."

"I see what you're saying. Joni didn't know about the secret safe, or else she would have found and probably removed the address book after her father's death. But how significant is that? How does it relate to her death?"

"I don't know," Scotty said.

An internal voice was telling Sam there was a connection here. But she wasn't able to see it. It was still an elusive, dangling string.

"Mind if we get out of here? It seems a bit stuffy. Maybe a short walk?" Scotty asked.

Sam got up and headed with him toward the door. It was a good suggestion. She had been sitting all day. They paid their bill and emerged into the night air.

"Where to?" she asked.

Scotty seemed to interpret her question as though it referred to the case. He led the way along the sidewalk that circled the restaurant and motel.

"Last night at dinner," he said, "we began a hypothesis testing. I think it would be worth pursuing."

"Where were we, do you remember?" she asked.

"If I recall correctly, we were trying to determine why Joni Wilson might have wanted to become Jane Williams."

"Yes. And now that you've refreshed my memory, what if Joni Wilson wanted another identity so that she could disappear?"

Her question wasn't surprising. It had occurred to him, too. "Let me play devil's advocate. Disappear from what? To where?" Scotty asked.

"Well, let me see. Remember Chapell's records on Joni's finances? They show regular withdrawals from her several accounts until they were depleted. She had taken out a mortgage on the house. Even applied for a credit card. About all she owned were the few clothes in her closet and the Rolls-Royce she was driving on the night of her death."

Sam sighed before her next admission. "Of course, if I'm wrong and she gambled it all away, she couldn't have disappeared very far. But if I'm not wrong and the money wasn't gambled away, she would have had the world to disappear in.

"But maybe we're missing a better question here. Why disappear at all? What was it about Joni Wilson's life that could have made her want to become someone else?"

"I wish I knew," Scotty said. "By the way, did you get the medical records on the deaths of her father and mother?"

The sidewalk was deserted except for them. They had walked about a block beyond the motel's parking lot. Scotty's voice suddenly seemed to echo in the darkness of the still night.

"No. I didn't request them. They're so far removed in time, I haven't looked for an association. But I can get them and I will. What is it? What do you hope to discover?"

"Just fishing. I keep wondering, too, where her money is. After talking with Julian Harris, I know your instincts are right. Joni was a gambler, but she wasn't broke. Chapell lied when he told you she squandered her money," Scott said.

"You know something?"

"Nothing conclusive. But I'm beginning to get some ideas. Everyone is saying Joni Wilson's money is gone.

There is no evidence of it, ergo it must no longer exist. But what if it's being hidden? What if we could find her money? What if we could prove Joni Wilson didn't squander it?" His deep voice had become excited.

"Then there must have been a motive on the part of those who denied its existence. Somehow they intend to get their hands on it," Sam answered.

"Exactly. And Chapell is the logical choice. Probably would be well versed in the clandestine dispersal of funds. And that could be the reason their meetings were being kept secret. Although I think the animosity between them was real, which makes their relationship a strange one. But maybe that's the motive—" Scotty began and stopped suddenly.

Sam turned in his direction. "What about the motive—" She didn't get a chance to finish.

"Get down!" Scotty yelled in her ear as he knocked her down.

Sam landed jarringly on the ungiving concrete, and for an instant there was an unfamiliar ringing in her ears as though her head had struck, too. No, it was more like the buzzing sound of a bee. Suddenly, Scotty's body jerked once, twice, and then collapsed as a dead weight on top of her.

"Scotty?" she whispered. "Scotty?"

There was no response. Then she realized what had happened in that instant of time. Someone had fired at them. With a silencer. And Scotty had been hit.

Chapter Twenty-seven

Sam moved her hand that was pinned under Scotty's un-conscious body. Slowly she groped for her purse that had fallen beside her, the shoulder strap still circling her arm. She found it easily, opened the clasp and slid her hand around the cold, comforting piece of steel. It was out and free at the side of her body when she heard the footsteps.

They were cautious. Padded. Coming closer, but she couldn't tell from what direction. She tried to get her bearings in the moonlit night.

She and Scotty had fallen on the sidewalk next to a scraggly bush, half a block from the motel. A side street was to their right, a vacant lot with dumped trash and other debris to their left. A tall hedge marked the property line surrounding the motel. The footsteps were coming from the left. On the soft dirt of the vacant lot along the shadow of the hedge.

The streetlight was behind them, illuminating their forms. Whoever it was had the advantage. The hunter was in darkness while Scotty and she lay in light. And like any hunter, he or she was moving in, slowly and cautiously, to make sure their prey was dead, not just wounded. The padded feet could stop at any time and take another shot. Sam would have just one chance.

Her heart was pounding in her chest. It wasn't going to be easy. With one hand over Scotty's body, she would have to shoot into the darkness at a moving target she couldn't see from a supine position. But it was the only chance they had. The footsteps were coming closer.

Years of discipline took over. Her hand steadied itself on Scotty's motionless back. She turned her head ever so slowly, directing it at the sound of the footsteps, mentally drawing a picture of a body and a hand with a gun. She exhaled deeply. Then she began to gently squeeze the trigger.

As always, Sam was surprised to see the flash and hear and feel the loud report of the gun at the instant it fired. But apparently she wasn't nearly as surprised as the hunter, whom she heard curse in sudden pain. Then the sound of feet noisily running on the soft dirt away from her and Scotty.

"Scotty? Scotty?"

He didn't move, and for the first time, real fear filled her heart. She moved her cheek next to his mouth and was relieved to feel the faint breath. But she couldn't do anything for him from her current position. She struggled for a minute to free herself from beneath his unconscious body.

As she knelt next to him on the cold pavement, she saw the dark stains close to each other on the right side of his shirt and reached out to feel their sticky wetness. She pulled a scarf from her purse and attempted to bunch it up and apply pressure to one wound to stop it from bleeding. She had nothing for the other wound except the palm of her hand. But despite the constant pressure she exerted on the wounds, there was still too much blood. Her scarf was soon soaked and useless.

Perspiration drenched her skin. A sickening dread ate at her insides. She needed help. Yet she couldn't leave him. And nobody had come running at the sound of the gun. She looked around desperately for an answer. And then she saw Scotty's rental car at the edge of the parking lot.

She momentarily moved her hands away from Scotty's injured side. The .45 was back in her hand. Discipline took over. She took aim and slowly pulled the trigger.

The car's burglar alarm broke into the warm, quiet night like a magnificent screeching eagle, bringing out a young gas-station attendant from across the street. He was heading for what seemed to be his own car, probably thinking it was the one broken into. But his path led right past Sam and he stopped dead when he saw her kneeling on the pavement. She didn't give him time to ask any questions.

"I'm police. This is an emergency. Call an ambulance immediately. This man has been shot."

Her hands were covered with blood. They were back on Scotty's side, applying pressure to the two bullet holes. The scene couldn't have been any clearer for the youngster. He nodded his head in understanding and ran back to the station.

A man and a woman came by a minute or two later, obviously attracted by the alarm, and asked if they could help. At Sam's direction, the woman took off her sweater, rolled it up, and put it under Scotty's head. Then she saw Sam's gun on the ground and seemed to become afraid. She hurried her companion away, leaving from fear of the unknown.

Sam knew she should have assured the woman and her friend that they were in no danger. But the effort of kneeling on the cold, hard pavement and tending to Scotty was having its effect. Her mind was becoming numb.

An eternity went by. She heard herself telling him help was on the way, that he was going to be all right. And at some point, she humbly began to beg him not to die.

"DON'T WORRY, Sergeant Turner. He's going to make it," the doctor, a woman, told her two hours later.

Sam sat back down in the waiting-room chair and put her head in her hands. "Thank you, Dr. Mooney. I...thank you so much," she said with a sigh.

"He's a tough, seasoned soldier who's been shot up before—and a lot worst than this, judging from the scars. The bullets are out and he's lost a lot of blood, but his vital signs are steady. He'll probably be out of here in a couple of weeks ready to dodge some more bullets. Why don't you go home now and get some sleep? You can come back in the morning.''

"I'd like to see him now."

"That's not possible," the doctor responded, not un-kindly but with undisputed authority.

Sam stood and faced the surgeon. "Look, he used his body to shield me. He risked his life to save me. I'd like to see him now."

"He's in the recovery room and not yet out of the anes-thesia. If you wear a mask and don't stay any more than a minute, I'll let you see him. Come along," she said.

Sam stood next to the tubes attached to Scotty and reached up to gently stroke his hair. It felt soft and fine be-tween her fingers. She leaned down, kissed his cheek and thanked God he was going to make it.

Half an hour later, the taxi from the hospital dropped her back at her rental car next to the motel. She unlocked it and reached into the glove compartment for the flashlight. Then she made her way along the sidewalk to where the shooting had taken place.

The area was roped off. The crime-lab technicians were still at work under bright searchlights. Men and women with white coats and sophisticated gadgetry scurried around. Uniformed police stood on the periphery to discourage passersby from stopping. Her boss was there. He turned as she approached.

"The boyfriend going to make it?" he asked with what sounded like nothing more than clinical interest.

Sam nodded.

"You were right. You got a piece of the guy who shot at you. We just found what is probably your spent slug. Lab guys say there's some blood on it. The wound must have been superficial, though. Let's have your gun. We'll need it for ballistics," Mansfield said.

Sam handed her weapon to the lab technician and watched as he placed it carefully in a plastic bag and wrote her a receipt.

"You said 'guy.' Can you be sure it was a man?" Sam asked.

"Appears to be. Only fresh footprints near this hedge were from a man's shoe."

"What size?"

He looked at her and frowned. "You tell me," he said.

"I don't know."

His frown quickly turned into a scowl. "I'm not buying that garbage!"

Sam had too much experience to be caught off balance by the challenge in his words.

"Maybe it was a sniper selecting a random target," she said. Even without the sarcasm in her tone, Sam's words made Mansfield's face turn red. She braced herself for what she knew was an impending explosion.

"Snipers don't get close enough to get shot at. Whoever it was knew exactly who he was shooting at, Turner, and you know it. You'd better stop trying to con me. It's the Wilson case, isn't it? You fought me on arresting that cousin. And don't think I don't know all about your little visit with Taswell in jail. Just like you to continue to investigate behind my back. Come clean, lady, or you're going to find yourself in the motor pool for the rest of your career."

Sam was angry. More angry than she would normally be, and under less control than she was used to exerting. But it had been a night of strong events and emotion, and they were having their effect. When she spoke, it was before she considered her words and restrained her feelings. Her anger carried her voice to all the other police personnel and lab technicians on the scene.

"I don't know who it was. If I did, I sure as hell wouldn't be wasting my time standing here talking to you. And of course it's all related to the Wilson case. Only a moron couldn't figure that out. Only a moron who insisted on putting the wrong man in jail so a murderer could be out shooting cops!''

Sam turned and walked away from the hushed group of men and women, hearing only the sound of her footsteps on the pavement as she made her way to her car. She kept the flashlight on while she attempted to fit the key in the lock. But she was making clumsy work of it because her hand was shaking so badly. Finally, she succeeded, opened the door and slipped onto the seat.

She closed her eyes and rested her head on the steering wheel for several minutes trying to control the shaking of her body. When it subsided somewhat, she put the key in the ignition, started the engine and began to drive away.

She felt the eyes of her fellow police officers following her retreating car. Sam knew what they must be thinking. She realized what she had done. Without looking back, she headed for an all-night gun shop.

It might take a while before she got her weapon back. If she ever got it back. And this was definitely not a time to be unarmed.

Chapter Twenty-eight

The pounding was relentless.

When Sam opened her eyes, she had no idea where she was or what time it was. All she could think of was the pain that racked every bone in her body. She was surprised to discover that she was lying fully clothed on a motel bed with a strange gun in her hand, until memory invaded the ache in her head.

Sam sat up, almost wishing she hadn't, as sharp pains drilled up her spine. But then her attention was diverted again by the sound of pounding. She reluctantly climbed off the bed and made her way to the door. A gaze in the peephole told her it was Manny. She let him in.

"You look like hell," Manny said, closing the door behind him. "Do you know you've got dried blood and dirt splattered all over your face and clothes?"

"Are you always this charming in the morning? You must be a delight around the breakfast table," Sam said.

"Only when the children haven't washed their hands and faces," Manny replied.

Sam chose to ignore his good-natured gibe. "They have complimentary coffee down the hall. I need to take a shower," she called back over her shoulder as she picked up one of her shopping bags and headed for the bathroom. When she started to wash her face with cold water, she found she was still holding her gun. She put it unsteadily down on the sink.

Ten minutes later she emerged, dressed in fresh clothes and feeling somewhat better. Manny had a cup of coffee ready for her and had also brought back some sweet rolls.

"Want one? They're lemon-filled. I got four."

"No. Help yourself. Coffee's enough for me."

He munched contentedly a few minutes before he got down to business.

"That was quite a little scene you and the boss had last night." He licked a drop of lemon off his fingers.

"You were there?"

Manny nodded. "As was at least half the department."

He looked at her tentatively. "You know, if I had called Mansfield a moron, I'd have been fired."

Somewhat surprised, Sam met his look. "You mean I'm not?" she asked, feeling some hope after a hopeless night.

"I know the boss was hard on you. Probably harder on you than he would have been with the rest of us. But that's because he has this thing for you. You know that. Hell, the whole department knows that."

Sam looked at him sideways. "Did he send you here this morning?" she asked.

Manny just nodded as the last piece of his sweet roll headed for his mouth.

The aspirin Sam had swallowed hadn't taken effect yet, and the pain in her head and elsewhere was distracting her from full comprehension.

"I'm not fired?"

"No. Frankly, you were lucky. Only way I can figure it is you made him happy because for once you showed anger. Lost your temper and made him feel superior for controlling his. Anyway, he excused your actions last night. Told us all it was just shock, reaction from having been fired at. He said you were upset because your friend had been hurt. And you had shot a man."

"Well, I'll be—" Sam began.

"What you'll be is on suspension for a week. Starting right now. You, ah, didn't leave him much face to save last night. I think he needs to forget you exist for a while."

"And the Wilson case?" Sam asked.

"Give me what you've got. I'm taking it from here."

"He's not closing it up with Taswell's arrest?"

"Now come on, Sam. He's a stubborn old goat, but he's not a fool. If someone shot at you last night because of what you're uncovering on this case, he wants to know."

Sam wasn't so sure. She drank her coffee and gave Manny's words some thought. Her companion took her silence for acquiescence.

"So who was it that used you and your friend for target practice?" he asked.

"I wasn't lying to Mansfield. I don't know."

"But you have some idea?"

"Not really. But I'll think on it and let you know later today back at the office. Right now I have to get to the hospital to see a friend," Sam said, as she rose and went to get her purse.

Manny was a bit disconcerted.

"I told you, you're on suspension. Lieutenant's orders. He doesn't want you downtown. Don't be a fool. You can't come to the office. If he sees your face—"

"So I'll sneak in," Sam interjected. "It's the only way. All my notes are in computer memory. And only I have the password. Lock up for me when you leave, will you?" Sam called, as she closed the door and headed for her car.

She left Manny with lemon filling on his face.

Chapter Twenty-nine

Scotty was trying to wake up, push aside the darkness. But the familiar sounds of a hospital were resurrecting nightmares out of the past.

He was back in the dark alley. He was crawling toward Jerry's body. But the deafening staccato of rapid fire kept coming. Ricocheting bullets swarming around him like angry killer bees. Finally, he was at his partner's side. But, it was too late.

Scotty's eyes gradually blinked open to his current surroundings. The images were fuzzy: white walls, bed, a tube coming out of his arm. Memories of the shoot-out were still vivid in his mind. But it couldn't be. That was a long time ago, wasn't it? Five years since Jerry and he had fought in that alley.

Current memory surfaced like a knife, stabbing him wide awake. Sam!

He reached for the nurse-call button and pressed it several times. He waited, but no one came. Then he noticed the phone at the side of the bed. He pulled on his IV trying to reach the receiver.

"Please Mr. Lawrence, lie still! You're about to tear that IV out of your arm. I'll get the phone for you. Now do as I say and lie still!"

The nurse who had finally answered the call button rushed to steady the metal arm that held the swinging IV tubes.

"Where is Samantha Turner?" Scotty asked.

"Turner?"

"Yes. The woman I was with when I was shot. Detective Sergeant Samantha Turner."

"You were admitted last night. I didn't come on duty until this morning. No one's mentioned a Turner."

Scotty's look was one of extreme impatience and agitation. The nurse obviously felt it.

"Perhaps if I got the doctor for you?"

She seemed glad of an excuse to leave. Scotty was just as glad she was gone. Everything was wrong. A nausea was churning his insides. What had become of Sam? Had she been shot, too?

He had to get to the phone. He pulled the tape holding the restricting IV in place, eased the needle out of his arm, then threw it onto the floor. He held his elbow up to stop the flow of blood and reached out with his other arm to grab the telephone receiver. He punched in her home number and listened to a disconnect recording. Of course, she had no home. He tried the motel where he had gotten her a room next to his. The line to her room rang on and on. She wasn't there.

He dialed her office number next, surprised at how easily he remembered all these numbers. It rang twice before a feminine voice said, "Homicide."

"Sergeant Turner, please."

"I'm sorry, but Sergeant Turner is unavailable. Can someone else help you?"

"What do you mean she's unavailable? Where is she?" Scotty asked.

"Uh . . . I don't know. She hasn't come in to the office today. Would you like to leave a message?"

Scotty never got a chance to answer the question.

"Mr. Lawrence. When we put an IV in a patient's arm, we expect to be the ones to remove it," the doctor standing by the door said loudly and none too happily.

Scotty hung up the phone.

"Where's Samantha Turner? The woman I was with last night? What's happened to her?"

"Sergeant Turner is just fine. Once she satisfied herself that you were going to be okay, she arranged for a twenty-four-hour protective guard at your door and went home to bed. Now let's see what we can do about getting you another IV. Miss Riverrum, if you will do the honors..."

"She wasn't injured?"

"No. As she informed me, you shielded her with your body. Pity you couldn't have found something a little less leaky. We used four units of blood on you."

If Scotty heard the humor, he ignored it. "But she's not at home. And her office said she didn't show up this morning."

Dr. Mooney sat on the edge of the bed to take her patient's pulse.

"I'm not surprised. She had a rough night. When you passed out on her, they tell me she had to shoot the maniac who was after you two."

Scotty felt somewhat better. Sam hadn't been hurt. The danger was past. But he still couldn't relax. "So, Doc, when can I leave?"

"Are you feeling any nausea? Any pain?" Dr. Mooney asked, ignoring Scotty's question as she probed his injury.

"A little."

The doctor directed the nurse to administer an injection to Scotty's arm.

"My name is Mooney," the doctor said.

"All right. Dr. Mooney, when may I leave?"

"You've got a private room and bath. Clean sheets every day. Gourmet meals served to you in bed. All the television you can watch, including cable. And you talk about leaving. Maybe we should have X-rayed your head."

Scotty smiled but was not distracted. "That means I can plan on being out of here tomorrow?"

"That means you can plan on getting up and walking around the room for a few minutes tomorrow. It will help the healing process."

"Then I can leave the next day." It was a statement, not a question.

Dr. Mooney put her stethoscope on the tray next to Scotty's bed. "Look, you were shot twice in the side—"

"I assumed that's probably why I was in the hospital," Scotty interrupted.

"The only reason the bullets didn't penetrate a vital organ is because they hit a metal plate in your chest. A metal plate that's holding up your right rib cage. Or more precisely, what is now your right rib cage. A souvenir from your last visit to one of our white resorts, no doubt?"

"No doubt," Scotty agreed.

"Well, then, let me remind you, Mr. Lawrence, that the human body only has so much flesh and blood and, at the moment, you are far below regulation issue on both. So it would behoove you to follow the advice of your learned physician, which is to relax and get your strength back."

"All of which means you're not going to tell me when I can leave?"

"Mr. Lawrence, I assure you that because of the kind of patient you are proving to be, the entire staff of this hospital will be devoted to your earliest departure," Dr. Mooney said as she turned and left the room.

The nurse drew some blood from Scotty's arm and left. Soon, Scotty found both the pain diminishing and a deep lethargy beginning. He dozed off. A faint memory of Sam drifted into his consciousness. He seemed neither awake nor asleep. When he opened his eyes, she was there.

"Hi. How do you feel?" she asked.

"Great. I'm so glad you're all right. It's so good to see you. I...I..." Scotty found he couldn't continue because he was so happy to see her.

She leaned down to tenderly kiss his face. His arms came around her, holding her gently to him. As their lips brushed, she felt her whole being tingle with joy. In that moment, she forgot everything except his love.

"I'm sorry I missed our date last night. Our after-files rendezvous," he said softly in her ear.

She straightened and sat down on the bed beside him, taking his hand in hers. He couldn't miss the ready twinkle in her eyes.

"It's amazing what lengths some people will go to just to avoid losing a pillow fight. What's the matter, did you decide the competition was too stiff?"

He managed a chuckle. "As I recall, it wasn't my pillow that lost its stuffing. The score is one-zero, my favor. In case you had forgotten."

Sam's face wore a look of feigned disdain. "Which only goes to prove I was supplied with an inferior weapon. Devious trick. I suppose next time you'll be expecting a handicap?" she said.

"Me?" Scotty's face was indignant. "A handicap? Never. I'm a pillar of strength."

Sam couldn't help laughing at his choice of words. "Seems I've heard that boast before. And we both know just what a pillar of strength you proved to be!"

She watched the color returning to his face. He reached for her then, and she let herself be caught in the warmth of his arms, snuggling up as close as she could without touching his injured side.

"Uh, Mr. Lawrence. Ma'am. Excuse me, but it's time for Mr. Lawrence's shot. And I need to draw some blood. Then maybe a little jelly dessert?"

It was the nurse who had interrupted them. To Sam's embarrassment, she found herself virtually lying on Scotty's hospital bed. She sat up quickly, but Scotty's arms restrained her from going far.

"Go away!" he yelled to the nurse.

"Now Mr. Lawrence—" she began.

But Scotty didn't let her finish. "Now where were we?" he asked Sam loudly, ignoring the nurse. He began to draw Sam to him again.

The nurse quickly scurried out of the room, threatening to get the doctor.

"I think we were just about to open one of your stitches," she said, resisting the pressure of his arms.

He sighed in disappointment and relaxed his grip. "I won't always be at this disadvantage, Detective Turner. I intend to continue where we left off. And you'd best be forewarned. A pillar of strength I may not be, but I heal very quickly."

Sam smiled at Scotty's warm, gray eyes. "I have no doubt, Mr. Lawrence. You definitely appear to be on your way to mending."

"Your medicine," he said, caressing her hands.

"What is this I hear? Yelling at one of my nurses?"

Dr. Mooney's voice was coming from outside the hospital-room door. Sam suspected her overly loud voice was being used to announce her impending presence. A moment later she came bustling through.

"All right, explain yourself, Mr. Lawrence."

A look of total innocence descended on Scotty's face. "Can't imagine what you could be talking about. All I'm doing is lying here trying to get well as my learned physician ordered."

"Detective Turner, visiting hours for this patient are over. Wait for me outside. Miss Riverrum, come in here, give your patient his injection, draw his blood and prepare his lunch. Mr. Lawrence, the head of the psychiatric wing is a good friend of mine. Gives me all the strait-jackets I could ever want. They are close at hand for difficult patients. Now let's take a look at you."

Sam left Scotty's room as directed and waited for Dr. Mooney. She used the time to question the police guard, but all had been quiet. With the exception of herself, only the night nurse, Miss Riverrum and Dr. Mooney had requested and been granted entry. At least whoever had shot at them would have a very difficult time getting to Scotty here.

Finally Dr. Mooney emerged from Scotty's room.

"How is he?"

"Doing quite nicely. I've had Miss Riverrum give him something to keep him asleep for a while. To make sure he rests."

"And his injuries?"

"Wounds look clean and free from infection. His pressure and pulse were a bit erratic a few hours ago when he regained consciousness. But they seem steady and strong now. Your visit's been good for him. I don't think he quite believed my earlier assurances that you were all right. He needed to see for himself."

"You don't mind if I come back later then?"

"I doubt if it matters what I answer to that question. You're still going to do just what you please. Just like Mr. Lawrence. But, no, I don't mind if you come back later. In fact, it will be good for him."

"You're sure he's out of danger?" Sam asked.

"His red blood-cell count was still low when we took it a few hours ago. He's had another transfusion of whole blood since then. If this last transfusion has brought his count into the normal range, then it's just a question of time before he's as good as new."

Sam was about to leave the hospital when she was beckoned to the front desk to take a telephone call. It turned out to be Manny.

"I'm sorry, Sam, but I have to ask you for your badge."

She knew it was coming, but the words still made her feel as though she was being punched in the stomach. She had never been on suspension before. She had never had her badge taken away, even for a little while. Her throat was tight when she spoke.

"All right, Manny. I'm coming in."

Chapter Thirty

"Is this all you've got?" Manny asked.

"You watched me ask for the Joni Wilson murder case. You saw me request a print of the entire file. And you watched it printing out. What more could there be?" Sam asked.

Manny picked up the stack of computer paper. "It's a thick file, all right. No reason to suppose you'd be holding anything back, except that I know how proprietary you are. I can't see you giving this baby up without more of a fight."

Sam looked over at her companion. She had borrowed Mona Lisa's smile. "Would I win?"

Manny shook his head and grinned like Leonardo da Vinci might have at the subtlety of his masterpiece. "Nope."

Sam returned her attention to the computer screen and entered a floppy disk in her A drive. "That's the way I see it, too," she said as her fingers zipped along the keyboard.

"Hey, what are you doing there?" He seemed suddenly uneasy at her activity.

"Just backing up my hard disk onto some floppies. You should have volunteered like I did when we were asked to try out this new down-loading system from the mainframe to the individual personal computers. Makes the job a lot easier."

"Well, I really don't like to use computers much. Don't really understand how they work. I give the information of what I need to the office personnel. They type in my reports and get the printouts I need. That's easy enough for me.''

It was what Sam had suspected. She smiled at Manny and picked up the phone to enter a dialing code and then a telephone number.

"Who are you calling?" Manny asked. His nervousness was all too obvious.

"What's wrong with you? I'm just sending my calls to the clerk's line while I'm gone. What do you do when you're going to be out of the office for a while? Let your phone ring off the hook?"

"The clerical force handles those things for me," he said defensively. "Maybe you should train yours to, also. Save you lots of time."

Sam ignored Manny's remark and replaced the cover on her computer. "Will you try the doors on those file cabinets over there and make sure they're locked?" she asked.

He turned around to look at the cabinets she was pointing at. And in that instant, Sam put several floppy disks into her purse.

"Those?" said Manny. "I saw you lock them a minute ago, remember?"

"Oh, right. Forgot. Well, I guess that's everything. See you in a week."

She was back at her motel room within forty minutes, sitting at the new computer she had bought that morning and setting up its configuration to match the one in her office, loading in the necessary software. She had forwarded her work number to the phone in her hotel room. This way, if she needed to have someone call her back with information, they'd never know she wasn't in her office.

She knew the killer was still out there. Yet she was fairly sure he had not yet found her motel. He probably had tailed her from the office yesterday to the restaurant, but she doubted he had discovered she was staying so close by. The motel personnel had sworn they had told no one she was registered. She was safe. At least she hoped she was.

She began to load her office files into her computer. She tried out a few commands and smiled. It was going to work. The data she needed was there.

She was not a windmill fighter. Which was exactly what arguing with her boss about giving up the case would have made her. She wouldn't have won. She could put up a good fight if there was even a slim chance of winning. But she had learned long before that noble gestures were a waste of her time. And everybody else's. It was much better to think of a way around obstacles. Reasonable alternatives to smashing against brick walls. Because she wasn't going to give up the investigation she started.

Once again she saw Scotty lying on the concrete sidewalk. The memory created new anger to feed her determination. The same person who had killed Joni Wilson had tried to kill Scotty and her. Twice. She was sure of it. And she meant to find out who.

She worked at the keyboard for more than a hour, periodically stopping to check her progress on the screen. When she was satisfied, she hit the save and print keys in succession.

The printer she decided she could afford wasn't as fast as the one at the office. It would take a while for the request to be completed. She began to devour the sandwich she had picked up on the way back to the motel as she sat listening to the steady clicking of the dot-matrix mechanism. It was a rhythmic din. Soon she found she was almost falling asleep to the repeating clatter.

She sat up straight, annoyed. But her annoyance wasn't just tiredness. It was the lack of clues to who had broken into her home and later bombed it. And who had shot Scotty.

The lab reports were conspicuously uninformative. The bullets that had been removed from Scotty's chest were too mangled. They had smashed against the metal plate that was part of his rib cage. There was no way even to be completely certain of the caliber of gun used. And not one of the suspects had a record of owning a handgun.

If only she could pull in her suspects and have them medically examined for a gunshot wound. But no judge was likely to grant such a warrant for any individual without additional, incriminating evidence. And she didn't have it.

Or did she? A murderer was after her for some reason. The answer had to be in the information she had gathered. She had to look over the new printout carefully. The printer was still clicking away.

Her impatience began to build. For the next twenty minutes, she occupied herself with cleaning and reloading her newly purchased gun.

She watched the pile of computer paper begin to mount. It was an updated file, not the old file she had printed out for Manny. And it was going to be at least twice as thick. Including a copy of the reports on the break-in at her home and the shooting attack the night before. And there were going to be two copies. One for Scotty and one for herself.

The idea of going on without involving Scotty further had crossed Sam's mind. He was going to need a lot of rest to mend. But on reconsideration, she had put herself in his place. If she had been the one shot, would she want to be cut off from any progress? Left out of the pursuit of the attacker who had tried to kill them? No way.

Besides, Sam couldn't imagine continuing the investigation without Scotty. She liked bouncing ideas off him, listening to his responses and suggestions. He was sharp, quick. Yet steady, consistent in his logic. He had helped her keep on track. And through him, she had learned a great deal more concerning the suspects in the case.

Of course, that wasn't the primary reason she didn't want to exclude him. The thought of being away from him for any length of time made her feel lonely.

Strange. She had only met him Friday. Six days before. Their relationship had started as a business one, but the attraction had always been there. An attraction that had quickly grown into love.

The printer ceased, and an empty quiet filled the room. Sam got up to review the material, readjusting her thoughts to the problems at hand. Later she and Scotty would have time to be together. Right now she needed all her concentration to find a murderer.

She looked over the new information that had come in since she had last reviewed the file.

The blood types of all the principals in the case were listed. She had requested the information hoping to get lucky with a match to the blood type of the individual who had shot at her and Scotty. But it didn't look too hopeful. Their assailant had A-positive blood. And, so it seemed, did almost everyone.

Julian Harris, Monty Larkin, Colin and Claire North, Isabel Kane, even the deceased had an A-positive blood type. Only Rebecca Myers and Walter Chapell had other types. For the moment, it appeared a dead end.

Sam turned to the hospital records, both on Joni Wilson's birth and her mother's subsequent death. The notes were more complete than most she had seen. Possibly because of the importance of the parents and the complications that arose.

Debbie had had two aborted pregnancies before she finally brought a child to full term. Her successful labor had been long and difficult and had taken its toll. She'd spent almost a month in the hospital. She had been given numerous units of blood during and after the protracted delivery because of her own blood loss and weakness.

Interestingly her doctors had to put out a special search for the blood replacement since Debbie Wilson had AB-negative blood, a fairly rare type.

Sam tried to recall the significance of the Rh-negative factor. If she remembered correctly, problems could arise if the mother was Rh-negative and the fetus Rh-positive. But the mother would not be at risk in the situation. It was the baby who could be born dead, or jaundiced.

Scanning the records more quickly, Sam found what she was looking for. Joni Wilson had not been born with a problem. As a precaution, the doctors tested her blood type at birth and found her also to have AB-negative blood, just like her mother. Inheriting her mother's blood type had kept Joni Wilson out of danger.

Sam was about to go on when suddenly something she read just a few minutes before registered. She flipped back a couple of pages and located the blood types once again. There it was. According to the dentist who identified the deceased teeth as belonging to Joni Wilson, his patient had A-positive blood.

But how could that be? The hospital records clearly indicated she had AB-negative blood. One was a mistake. But which?

A crazy thought had just occurred to Sam. She looked quickly through the inventory of the Wilson woman's personal things: receipts for the paste jewelry, a dentist visit, and a family album.

The dentist on the crumpled receipt from the study's desk was a different dentist from the one listed in the black address book found in the secret safe of the deceased's car. And, the bill in the desk was dated about two and a half years later.

Normally blood type was something a patient voluntarily entered on a medical-history record. Included as a precaution in case of sudden complications. It could have been transcribed incorrectly by a busy dental assistant. But what if it wasn't? What if...?

The contents of each of the deceased's personal items were specified in Sam's reports, but since the actual items weren't considered evidence, they were still at the Beverly Hills estate. She would need to go there next.

But first she needed to put in a call to the dentist whose receipt was found in Joni Wilson's desk. She needed to find out what blood type his patient had.

Sam reached for the phone just as it began ringing.

"Sergeant Turner, please," the woman's voice asked.

"This is Sergeant Turner."

"Ms. Grenville, Heritage Insurance Company. I'm calling about the Joni Wilson murder."

"Yes, Ms. Grenville. What interest do you have in the case?"

"Only a small insurance policy on the deceased. I became somewhat concerned when I heard on this afternoon's news that my investigator, Scott Lawrence, had been shot and that you, too, had been the target of a gunman."

Shocked into sudden silence, Sam stood holding the phone.

"Detective Turner? Is everything all right?"

"Yes, fine. And Mr. Lawrence will recover. I'm sorry for the lapse in attention. But your investigator did not identify himself as such when we met. I had the impression he was a private investigator out of San Francisco. His working for you . . . surprised me."

"He's not on salary. Mr. Lawrence took this case on commission and will only get his percentage if he discovers we aren't liable. Save me some money and prove that yourself, will you?"

Sam felt as though the floor was sinking, pulling her down. She couldn't think straight. She couldn't quite grasp the significance of what this woman was saying. Scotty was working for her? Scotty was going to get a commission?

"Detective Turner?"

"If it's true, I'll prove it. It's what you pay your taxes for." Sam's tone was as dull as her senses. She mustn't draw any conclusions yet. She must investigate this.

She was about to hang up the phone when a thought pressed for recognition in her numbed brain. "Just one thing, Ms. Grenville. Who is the beneficiary on that small life-insurance policy and exactly how small is it?''

"Isabel Kane, and the amount is one hundred and fifty thousand.''

Chapter Thirty-one

"I don't want the money, Sergeant Turner. If that's the only reason you wanted to see me this evening, you're wasting your time. Some of Joni's friends are coming tonight. I have a lot to do. Now, if you'll excuse me..." Isabel Kane said.

They were sitting at the table in the crisp, white kitchen with its shining floors and gleaming dishes. The aroma of fragrant, fresh-brewed coffee curled from their cups into the coolness of the air-conditioned room.

Sam wasn't often surprised by people, but Isabel was proving to be an exception.

"You knew about the life-insurance policy?" she asked.

"Yes. Joni told me about it when she took it out. It's a mistake. All a mistake."

"Why didn't anybody else know?" Sam asked.

"Joni wanted it that way. She gave me the papers and told me to keep them safe. I threw them out."

"You're entitled to the money. Why won't you take it?"

Isabel sat in the straight-backed chair with her long, slender fingers resting around the saucer of her cup. Almost as though they circled a part of her life that she fought to protect against prying eyes.

"I raised Joni. She was as close to me as my own daughter. How can you think I would allow myself to profit from her death?"

The tears were shining like jewels in her eyes. Sam didn't like what she was about to do. But she had no other choice.

"Joni wanted to thank you for your love, your care of her. She wanted to insure that your future, and that of your daughter, was financially secure. It's not wrong to take money given in that spirit."

Sam was pushing for a response, hoping for a reaction. There was something unseen here, yet almost tangible. She could feel it. Isabel's eyes dried up in what seemed like a sudden flash of torture, or guilt.

"Spirit? How can you presume to know the spirit of this gift?" she began, then stopped abruptly.

Sam waited patiently. She watched the pain on the woman's face. Isabel rubbed her fingers together almost as though they had been singed.

"You didn't even know Joni. You didn't brush the dirt from her scraped knees, the tears from her sad eyes. You didn't sit up with her all night through the measles and the mumps. You didn't applaud her hard work when she got an A on her report card. You didn't . . ."

Isabel's head went down. Sam knew if she had a choice, she would leave. But she didn't. She had to have answers now. Answers only Isabel could give. She laid her hand on the woman's arm. "Do you have a picture of Debbie? Joni's mother?"

Her urgency must have communicated itself to the crying woman. Isabel lifted her head with an effort and reached into her pocket for a tissue, still hiding her face from Sam's penetrating gaze.

"A picture of Debbie?"

"Yes."

"No. There aren't any pictures of Debbie."

"What about a picture of Jessica?" Sam asked.

"What? My daughter?"

"Yes. Jessica," Sam repeated.

Isabel finally seemed to make the transition in subjects. Her eyes looked at Sam a little warily.

"There's one in my room."

"May I see it?"

When the woman didn't respond to her request for a moment, Sam thought she might be thinking of refusing. But whatever precipitated the internal struggle, Isabel finally gave it up.

"All right," she said, then rose slowly and left the room.

Sam stood up, nervous excitement pushing her into movement. She felt both anticipation and foreboding. When the picture was handed to her, she studied it closely.

It looked a few years old. Not professionally taken, but it was a close-up shot, under good lighting. Sam immediately noticed the same dark hair as Isabel's, and the same blue eyes. But the resemblance ended there. The nose was a tiny button. The face was delicate, heart-shaped. The eyes were vacant, unfocused.

"Where is Jessica now?"

"She's at Peterson's Academy, a special school in Monterey. Joni took her there six months ago. To . . . to help her become more confident. Teach her how to be more self-sufficient."

"It's a school for the mentally retarded?"

Isabel nodded.

"May I have this picture?"

"If you wish."

Isabel's frown made it obvious it wasn't her wish.

"I'd like to see Joni's room now, if you don't mind?"

It was clear from her look that Isabel did mind, but she led the way up the stairs just the same. She then left Sam alone.

The room was as she remembered it on the night she and Scotty had stopped by. Sam knew precisely where to find the family album. The dresser drawer opened silently. She moved aside some monogrammed handkerchiefs, fingering the embroidered JW. By adopting the name of Jane Williams, the deceased wouldn't even have had to change her monogram. Sam reached for the black leather book.

The album must have been started by someone when Joni was just a baby. There were several snapshots of her on a blanket when she couldn't have been more than one month old. Then there were a couple of more shots when she was probably a few months old, crawling on her tummy. Then some standing beside her crib.

Sam guessed Joni was about ten in the next picture. She stood, solemn and frowning, next to her father in a pose that looked extremely uncomfortable for them both: straight and at attention in their Sunday clothes. She had the slightly square shape of her father's face. His light blue eyes. There was no question she was his daughter.

Most of the rest of the scrapbook was filled with pictures of Joni as she excelled through grade school, high school and college. Her vaccination records. Her report cards. Some awards for achievement in math and sociology.

She hadn't posed for any more pictures with her father. But every so often, Joni and Jessica were shown together. Swimming in the backyard pool. Dressing up in clothes much too big for them. Singing Christmas carols in front of a decorated tree. Two girls. In some ways so alike, and yet so different.

When Sam got to the last page, she found a copy of the same picture that had accompanied the television news story of Joni Wilson's death. The professional lighting emphasized the tanned skin and confident blue eyes.

While she was studying the picture, Sam's attention was suddenly drawn to a slit in the binding of the photo album. Her fingers explored beneath the leather and brought out an old picture hidden there. As she stared at it, many things began to make sense.

It was about time she made a call to the place where Jessica Kane was being kept. She went to the phone in the hall and got the number of Peterson's Academy from Information. She spoke to the person in charge and identified herself as a police officer.

"You have a student, Jessica Kane?" Sam asked.

"Yes. Miss Kane is a resident here. What is this in regard to?"

"I need to know if Miss Kane left the school grounds last Thursday."

"I don't know offhand. Just a moment, I'll check the records."

Sam tried not to think about anything as she held on the line. The seconds seemed like hours. Finally the voice came back.

"Yes, Sergeant Turner. As a matter of fact, Miss Kane was gone most of Thursday and Thursday night."

Sam listened to the administrator for several minutes, getting the particulars of Jessica Kane's absence.

"Get her ready," Sam said. "She's going on another trip."

Sam hung up the phone. All she needed was confirmation. She looked at her watch. Four o'clock. Time to cash in some favors from the uniformed squad. They could arrange for the woman's pickup. It would be light until at least eight. They should also be able to find the academy if they started right away. She reached for the phone again to make the necessary arrangements.

Minutes later, as she pulled away from the Wilson home, she had a strong desire to see Scotty. To share with him what she had learned. But she fought it. He hadn't told her about his real interest in the case, or his percentage arrangement with the Heritage Insurance Company. He had pretended to care for his own personal gain.

Her experience with John Bateman hadn't been enough. She had been taken again. Her trust betrayed. It felt as though she had swallowed cut glass that was tearing up her insides. She could no longer hold back the pain.

Tears raked her cheeks. Gone was her resolve to keep them at bay. Damn! How could she be hurting so much more than the last time?

The road was a blur before her. If she didn't get ahold of herself soon, she was headed for an accident. Pulling off onto the shoulder, she wiped her eyes with the back of her hand. She had to concentrate on her work. It had saved her once. It would save her again. There wasn't anything else.

Perhaps the worst thing was that she didn't want to let go. Even now she wanted to believe Scotty cared. After all, wasn't he lying in a hospital bed because he had shielded her? Wasn't it he who had uncovered so much concerning the suspects she'd had such difficulty in seeing? And hadn't he shared everything about the case with her?

No, not everything. Not the life-insurance policy and its beneficiary. Two important facts. If only he'd told her! She bit away her tears of disappointment. They weren't going to help. She had only herself to count on. The department had withdrawn her from the case. And Scotty couldn't be trusted.

Sam would see he got a copy of the latest file. After all, he had helped her. Even if he had deceived her. If he could figure a way to make his commission from the information, well, she would not stand in the way of his getting it. But she would never see him again. And if she lived to be a hundred, she would never trust another man.

She took a deep breath. Checking her mirrors, she pulled back onto the roadway. She had a plan. Its proper execution lay squarely on her shoulders.

It was the kind of responsibility she had always loved. To be the master of her fate. In total control. Having to depend on no one but herself. It was the kind of responsibility that gave her a zest for life, which tapped her strength and always found more in reserve than she would ever need.

But somehow, today was different. Today it was the kind of responsibility that made her feel absolutely alone.

Chapter Thirty-two

Scotty was uneasy. Ever since he had read the afternoon paper concerning the shooting, he had become extremely restless. Their assailant was still mobile and at large, which meant Sam was still in danger.

Warren had called earlier, said Sam had phoned him that morning at the San Francisco office with the news of the shooting. His partner offered to fly down, an offer Scotty refused. There was only one person he wanted to see.

He had tried her number both at the motel and at the office, but had gotten no response from either. For the past few hours, he'd expected her beautiful face to be popping through his door. When it hadn't, he tried to remind himself she was working hard on the murder case.

But being out of contact with her, confined to the hospital bed, was driving him crazy. Which was why, when the package from her finally arrived, he almost felt like kissing the guard who delivered it.

He tore it open, but was disappointed in her cryptic message, which said only: "Updated file for your perusal. Good luck." He turned the short note over looking for a more personal communication, but there was nothing.

"Oh, Sam," he thought aloud. "I wasn't necessarily expecting you to sign it 'love,' but no signature at all?"

He decided at that moment that women just weren't romantic. The only thing he could do was to read through the material. At least it would keep his mind occupied.

He noticed the updates contained a lot of financial background on the suspects. Walter Chapell was heavily extended. Venture-capital losses over the previous tax year appeared substantial.

Julian Harris was down a couple of million himself, but Scotty couldn't determine where the money had gone specifically. It looked like gambling losses. Had he been lying when he'd talked about his limit? When he left the impression he won more than he lost?

The Larkin family fortune had been dwindling yearly. Monty must have traded on his family name to gain access to the wealthy homes in which he proved a frequent guest. And yet, about four months earlier Monty's mother had begun to renovate their old family home in Boston. Just about the time Monty and Joni had become an item. Had the woman been anticipating a wealthy daughter-in-law?

The Norths were in very bad shape. Colin had recently taken out several million dollars from the fledgling franchise operations of his hot-dog chain and left the capital investment absolutely bare. Sales had fallen off, and no cushion remained to carry him through the lean times. He would lose the business unless he could replace the several million. Scotty wondered where the money had gone. Was he a gambler, too?

Rebecca Myers came from a well-to-do Beverly Hills family. She held the position of finance officer at Hollywood Savings and Loan. Her bank account was comfortable, but her net wealth had gone down close to a million over the past year. Coincidence?

Was there anything in the records that might give a clue?

Scotty spent some time reviewing the information, looking specifically for something unusual. From the receipts, it appeared as though Joni Wilson had gambled away her fortune. Because after every large withdrawal, she took a trip to one of Europe's gambling centers and paid for her airline ticket and hotel room by credit card.

Scotty looked back at the credit-card receipts. Suddenly it seemed to him she had deliberately left an audit trail to try to substantiate her losses. It had been Joni Wilson's plan to make her money seem to disappear!

But where did it go? No American Bank showed . . .

Scotty quickly turned over the computer printout and sketched a map of Europe. Then he marked an X at the casinos where the credit card had been used. Next he looked at the airline tickets that had been charged, tracing their routes. The answer lay there at the point of converging lines.

One place was always a point of departure from Europe. On each occasion, no matter where else was visited, the return flight made a stop there. Switzerland. Famous for its anonymous bank accounts. Surely an old game of tax evasion. One the IRS had come up against before. One they would surely have discovered eventually. Unless the tax evader died before they had a chance to investigate.

What had he and Sam been discussing just before the shooting? Oh, yes. How Joni Wilson's money might be hidden away somewhere and who might have killed her to get it.

Maybe the more important question was who had hidden the money away.

Scotty jumped when the phone rang. When he grabbed for it eagerly he anticipated it would be Sam. His face fell at the sound of the voice on the other end of the line.

"Mr. Lawrence? It's Ms. Grenville of Heritage Insurance. How are you feeling?"

Scotty tried to sound grateful for the woman's interest. "Fine. Good of you to inquire."

"I hope this isn't too late to call, but I forgot to get the name of the hospital you were in when I spoke to Detective Turner this afternoon. It wasn't mentioned in the newspaper. Protection, no doubt. But as you can see, I have my sources."

Scotty's stomach turned in a sudden queasiness. "You spoke to Detective Turner?"

"Yes. One of the reasons I'm calling you. I'm afraid I let the cat out of the bag. I didn't realize you weren't going to tell her of our arrangement. Of course it can't matter much now since you're incapacitated and off the case anyway."

Scotty spoke to Ms. Grenville for a few more minutes completely unaware of anything he said. His responses were on automatic. As soon as she hung up, he tried desperately to reach Sam at both her numbers. But once again, no answer.

No light was escaping from around the heavily draped hospital window. He looked at his watch. It was a few minutes after eight. He got out of bed and went over to the door. The guard was sitting immediately to the right reading the *Los Angeles Times*.

"Hi. You remember the package that arrived for me this afternoon? Who delivered it?"

"Why, Detective Turner gave it to me personally. Is something wrong?"

"No. I just haven't been able to locate her. Was she assigned to a new office? For protection maybe?"

"Don't worry. She's safe. Detective Turner's no longer even on the case. The lieutenant pulled her off this morning and put her on leave."

Scotty returned to his bed. His legs were wobbly and he felt dizzy. Even walking over to the door and speaking with the guard had proved to be an effort.

He had to think. Sam now knew about his affiliation with Heritage Insurance. But she couldn't have known that, from the moment they met, he had no intention of trying to undercut her investigation, or use her to make his percentage. So, she must think the worst. No wonder she didn't call or come to see him.

And on top of losing faith in him, her boss had taken her off the case. Scotty knew she must be feeling pretty rotten. He had to talk with her. Where was she?

A cold shiver suddenly climbed up his spine. He picked up the computer sheets in front of him and looked at the print date and time. They were from this afternoon. And the guard had said she was taken off the case this morning.

Of course! He should have realized immediately. She wouldn't meekly stand by and be pushed off her case. She would continue the investigation. Just as he would, alone and with no backup. With a murderer waiting to get her in his sights.

He sat back and forced himself to read every report. Every word. He wanted to know everything she knew, because he would need that information in order to guess her next move. It was taking an eternity. But he clamped down with hard discipline. He would do what had to be done.

When he had digested it all, he had a faint glimmer of hope. He would need to make some calls. And if they confirmed his suspicions ...

He got up to check the window. It opened from the inside. A fire escape was just to the right. One floor down and he would be on the pavement. A major hotel was just down the street. He could get a taxi there.

Scotty went over to the closet and reached for his jacket. His clothes had apparently not been searched. The loaded gun was still sealed inside its secret pocket, undisturbed. He drew it out.

Chapter Thirty-three

It was just after nine that night when Sam picked up her second passenger at the airport and drove out to the Wilson estate. The lights seemed to be on throughout the house as music and voices drifted to the front stairs. Sam's ring brought Isabel almost immediately. The housekeeper's surprise was evident at their arrival, but she took her instructions without comment.

Sam stood in the darkness of the entryway for a moment, studying the people gathered in the living room. Colin and Claire North were sitting together on a love seat. Claire was sipping her drink and laughing, not at all like the shaking woman Sam had interviewed.

It was all so clear now. Why hadn't she seen it before?

Rebecca and Julian were sitting on the larger sectional, laughing at something Walter Chapell had said, as he stood before them, waving a drink animatedly. And Monty Larkin had just walked over to the mantel, to pick up some matches to light his cigar.

Sam stepped into the center of the room feeling like she had just gone on stage in a Broadway play. She had the basic idea of her part, but soon she would be required to ad-lib as the others played their roles.

There was an immediate hush as her presence registered.

It was finally Julian Harris who stood and approached Sam. She didn't miss the edge to his voice.

"Well, if it isn't Sergeant Turner come to crash our little party."

"Sergeant?" a high voice repeated. Claire North betrayed her surprise at Sam's title.

"Yes. Our friendly police interrogator, Claire. Be a gentleman, Julian. Get her a drink," Monty said.

But Julian apparently didn't feel like playing host. Quite agitated, he stood in front of Sam. She believed part of his unease came from the fact that she was a good deal taller than him.

"You know trespassing is a crime, Sergeant," Julian said. "I'm afraid I'm going to have to report you to the authorities."

Sam deliberately stared down at him. "Really, Mr. Harris? Are you sure I'm the one who is trespassing here?"

"This is a private party. In a private home. You have no business busting in—" Rebecca began, standing up.

"Yes," Sam interrupted, her gaze taking in the woman's indignant look. "This is a private home. But I think you have all forgotten whose."

For the briefest of moments, Sam saw her words register, then the uncertainty. Julian turned and headed for a drink. Rebecca sat back down again. Claire clutched at her husband. Monty laughed.

"Well, she's got you there, Julian ole boy. I told you you should have just gotten the sergeant a drink."

It was Walter Chapell's turn to make a stand.

"As executor of the Wilson estate, I have every right to be here to take inventory of her personal effects."

Sam picked up his drink. "And is this part of the inventory you're going to show as missing?"

He snatched his drink out of her hand, knocking an ice cube out of his glass and onto the floor.

"What makes you think I don't have permission from the beneficiary?" he said.

"What beneficiary?" Sam asked.

"Peter Taswell, of course!" Chapell said.

"Mr. Taswell is right here, and the only one he has granted permission to enter his home is me," Sam said, beckoning Taswell into the room.

He came in smiling, obviously happy with his introduction.

"That's right. You're all trespassing," he said.

Sam watched the faces of the others as Taswell entered. They were all surprised and uncomfortable. And angry. Even Monty came unglued from the fireplace mantel, a frown disrupting his previous cool. Colin was the only one foolish enough to voice his thoughts.

"Everyone knows a person can't profit from a crime. The state will never let Peter keep this house—since he killed Joni to get it."

Sam turned to look Colin squarely in the eyes. "Now I'm glad you've brought up the state, Mr. North. Because you're right. Criminals are not allowed to profit from a crime. But a person is not a criminal until a jury of his peers so decides. And no jury has decided Mr. Taswell is one. So that same state presumes Mr. Taswell innocent."

Monty banged his glass on the mantel. For the first time, Sam heard an edge in his voice.

"All right. You've sprung Peter and barged in here. Obviously you've got something on your mind. Let's hear it and get this over with."

"As you wish, Mr. Larkin." Sam motioned Peter to have a seat. "But I don't think I'll begin at the beginning. Instead I'll start with the death of Greg Wilson two years ago."

Sam deliberately moved a couple of paces to her right, where she could be in shadow. Her voice now seemed to come out of the darkness. Disembodied. Eerie.

"When Greg Wilson died," she went on, "his daughter learned something that caused her a great deal of anguish. For weeks she pondered the problem. Then one morning she devised a solution. A solution that meant she must assume another identity. But first she had to appear to die."

Sam paused a moment to look at the quiet, upturned faces. None showed surprise. She continued, "But before she could 'die' in the eyes of the world, she had to arrange it so that she would still possess the money she held as Joni Wilson. She was determined to take it with her. So she sought the aid of her lawyer and friends in making it appear as though she had lost her considerable fortune gambling. All the time, this money was being transferred into a Swiss bank account for her use when she assumed her new identity."

"Colin!" called a breathless voice from the couch.

It was Claire. Her face was quite flushed, but the rest of the gathering was made up of quiet, immobile features. Waiting.

"She knew that her death would not be accepted unless a body was found," Sam said. "A body that would be identified as hers. So she arranged for a young woman of her size and coloring, using the name Joni Wilson, to visit a dentist—to establish the records for subsequent identification. Then she carefully planted these records in the back of her desk to be conveniently found after her 'death.'"

Chapell stood up in protest. "This is crazy. Why should we listen to you?"

Sam's look met his, causing the lawyer's eyelids to blink. Her next words caused him to sit down.

"No use, Chapell. We know about the car pulled off the road under a thicket of trees and heavy brush. The one Joni had all packed with clothing just waiting to take her to the airport where she had booked a flight to Switzerland.

"Of course, she'd intended it to look like an accident. Her paste jewelry would be found on the badly burned body. The dental records would be checked. The body would be identified as Joni Wilson, accident victim. The last thing she wanted was for it to look like murder. Although that is exactly what she had planned to commit. A murder."

Sam's pause was again deliberate. She looked at each one of Joni's co-conspirators, reading the knowledge of their complicity all over their faces.

"Isabel, please bring our guest in now," she asked.

Isabel moved from just outside the entrance to the living room and beckoned a dark-haired woman into the room.

The young woman's face was in shadow at first. Then she stepped into the light. The fake jewelry surrounding her neck and wrists gleamed. The long dark hair curled at the ends. The light eyes looked ahead, a bit confused and unfocused.

Claire North immediately stood, pointing her finger in surprise. She had obviously been expecting someone else.

"It's Jessica!"

"Then who...?" Rebecca Myers asked, then stopped as her eyes opened wide in what looked like horror.

A choked sound came from the throat of Colin North. Monty Larkin appeared to move involuntarily toward the dark-haired woman from his position by the fireplace.

Chapell grabbed hold of the arms on his chair. "It can't be!" he breathed.

Julian unconsciously brought Rebecca's hand to his side as though he needed reassurance she was still there. "Joni can't be dead!" he said. "She was the one who was going to... Someone's killed Joni!"

Chapter Thirty-four

The exclamations and uproar that followed the appearance of Jessica Kane frightened the young woman. Isabel rushed to her side to comfort her.

Samantha was working at getting the group to settle down. "So, now you realize the wrong woman went over the cliff in Joni Wilson's car that night. At least, wrong for your friend's scheme. She had planned to send her childhood companion, this mentally slow woman, to die in her place. That's why she took her to a dentist under the name of Joni Wilson. Yes, the dental records found in the drawer of Joni Wilson's desk match this woman's."

Julian Harris's face was flushed. He looked ready for a fight. Trouble was he couldn't seem to find an adversary. "But how could the body have been identified as Joni's then? She destroyed all other medical records. I know. I watched her!"

Rebecca looked alarmed. She tried a warning glance, but when she couldn't catch Julian's eyes, she said, "Julian, don't!"

Sam put up her hand. Everyone in the room stared at it as though something was written on the palm. "Julian's right. All the medical records she knew of were deliberately destroyed."

"Then how were you able to identify Joni?" Chapell asked.

"It was the secret safe in Greg Wilson's car. He had it installed. Only he knew of its existence—until his car burned, exposing the secret compartment. It was also where he chose to keep his personal address book, a book that listed the Wilsons' family doctor and dentist," Sam answered.

Colin North had his arm securely around the broad shoulders of his wife, much like one of his self-sealing hot-dog buns. "Joni never mentioned it," he said, "so she couldn't have known about it. And we thought the police had found the phony records."

"It was a queer twist of fate," Sam said. "Like the murder of your friend."

Monty Larkin was moving suddenly toward Peter Taswell, like a bull ready to charge. The deep tan of his skin appeared even deeper because of the rush of blood. He began to advance on the thinner, much smaller man with clenched fists.

"You creep! You killed her after all, didn't you!"

"That will be enough, Larkin!"

Sam's loud voice was effective. Larkin paused, but when she stepped between the two men, his halt did not include a retreat.

Peter's thin body shook. "I didn't kill her!" he whimpered. "I never even talked to her that night. Ask Chapell—he was with her. I saw his car. I tell you I saw his car!"

Everyone turned to look at Chapell, and his small dark eyes seemed to shine eerily, as though lit from within. His pointy nose snorted in denial.

"No. This is ludicrous. It wasn't me! I was just giving her an account of the funds she had left, verifying what was in the Swiss account. I didn't even know she was planning her phony death that night. You know she always kept that a secret. The when, I mean. I was just helping her to get the money out of the country, hiding it from the IRS."

"But you have access to that Swiss account now that she's dead, don't you Walter?" Julian asked.

The quiet in the room told Chapell that Julian wasn't the only one who was wondering about the money. His two front teeth chattered away like they were hewing the wood for the cross over his grave.

"I didn't do it! I swear! I was only at her place about twenty minutes. All we did was go over the current figures in her accounts, I tell you. Then I left. Damn it, I left! She told me to go because she was expecting Rebecca!"

Chapell's short arm was pointed at the chestnut-haired, deeply tanned woman. In unison, everyone turned to look at her. Sam watched in fascination. The once tight-knit group, joined closely in a murder conspiracy, was finding itself being pulled apart at the unexpected revelation of the death of its leader.

It was Rebecca's turn to see the accusing eyes, to be the focus of the hostility. She reached out and grabbed Julian's hand for support. "No! I didn't see Joni. I phoned and told her I couldn't come. I forgot Julian and I were going to this comedy club, you see. I had told her earlier I would drop by. So when I remembered she expected me, I called her from Julian's car phone."

The stares continued.

"She and I were close friends! We were to meet in Europe in three months. You remember her telling us. She had over a million of my own money. Keeping the interest it was earning safe from the IRS. I would have been a fool to kill her. How could I get it back? I tell you I was with Julian all night. Tell them, Julian, tell them!"

Julian didn't have a chance to confirm or deny. Monty was too primed for a strike. "Come on, Rebecca," he snarled. "We know he'd swear to anything you asked him to."

Apparently any physical relationship Monty and Rebecca had shared had not led to loyalty. Sam knew his implied accusation couldn't have been more blatant, as was Rebecca's retort.

"When it comes to swearing, Monty dearest, you're going to be out of luck. Because all I can swear to is that when I went into the kitchen for some milk around midnight, you weren't on the couch passed out like you've claimed!"

Monty's fists clenched again. He took a step forward only to suddenly find Julian in his way. Julian's look was fierce. He seemed ready and even eager for a physical confrontation with the much bigger Monty.

"Come on, you guys. Lighten up," Colin said.

It was a mistake. Neither man was in a mood to be reasonable.

"Don't give me any of your sanctimonious lip, North," Julian said. "Joni told me you had tried to get the money back you had put into our little community pot. And she had told you no. Is that why you decided to kill her?"

"That's not true!"

It was Claire who made the protest.

"Colin just needed to put a little money back into the franchises. But he told Joni he'd wait a week or two until she could arrange it. And besides, he was with me all night."

Sam found herself almost enjoying this falling-out among these co-conspirators, though she was still finding it hard to understand how they could have condoned a cold-blooded killing. Had their friend been a magician to have convinced them all? Or was it simply basic greed that motivated them?

She was tempted to let them continue. Rake one another sufficiently to be sure the group would never close ranks again. But the flying accusations were getting too far off the target. It was time for Sam to refocus the discussion.

"You're all laboring under a misconception. Joni Wilson is not dead. Her body was not the one found in Greg Wilson's Rolls-Royce."

The silence that followed that bombshell was almost tangible. Blank stares met Sam's eyes.

"But who...?" Julian voiced the question that was on almost everyone's mind. He sat down and Monty moved back to his place by the mantel. They were like two moving toys whose batteries had run down. Sam went on to explain.

"I began this story with Greg Wilson's death two years ago. Now I would like to take you back twenty-four years to the real start of the events that led to a young woman's murder. The birth of two baby girls. Two different mothers. The same father—Greg Wilson."

"Isabel was—" Claire began.

"Isabel was a young girl—only sixteen. With no parents or relatives. She hired herself out as a maid to earn enough money for her keep. Unable to protect herself, she became the victim of her employer's abuse," Sam finished.

Isabel sat next to the frightened woman-child she held in her arms. She said not a word. But a silent tear began to make its way down her cheek as Sam went on.

"Two sisters. One the image of her father; the other bearing a close resemblance to her mother. Both born healthy, but not equally.

"Very early in childhood, the slower development of the child who resembles her mother is noticed. Her mother has her checked by doctors, and it is found she will not mentally progress.

"But it isn't the maid's child who is found to be slow. It is the heiress to a fortune. Debbie Wilson's daughter— Joni—the young woman sitting here with Isabel, who raised her like her own daughter. The young woman you know as Jessica Kane."

It was Rebecca who found her voice first. Heavy with shock and dismay as though she had been the recipient of a cruel joke. "The children were switched! Joni wasn't Joni, after all."

Claire leaned forward, her expression bewildered.

"The Joni we knew is dead?"

"Yes. The woman you knew as Joni Wilson, your friend, was the one found in the destroyed Rolls." Sam could feel the thin tree behind her back that was Taswell once again begin to shake in protest. "This is nonsense. I've known

Joni since she was a child. She was bright, fast. I couldn't be related to this creature. I don't believe this story. It's been fabricated to let this maid's child get my money," Peter Taswell said.

"Actually, Taswell is within his rights," Chapell said. "What proof do you have that the babies were switched? Greg Wilson accepted the woman I've known as Joni Wilson as his legitimate child and heir. How can we be sure what you say is true?"

Sam shook her head. Greed made strange bedfellows. Now, Chapell and Taswell were siding together.

"There is proof. This is a picture of Debbie Wilson I found this afternoon. Look at the woman's delicate, heart-shaped face. The tiny button of a nose," Sam said as she handed the worn picture around. "And then look at this young woman sitting beside Isabel. The same face as Debbie's. The same nose."

Julian was the first to view the photograph.

"A physical resemblance exists, I grant you. But that isn't proof," he said.

"Not definitive proof. But that exists, too, in the hospital records at the time of birth. Joni Wilson's blood type was unusual. She inherited a rare AB-negative from her mother, Debbie—the same as hers." Sam gestured at the young woman at Isabel's side. "However, according to the dentist listed in Greg Wilson's address book, the woman being passed off as Joni Wilson all these years had A-positive blood. She was not the child of Debbie Wilson."

Quiet ensued, during which everyone appeared to be digesting the last bit of information. Sam watched the distraught faces without sympathy. Her heart had no room for a bunch who would have stood by and let a gentle, harmless young woman be murdered.

"Did Joni, I mean the woman we knew as Joni, know about her relationship to Jessica?" Rebecca asked, finally breaking the quiet.

"I think she knew the other girl was her half sister—her father's illegitimate daughter. And I think she used that information to gain a hold over her father. I think that's why she always insisted on keeping her half sister around. As a taunt to him, maybe even as a threat."

Colin North shook his head.

"No. What you say can't be true. Greg Wilson would have known which daughter Joni was. If she was the illegitimate one."

Sam's eyebrows raised along with the inflection in her voice. "Would he? He literally ignored his daughter until she was an adult. Then he only seemed to show interest because she was pretty and clever. And his friends had noticed her. Do you think he would have admitted, even to himself, that she was not his legal heir?"

Chapell's arms crossed over his barrellike chest. He frowned in obvious disapproval.

"You really want us to believe that the woman we knew as Joni had no idea who she was all these years? And suddenly a light turned on?"

"It's not so farfetched. The only thing that might have tipped her off sooner was a picture of Debbie Wilson. Had she seen one, she might have noticed the similarity in the face of her half sister and put two and two together.

"But since Isabel kept such pictures from her, I would guess she didn't know she wasn't the real heiress until after her father's death. I believe it was then that Isabel confessed to the switch and produced the picture of Debbie. It would explain the depression she suffered. Her fear of being discovered somehow—her sudden decision to kill off the real Joni Wilson and live her life abroad as someone else," Sam said.

"But why did Isabel tell her then? What was the point after all those years?"

"It was Debbie Wilson who asked Isabel to switch the babies. To keep her husband from getting her money. And maybe even to protect the life of her child. She feared that a retarded child could be controlled, manipulated by her father when she turned twenty-one and inherited her mother's money. Then he would have control over that money to do with as he pleased.

"But once Greg Wilson was dead, there was no need to keep up the charade. At least, that was probably Isabel's thought. I doubt that her daughter saw it that way," Sam said.

"I never knew she was planning on becoming someone else. I just thought she was hiding her money," Claire said. "I know she talked about faking her death and living in Europe. But somehow it seemed so unreal, like a part she was going to play. Now she's dead, and nothing is as it seemed."

Julian Harris seemed to recover from his initial shock at Claire's words. "Except she is dead. And someone killed her. We're forgetting someone killed her. Someone after the money," he said.

Rebecca picked up Julian's lead. "Yes. Someone who must have wanted all our money, too. Someone who thought killing her would be the way to get it. Someone who lured her to that place off Mulholland Drive."

Sam stepped in once again. "No, you're wrong. Jessica Kane, the one you thought was Joni, wasn't lured there. She went voluntarily so she could put the real Joni in a car. To set it on fire...to push it off the cliff. But someone followed her. Someone who stopped her. Isn't that how it happened, Isabel?"

Tears flowed from the maid's eyes as she stared straight ahead, at first appearing not to have heard Sam. But after what seemed to be a long time, she responded in a curiously flat tone.

"I just happened to get up for some milk when I saw Jessica leaving the house with Joni. I knew something was wrong because Joni was supposed to be at the school. I wondered where Jessica was taking her and why she was wearing all those fake jewels.

"Then suddenly, I realized Jessica must have arranged to get Joni. That's where she had gone that morning when she left the house. I didn't know why she'd want to bring Joni home. At that moment, I just had a vague uneasiness. So I called out to her."

Isabel paused for a second, and when she resumed, her voice had a melting sadness.

"Jessica told me what she was going to do. Had it all worked out so everyone would think it was an accident. She told me she had provided for me with an insurance policy. I was not to worry! She was going to kill innocent little Joni and I was not to worry!"

Sam suddenly felt as though she had betrayed Isabel Kane. To have her bare the tragedy of her life in this room of unrepentant people. As though locked into that moment of understanding, Isabel's eyes, disrobed in tears, turned to stare into hers.

"I was struggling with Jessica over the gasoline can. Suddenly she pulled hard, and I lost my hold on the can. Jessica lurched backward, hitting her head on the car door. She fell to the ground, still clutching the can of gasoline. The top of the container had opened, drenching her clothing.

"I had to stop my daughter. I swore to Joni's mother on her deathbed that I would watch over her baby. Not let anything happen to her, protect her like my own. I swore it. Oh, dear God, I swore it!" Isabel Kane cried as she rocked the bewildered child of her only friend in her arms.

Chapter Thirty-five

"Isabel killed her!" Peter shouted.

"No!" Sam said. "It wasn't her. It was someone who followed Jessica and Isabel out to the spot on Mulholland Drive and saw the two women struggling with the gasoline can. Someone who watched Jessica fall to the ground and Isabel drive away. Someone who took the opportunity to murder."

She turned toward Taswell. "Didn't you say there were two cars at the Wilson house that night? Chapell's Mercedes and another car around the side, which you couldn't identify?"

"Yes. That's right."

Sam knelt next to the maid. She took hold of her wrists, an act to convey the importance of her questions. "Isabel, you've been lying about the night Jessica died. All this time. Because you thought you were responsible for your daughter's death?"

The maid's affirmative response was more like a shudder. Sam's voice became an insistent urging. "Tell me what you thought? Tell me about it now."

Isabel's expression was drained. Defeated.

"Jessica must have gotten up, but she would have been dazed and disoriented. Somehow she must have gotten into the car, tried to start it ... and it lurched over the side, catching fire on its way down. My pledge to Debbie to protect Joni made me leave my own daughter to die."

Isabel's head sunk once again in torment and guilt. Sam shook her shoulders hard. "No, Isabel. Jessica's death was not an accident. Someone put her in that car and shoved it over the cliff. Think back. Before you went to bed, Jessica had a visitor. Who was it?"

"Mr. Chapell. They were in the library going over some documents."

"And did Mr. Chapell leave?"

"Yes. I heard his car. My room is toward the front of the house. I remember I heard his Mercedes start up."

"Did you hear another car arrive?"

Isabel seemed a little confused for a moment as she sought to recall. The room was as still as a stopped clock.

"No. Mr. Larkin had arrived earlier. Before Mr. Chapell," she said, obviously thinking aloud.

"And did you hear Mr. Larkin drive away? Before Mr. Chapell arrived?"

Isabel seemed surprised. Not at the question, but at the answer she was about to give. Her eyes became suddenly alive.

"Why, no! He had parked his car around the left side of the house near my room as was his custom. I'm sure I didn't hear him start the Porsche. It was Mr. Larkin! He must have followed us. He must have been the one to kill Jessica. He killed my daughter!"

All eyes stared at the tall blond man leaning against the fireplace.

He was calmly forming and releasing a smoke ring into the deathly quiet room. It floated up sideways, caught by a current of the air-conditioning. Then, strangely, it hit another current, which brought it back directly in front of him, like a malevolent spirit coming back to haunt him. Monty's gaze fixed on the smoky apparition of his own making.

His voice was even and conversational between his puffs on the large cigar in his mouth.

"We were going to get married. I had asked her on my knees and she had condescended to share her wealth. She, the illegitimate granddaughter of a real-estate agent, had finally decided to stoop so low as to marry me. A Larkin! With a family name traceable to royalty! What a joke.

"And then I called her from Rebecca's that night and she told me it was all over. Said she had gotten suspicious when I wouldn't contribute to the common fund being hidden from the IRS. Told me she'd had me investigated and found out I was broke. She said she knew I was only trying to marry her for her money. She even had the nerve to tell me she had no hard feelings."

Monty puffed hard on the strong-smelling cigar.

"Well, I had a lot of hard feelings. Time had run out. All the money my family had left, I had spent on the relationship. I had even told Mother to go ahead and fix up the house. I had told all my friends back in Boston about the marriage. I—"

Monty stopped, suddenly seeming to remember where he was.

"I didn't believe it," he continued after a moment. "I never believed the scheme of substituting the dumb kid for her. An heiress had no reason to disappear. And I didn't believe she could just kiss me off. So I drove to her place. I had just started to look around the house for her when Walter arrived. Their meetings were always so clandestine. I got curious, so I hid in a back room and listened in."

Monty raised his hands wide, as though he was about to open the door to a hidden room.

"I heard it all. She had over thirty-five million in that Swiss account! She had blackmailed Walter into helping her transfer the bulk of her inheritance by threatening to tell his wife about some indiscretion. And she was insuring his cooperation by promising to cut him in for five percent. But she lied. It wasn't true.

"When she followed Walter to the door, I found transfer slips on her desk. They were already filled out. She was going to take the money out of the account he had started for her and put it in a separate, numbered account where only she would have access."

Monty looked around impatiently. "Well, don't you see? She was cutting him out. And us all. She didn't care anything about any of us! She was going to disappear for good, with all the money. Knowing by the time we found out, we wouldn't be able to say a thing. Because from the start, we had known who really died in the accident."

"Except it wasn't an accident, was it Monty?" Sam asked.

He turned toward her and smiled. A smile that left Sam chilled to the bone. He puffed on his cigar and seemed now to be talking only to her.

"I saw her pack her bags and leave with the other woman. I knew she was going to fake her death. Right then. So I followed and watched the struggle. I saw Isabel take the other woman away. Obviously Joni, I suppose now it was Jessica, had tried to kill her. And Isabel had stopped her. And then, well, it all seemed so clear. It would be such poetic justice for her to go over instead."

Monty flicked the ash from his cigar onto the carpet. He ground it in viciously with his shoe.

"She was half-unconscious, moaning there in the dirt, soaked with gasoline. I just dragged her behind the wheel, released the hand brake, lit a cigar and threw the match on the seat.

"The flames caught immediately. She had already pulled up close to the edge. All it took was a shove. I remember thinking, as I watched her falling down the ravine, what a waste of a good car."

The unlined face suddenly contorted into a sneer. Monty reached into his pocket for what looked like a handkerchief.

"I thought she was a real heiress. With her out of the way, I knew Chapell and I could come to terms and divide the money. Damn woman. Couldn't even turn out to be who she was supposed to be. She was always playing stupid games. Just like you," Monty said as he pointed the barrel of his gun at Samantha.

Chapter Thirty-six

While a surge of adrenaline pumped wildly through her body, Sam stood perfectly still in front of the cold steel pointed at her. She hadn't anticipated Monty's having his gun on him. She'd been taken unaware. A serious mistake. And one she would have to attempt to rectify fast.

"It won't work, Monty. My backup is outside waiting for my signal. If he doesn't get it in five minutes, he'll call in an alarm and come in shooting."

Monty shook his head and smiled.

"You don't have any backup. I know you were taken off the case. Everything you've said and done here tonight has been your own idea. You and the other one are alike, you know. She thought she had all the right moves, too. But as you'll recall, I had the last shove."

He reached over and eased the strap of Sam's purse off her shoulder and replaced it on his. His gun was pointed unwaveringly at her heart.

She saw the cold look on his face. The handsome face that housed such an ugly soul. He was a killer. And she was to be his next victim. Fear clutched at her spine. She tried to face the fact of her death. But her mind refused. She had to try to play for time. She had to try to think!

"If you kill me, you'll have to kill all the witnesses in this room."

The smile didn't leave his face.

"Why? I'm not going to be around to get arrested. And besides, I've already killed once. If they catch me, once more won't put any more fumes in the gas chamber. Come on, Walter, we have a date in Switzerland," Monty said.

Chapell eased away from the rest of the group and joined Monty. She knew she had to try to get to the lawyer. Let him see he was being used. Try to turn him against Monty.

"You're a fool, Chapell. Once you give him access to the Swiss account, he'll kill you," she warned.

Chapell's woodchuck countenance didn't look too happy at her words. His eyes darted nervously to Monty's face. The tall blond man laughed.

"Take it easy, Walter. Just an old police trick—divide and conquer. Just start backing up slow and easylike out those doors. Unless, of course, you want to go back to that hooked-nose shrew you call a wife."

Monty's words apparently suggested a more serious fate than even Chapell's death. He did as he was told. Sam could feel the sick pit in her stomach growing into a watermelon as the tall man issued his orders.

"Now this is the way it's going to be. I'm going to cut the telephone lines. I'm going to shoot holes in all your tires. And then I'm going to shoot holes in the sergeant here. And I don't want to hear a word out of anybody. Not now. Not ever. Because if I do, I'll be sending you greetings in the mail. Loud greetings, guaranteed to blow you away."

"You're going to kill her?"

It was Claire's voice, her tone almost curious.

"Oh, yes. It's because of her all this has come out. I thought she must have some evidence about the Swiss account. Something she found in the secret car safe that kept her investigating. I even thought once she might be after the money herself. So I placed a little packet in her mailbox.

"She was lucky that time. And she obliged me by arresting Peter. For a while I even thought of passing on her. But she refused to be satisfied with Peter, kept snooping around with that insurance guy. And when I overheard them talking about Walter's possible involvement, well, I had to discourage her. Walter would have led her right to me."

Monty pulled Sam suddenly to him and ran the barrel of the gun across her cheek. When she flinched she heard his small, satisfied laugh. He tightened the arm around her chest.

"But she's been very hard to get rid of. Left me with a nasty gash in my arm last time we met, which still hurts like hell. I'm going to delight in killing her. Shame I don't have more time to do it properly."

His arm was crushing her ribs. Sam had no more time to be afraid. Her gun was in her pocket. At least she'd had the presence of mind to take it out of her purse and place it where it would be more accessible. If Monty was going to cut the phone lines, she just might have a chance to reach for it while his attention was diverted. She stood ready.

"Walter, get some wire clippers out of the drawer there. Bring them along and I'll show you where the junction box is. Stay put everyone. Come on, you. Let's take a walk."

Monty pushed Sam ahead of him. She stumbled toward the door. She knew she was not going to go down without a fight. If he waited until they got outside to shoot her, she would have a better chance. It was dark. She'd make a break for it, turn and fire.

But as they walked out onto the porch, Monty grabbed her left arm, twisting it hard behind her back and pulling her viciously with him down the stairs toward the side of the house. Pain shot through her body. She bit her lip in an effort not to cry out. He was too close for her to make a run for it. Too strong for her to fight. Her options were dwindling rapidly.

"There it is, Walter. That rectangular box on the side. Yes, that's right. Now get on with it."

As soon as Chapell opened the junction box, he became animated. "Dammit! I just felt a shock. Must have touched the wrong spot. Monty, wait. I can see a vibration! Someone inside is using the phone. Monty!" Chapell called.

"Pull the damn wires, you fool!" Monty yelled.

Walter started pulling and clipping wires frantically.

"And when you're finished, bar the back door and get the plastic explosives from the trunk of my car. No house, no witnesses. We won't leave anything for the police to find."

Chapell headed for the car and Sam heard Monty's voice near her ear. "And now for you. Let me show you what it feels like to be shot in the arm."

In that instant, Sam knew it was now or never. She bent down sharply at the waist and pushed back as hard as she could into Monty's body, stamping on his right foot and swinging her right arm over her head at his face. Her palm jabbed his nose, and she heard with satisfaction his yelped curse as he loosened his grip on her left arm.

It was all she needed. She tumbled over onto the pavement and came upright with her gun drawn. But before she could fire, she heard a whistling sound and felt the burning of a bullet as it pushed her left shoulder back into the ground. Another whizzed by her right ear. She hadn't bought enough time. Larkin had recovered.

She rolled over quickly into the dark brush at the side of the house, trying to get out of his range of fire.

Before the pain starts, she thought. *I must fire before the pain starts.*

Her right hand came up at her thought, but her left hand was unresponsive. Her left side had lost its circulation when Larkin had pinned her arm to her back. It was now useless. And any moment the torn bone and tissue would register in her brain, shocking her into unconsciousness. She could wait no longer. She fired.

The report was loud, unlike his silenced gun. She could see Monty's right leg crumple beneath him. Her bullet had hit him too low. She had to fire again, but there was no time. His gun was already raised and directed at her chest.

In that infinitesimal moment before it happened, she was sure she was about to die. But she was willing her hand to aim and fire again. Willing her body to take him with her.

A deafening roar assailed her ears. Monty's face appeared before her like an apparition. White as a ghost in the porch light, with a large black hole between the eyes.

Just before she lost consciousness, she thought how strange to have shot him there! She had been trying to put a bullet through his heart.

Chapter Thirty-seven

Sam was aware of muffled sound. Indistinguishable sound. She tried to open her eyes, but there was no light. Did she still have her sense of touch?

She strained to make a fist with each of her hands. The exertion brought a sharp pain, but she couldn't tell from where. She was almost thankful. At least she could still feel. At least her brain would not be trapped in a paralyzed body. She fell back into oblivion.

When she awoke again the sounds she heard were clearer. A voice called for someone. By the time Sam opened her eyes, she was able to distinguish the round face of Dr. Patricia Mooney bending over her.

"I can see!"

"Brilliant deduction, Sergeant Turner. What an amazing detective you are! Of course you can see. You were shot in the shoulder, not the eyes," Dr. Mooney replied. Her tone was as uncompromising as ever.

"How do you feel?"

"Dull ache on my left side. Nausea."

"Hmm. You would think that at the rate you people get yourselves shot up that you would have the presence of mind not to eat at least twelve hours before. All right, nurse. Give the sergeant her nausea shot. And draw me some blood."

As the nurse followed directions, the world around Sam began to expand. She saw beyond the face of the doctor to the walls of the hospital room. She looked toward the window. The curtains were drawn. She realized she didn't know if it was night or day.

"What time is it?" she asked.

"About six o'clock."

"Morning? Evening?" Sam asked.

"Morning. If you feel up to it, there's a Sergeant Gonzales outside waiting to get your statement, and Mr. Lawrence is—"

"I'll see Sergeant Gonzales," Sam interrupted.

Patricia Mooney's face puckered into a surprised frown. She started to open her mouth to say something, and then appeared to reconsider as she turned and left without a word.

Manny's face was grim. Sam knew the news was bad.

"Tell me what happened," he said.

"No, you tell me," Sam answered.

"I've got a feeling only you can straighten out this mess. When we arrived at the Wilson estate last night, the whole place was in chaos."

"Who called you?"

"A Miss Kane, the housekeeper. She was putting through an emergency 911 call requesting the police when the line went dead. The emergency center had a record of the calling number, so they contacted us to dispatch a unit."

Sam smiled. She should have known. Isabel wouldn't have let the murderer of her daughter just walk away.

"What did she tell you?"

Manny watched Sam's face closely.

"Some wild story about your showing up and accusing the entire flock of Joni Wilson's friends of attempted murder and Monty Larkin of the murder of her daughter. And all the time she was clutching this daughter who was supposed to have been murdered. Except that she kept calling the daughter Joni Wilson."

"No one else backed up her story?"

"Oh, Peter Taswell said Monty Larkin was a murderer, all right. But his story was Monty had murdered Joni Wilson. He said the woman Isabel Kane kept claiming was Joni was her own daughter, Jessica Kane."

"No one else said anything? The Norths? Julian Harris? Rebecca Myers? Walter Chapell?"

"Walter Chapell wasn't even there. And no, the rest had nothing to say. Except they wanted to talk with their lawyers."

Sam just shook her head. No surprises from that bunch.

"Well?" Manny said. His notepad ready.

"You won't need that. I was wired. It's all on tape. You'll find it in my jacket over there. A pocket hidden under the right sleeve. I'd put out an all-points bulletin on Chapell if I were you. You'll most likely find him at the airport. Or already en route to Switzerland," Sam said as she pointed to the closet.

Manny looked surprised as he retrieved the small cassette.

"An illegal recording isn't evidence."

"It doesn't have to be. It will give you the big picture. All the information is verifiable. Jessica Kane's getaway car was found late yesterday hidden in the heavy underbrush near where the Rolls went over. A couple of uniformed officers had it towed to the lab for me. And I think you'll find Isabel Kane will be a good witness."

"What she said was true?"

Sam nodded. Suddenly she felt very tired.

"Too bad this won't help at your disciplinary proceedings. Mansfield is determined to throw the book at you. You gave him more than enough ammunition. Taking Taswell into your personal custody without any authorization by itself was sufficient to—"

"Just tell me one thing more," Sam interrupted. "Did I kill Larkin?"

Manny looked genuinely surprised.

"No, I thought you knew. Lawrence did. He's under arrest for suspicion of murder. That is, if he pulls through. We found him unconscious and bleeding all over you last night."

"I TRIED TO TELL YOU BEFORE but you cut me off. I repeat, he's going to be just fine. Now go back to your own room and get back into bed before you collapse."

Sam had made it past the police guard. Now it was only the formidable doctor standing in her way.

"I'm going to see him."

Dr. Mooney shook her head and sighed.

"Listen, why don't you two move to another state? Alaska, maybe. Then when you decide to get shot up again, you can go to some doctor who can just throw whale blubber at you."

Sam wasted no time on the doctor's retreating figure. She opened the door to Scotty's room. He was sitting up, trying to disconnect the IV securely attached on the bed and his arm.

Relief swept over her. She hadn't believed the doctor. And from the description Manny had given, Sam had pictured Scotty seriously hurt. Not sitting up in bed looking annoyed at some elaborate hospital apparatus, which was designed to keep his IV from being easily removed. Suddenly he looked up. When he saw her standing inside his door, his expression brightened considerably.

"Sam!"

It was an awkward moment. This was the man she had given her love to. The man who had both saved her life and betrayed her trust. It was the memory of how he had broken her heart that surfaced now.

"Scotty, I'm . . . sorry to have barged in. I just wanted to be sure you were okay. I . . . have to go now."

Scotty could see her hesitation, hear the formality in her tone, feel the distance that had come between them. He let out a deep sigh as his heart sank to the floor. Somehow he had to explain. So she could trust and love him again.

"No. Please, don't go. Sit down in this chair. You probably shouldn't be standing. Are you even supposed to be up?"

She hesitated. Her pride told her to go, but something stronger was pulling her toward him. Urging her to take the offered chair. The struggle within her was decided when her ankles began to shake. She knew she had to get off her feet soon or they were going to collapse under her. She rolled the metal bar that dangled her own IV tube to the chair at his bedside and sat down.

She was only a couple of feet from his bed. He wanted to reach out to take her hand. Just touch her. But he knew she wouldn't let him.

"Are you feeling all right?" he asked instead. He couldn't believe how hollow his voice sounded in his own ears. How defeated.

"I'm okay."

Her answer was a monotone, devoid of spirit. It seemed as though the void between them was widening. How could he close it? She had to still feel something for him. Otherwise she wouldn't have come to see if he was all right.

He leaned back against his pillow and tried to relax. At least she was here. He would give her some time, some space. And in the meantime, there was much he wanted to know.

"If you're feeling well enough, Sam, I'd like to know what happened at the Wilson place last night. I haven't been able to get a straight answer out of anybody."

Samantha avoided looking at Scotty. She focused on the metal bar at the back of his hospital bed as she thought about his request. He certainly had a right to know the finish to the Wilson business. She couldn't deny him that. If she could just keep her voice even....

She managed, but the events seemed strange to her as she related them. Almost as though they had happened to someone else.

"So it was Monty Larkin all the time. What pointed to him?" he asked.

"I kept remembering what the woman the world knew as Joni Wilson had said. That she would never marry a man with less money than she had. Her finding out about Larkin's lack of money had only been a matter of time. And it was obvious he had invested too much in his pursuit of her to give up easily."

"How did you know he could kill?"

"His political affiliations gave me an indication of his capacity for violence. That right-wing organization he belonged to was suspected of having sent several letter bombs. He was the one who sent me mine, of course. And shot you." Her voice had almost given her away then. She was thankful when Scotty spoke.

"I suppose Larkin approached Chapell after he murdered the woman he thought was Joni. He needed Chapell to get his hands on the money. The thirty-five million tax-free dollars. Do you think he told Chapell he killed her?"

"Hard to say," Sam replied. "Larkin might have just tried to make a deal with him to double-cross the woman they thought was Joni Wilson. Larkin knew the relationship between Chapell and Joni was strained. And although the lawyer may not have been in on the actual killing, he didn't seem too broken up about it when Larkin confessed. Chapell was still ready to go with the murderer to get his hands on the money."

"So she was really going to murder her own half-sister?"

"Yes. The school in Monterey told me she had come by and picked up the woman they thought was Jessica Kane the Thursday of her death. She told them she was placing the woman in another school and not to expect her back."

"But she did come back?" Scotty asked.

"Isabel flew her back on an early Friday morning flight after she stopped her daughter from her murderous intent. She just told the officials a mistake had been made and that Jessica would continue to stay with them, after all. It was after talking with the school that all the pieces seemed to fall into place."

Scotty looked at her still-averted head, the long dark strands of thick hair that surrounded her shoulders. Again he fought his desire to touch her.

"Nice piece of detective work, Sergeant Turner."

She tried not to hear the warmth in his voice. She tried to concentrate on the topic at hand. "To be honest," she said, "until Isabel verified it was Larkin's car Taswell had seen, I wasn't sure. Problem with this case was that everybody had a motive. Her relative, her lawyer and her friends. And they all seemed capable of murder."

She felt very tired suddenly. As though the telling of her story had taken all her strength. But before she went back to her room, before she left him forever, there was something she wanted to know. She inhaled as though some oxygen might help to get her through the next words.

"Scotty, how did you know I'd be at the Wilson house? How did you get there in time?"

He tried to catch her eye, but still she looked away from him. His voice reached out. "I'd been calling around trying to find you. When Isabel told me Joni's friends were gathering there, I knew that's where you'd head. To confront them with their conspiracy. You see, I had it figured that Joni Wilson was still alive. Hiding out under Jessica Kane's name at the school in Monterey. I called there, and they told me you'd had a policeman pick up the woman and fly her down to L.A.

"I hadn't figured out the switch in babies. I didn't know what you planned. But I knew you were alone. And in danger. I had just gotten to the Wilson estate when I saw you exchanging fire with Larkin. He was aiming for you again, so I . . . stopped him."

His voice had turned fierce, like it had once before. She remembered his pledge then. The one he'd made when he had held her in his arms after the bombing of her home. When he'd said he would get the creep who had done it. And last night he had made good on that pledge. Tears stung her eyes.

"Thank you. Thank you for saving my life. I know a thank-you is inadequate, but I mean it most sincerely."

He saw the tears in her eyes, heard the tremble in her voice. It made his heart hurt. He wanted so much to go to her, take her in his arms, kiss away her sadness.

"Sam, there's no reason to thank me. Don't you understand? I would do anything for you. Anything. I . . ." he began.

Sam wouldn't let him finish. Mustn't let him finish. In case she started to believe in him again.

She got up to leave, blinded by her tears. She felt his arms suddenly on her shoulders.

"Sam, listen to me. You've got to know. That Heritage Insurance business—I gave up considering any commission as soon as we started to work together on the case. My only thought was to help you, to protect you. I thought if I had told you about giving up the commission for your sake, you might have felt obligated. I didn't want that."

She looked up at his words. Could this be true? His face was pale. His eyes an anxious gray. Every cell inside her cried out to believe him. But a small doubt still lingered.

"Why didn't you tell me about the life-insurance policy? Knowing it proved so important in understanding the switch of the babies."

"I should have. I realize that now. But since you gave me every indication at the funeral that Isabel Kane couldn't possibly have murdered the woman she had raised as her daughter, I just assumed the life-insurance policy wasn't a related issue. That's why I didn't tell you about it. The only reason. Please believe me."

She saw the steady light in his eyes, felt the warmth of his hands flowing through her. She did believe him.

"Oh, Scotty! I've been so miserable."

He gathered her into his arms and held her close to him for a long while, not speaking. With each moment that passed, she felt more and more of her old strength returning. Finally she raised her head to look at him, reaching out her hand to stroke the sandy stubble on his pale cheek.

"You do deserve the insurance commission, you know. I'll tell Ms. Grenville so. It was only because of you that I checked into the hospital records on Joni Wilson's birth and learned the truth about the switch of babies. Since the insurance policy was on the life of Joni Wilson and since she's still alive, the insurance company is off the hook and owes you that money."

"What about you? What will the L.A.P.D. do?" Scotty asked.

"Nothing succeeds like success. When all of the evidence is in, I'll probably be let off with a reprimand, which makes me feel good. I don't want to leave under a cloud."

Scotty wasn't sure he had heard her right. "Leave?"

"Yes. I'm tired of fighting for the opportunity to do my job right. People with money and connections have too much power. Staying honest with myself gets more and more difficult every day."

"You fight for what you know is right. You've bought a set of standards and you won't sell out. I know you," Scotty said.

Sam smiled at his insistence. "Maybe. But the cost is getting too high. The Wilson case was the first time I released a prisoner without authorization, worked on a case in violation of orders. It was the handwriting on my career wall, etched deep and bold. I've gone against the rules, made the ends justify the means. That's no way to work, and no way to live. I'd best find another job while my good memories of police work still outnumber the bad."

Scotty felt a sudden surge of strength. "You're too talented to give investigation up, Sam. Too well trained and dedicated. And you don't have to. Just refocus your efforts into private investigation. Come work with me in San Francisco as my partner...as my wife."

"Are you sure?" She turned in his arms to see his face more clearly. "We haven't known each other long."

"Long enough to know I can't imagine living without you, darling. I'm not doing this very well, am I? I know I'm not saying the right things. I haven't told you about the great San Francisco Symphony Orchestra. I haven't even told you how much I love you."

Sam smiled. "Oh, yes, you have. So many times, in so many ways."

Epilogue

An October rain swept the narrow streets below her and brought in a cool capsule of fresh air through the inch of raised window. Sam inhaled deeply, willing the sweet cleanness into her lungs. Red brake lights blinked warm and friendly in the gentle, swirling mist.

She sat lazily at her desk in the new offices of the San Francisco detective firm of Riddle Investigations making only a halfhearted attempt to try to catch up on the backlog of mail. Contentment filled her being. A deep contentment, growing out of her love for Scotty and their life together.

It was their first day back after a short hospital stay and an extended honeymoon, which coincided with the firm's move to a new office and the initiation of a new partnership. Nothing could be more perfect. Except she wished her drive for work would resume its normal fervor.

A large stack of unopened mail littered the desk. She was trying to sift out what she thought Scotty and she should handle first when she came across an envelope addressed to Warren Preston. Just as she was about to put it in a separate pile to be forwarded to the new Hollywood address of Scotty's ex-partner, her eye caught the return address and name, then riveted on the postmark.

Sam sat straight up in her chair, every muscle in her body suddenly at attention.

"Scotty!"

He came with a bound from the next room, still holding some files in his hands.

"What, Sam? What's wrong?"

"Look at this."

He put down the files on the edge of her desk and reached for the envelope, realizing almost at once why Sam had called so excitedly.

"It's from Jane Williams!" he said.

"And look at the postmark. It was mailed just two weeks ago. At least a month and a half after the death of Joni Wilson—I mean, Jessica Kane. And, it was mailed from New Jersey!"

They looked at each other, aware they were both thinking the same thing.

"Do you suppose Warren would mind? I mean under the circumstances?" Sam asked.

Scotty was already tearing the letter open. He read its contents aloud.

Dear Warren,

I want you to be one of the first to know I'm getting married! And it's all because you were able to find my birth certificate.

You see, I'm afraid I didn't tell you everything about my situation when I consulted your firm last month. I was desperate to find proof of my birth because my fiancé's family was putting a lot of pressure on both of us. They're wealthy and were a bit skittish about the circumstances of my birth—not sure I wasn't the product of insane or gangster parents, I suppose!

I did stay over an extra day in San Francisco to see you again, and to tell you the truth. But when I started to come to your office, well, I guess I got cold feet, thinking about our day together and all. I'm sure you understand.

I'm so grateful to you, Warren. Locating my birth

certificate has put a stop to all my future in-laws' non-sense, and the wedding date has been set for November 15, as you can see from the enclosed invitation.

Please come, Warren. I want you and Charles to meet. I'm sending a photo of us both.

Warmest regards,
Jane

They sat in silence for several minutes just staring at the picture of Jane Williams and her fiancé.

"A vanilla ice-cream cone dipped in chocolate," Scotty finally said.

"What?"

"It's how Warren first described Jane Williams. I should have known from that moment the two women weren't the same," he said, shaking his head.

"But how? I don't understand," Sam asked.

"Jessica Kane, alias Joni Wilson, was a tanned Southern Californian. Jane Williams was from the East. Her skin was white, the way it is in this picture. The color of vanilla ice cream. If Warren had really seen Jessica Kane, he never would have described her that way. Her skin was too dark. I knew there was something about that description that bothered me all along. But until now, I didn't realize what it was."

Sam walked over to the window hearing the light rain laugh against the pane. As though some powerful, unseen force in the universe was having its joke on them.

"Scotty! So many of our assumptions about the case were predicated on the two women being one and the same. Our entire idea about the heiress trying to assume another identity. And even though we were wrong about her pretending to be Jane Williams, we were still right. The irony!"

"Yes, I know. But the mistake turned out to be a great stroke of good fortune for me. I met you."

She turned and smiled.

He came over to put his arms around her, sighing in happiness at the feel of her love.

His closeness began to stir desire within Sam. She allowed herself one deep, lingering kiss before she held him at arm's length, looking into the warmth of the wonderful gray eyes she loved so much.

"Scotty, I could go on kissing you all day, but she has a false birth certificate and she doesn't know it. And this guy she's going to marry is Charles Tremont. I recognize his picture. He's from one of the richest families in the country."

Scotty watched the tiny pinpoints of light come sharply into focus in her eyes.

"It's okay. I know what you're about to say," he said.

"You do?"

"Uh-huh. You're about to tell me we only have until November 15 to find out who *this* Jane Williams really is!"

Harlequin Temptation dares to be different!

Once in a while, we Temptation editors spot a romance that's truly innovative. To make sure *you* don't miss any one of these outstanding selections, we'll mark them for you.

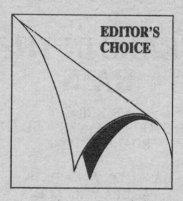

EDITOR'S CHOICE

When the "Editors' Choice" fold-back appears on a Temptation cover, you'll know we've found that extra-special page-turner!

THE

Temptation

EDITORS

TEARS IN THE RAIN

STARRING
CHRISTOPHER CAVZENOVE AND
SHARON STONE

BASED ON A NOVEL BY
PAMELA WALLACE

PREMIERING IN NOVEMBER

TITR-1